Thomas's Second Chance

Hillary Gauvreau Oat

Thomas's Second Chance © 2025 Hillary Gauvreau Oat

Produced and printed by Stillwater River Publications. All rights reserved. Written and produced in the United States of America. This book may not be reproduced or sold in any form without the expressed, written permission of the author and publisher. Visit our website at www.StillwaterPress.com for more information.
First Stillwater River Publications Edition

Library of Congress Control Number: 2025909837
ISBN: 978-1-965733-74-5
12345678910
Written by Hillary Gauvreau Oat.
Cover designed by John Oat.
Published by Stillwater River Publications, West Warwick, RI, USA.

Publisher's Cataloging-in-Publication
(Provided by Cassidy Cataloguing Services, Inc.)

Names: Oat, Hillary Gauvreau, author.
Title: Thomas's second chance / Hillary Gauvreau Oat.
Description: First Stillwater River Publications edition. | West Warwick, RI, USA : Stillwater River Publications, [2025] | Series: Oat, Hillary Gauvreau. Ogilvie family series ; bk. 2.
Identifiers: LCCN: 2025909837 | ISBN: 9781965733745
Subjects: LCSH: Muscians--Fiction. | Alcoholics--Fiction. | Man-woman relationships--Fiction. | Funeral rites and ceremonies--Connecticut--Niantic--Fiction. | Niantic (Conn.)--Fiction. | LCGFT: Romance fiction.
Classification: LCC: PS3615.A352 T46 2025 | DDC: 813/.6--dc23

Cover Design

It is a challenge to select a cover design that matches the tone of the story and catches the eye. Design artist John Oat, and I, brainstormed and poured over images until we finally settled on the bold image of a Scottish thistle. Scotland is in the Ogilvie family blood. The thistle is the national flower and symbol of Scotland. It is known for its beautiful flower and sharp thorns. Able to flourish on rough land, it's stubborn and resists efforts to remove it. It represents bravery, courage, and loyalty. It is the perfect symbol for Thomas Ogilvie.

Also by the Author

It's About Time

Dedicated to the invincible, honest, kind, and intrepid writing group I am grateful to be a part of. I could not have done this without you.

"He who learns must suffer. And even in our sleep, pain that cannot forget falls drop by drop upon the heart, and in our own despair, against our will, comes wisdom to us by the awful grace of God."
— Aeschylus

1

One Day at a Time

Thomas peers through the rain-streaked French doors of his stepmother's condo in Niantic, Connecticut. His mother, father, and now his stepmother, Bess, are all dead and buried. Earlier today, at Bess's memorial, people wondered how he was doing. Thomas is, after all, the sensitive son; the one with problems. People like to put air quotes around that last part. He knows. He's seen them talking.

Truthfully, he doesn't know how he's doing. Memories, like shards of glass in his psyche, are carefully packed away in bubble wrap to prevent further injury. Tamped-down feelings, like a Jack-in-the-box toy on its last crank, are ready to pop. Maybe people *should* worry about him.

Thomas's mother, Caroline, died when he was young. Bess once told him that losing a mother at a young age was a pain that would always linger. Thomas can't argue with that. Although it's been almost forty years since she passed, he still misses her. Throughout his childhood, things were going on in the family that Thomas had no awareness of. Bad things. His mother was a Grammy Award-winning musician, composer, and producer, so she was away from home more often than not. When Thomas was eight, the family attended the Grammy Awards to see her being honored. It was thrilling, and Thomas knew he wanted to be just like her.

His mother wasn't like other mothers, and that was tricky territory for Thomas. He was proud of her but missed her desperately. He wanted her to be home after school, smiling and asking about his day. That didn't happen much, and his disappointment shot out in angry bursts at his father, James. Never once was Thomas angry that his mother chose career over family. He didn't know that she had other reasons for staying away; James protected his sons from that mess.

When Thomas was fourteen, his mother came home after an extended absence. Something was wrong. Her clothes hung shapelessly on her bony frame. The mother that Thomas had always known, with her bright smile and sparkling eyes, was not present in this unrecognizable body.

In one painful year, his mother wasted away as lung cancer consumed her like a raging fire. Whenever she felt well enough, Thomas would curl up in the bed next to her. They would talk, sing, or watch television. He hated that she was sick, but he loved that precious time with her. Her death was a heartbreaking tragedy. She was gone, and she was never coming back.

At her funeral, Thomas sat between his father and Auntie Maura, keeping his head down to avoid everyone's sad eyes. Awash in grief, he wondered how his life could go on without his mother in it. Expressing that to well-meaning people felt impossible.

His older brother, Andy, sat stoically on the other side of their father. Always appropriate, Andy never cried. Thomas, on the other hand, was barely able to hold himself together. Sensing his emotional state, Auntie Maura held Thomas's hand. He welcomed the comfort, and Thomas was grateful that Maura was there beside him in the church. When his father saw Maura's tenderness, he edged a tiny bit closer to his son. Whenever Thomas's mother was away, his father devoted every free minute to his sons, but it was never enough. Maura had picked up the slack. Thomas didn't care if she wasn't a real aunt. He appreciated the attention.

As Thomas grew into adulthood, the painful hits kept on coming. When he was twenty-four, Thomas learned that Maura had been lying to him his whole life, turning him against his family. The betrayal cut him deeply. Then, when he was twenty-seven, his wife Lydia divorced him, not that he blamed her. He was a drunk and a cheat. The career he'd planned had fallen through. Everything he touched turned to shit. After the truth came out about Maura, Thomas and his father made an effort to reconnect. It was a fragile relationship that needed time and attention, but Thomas preferred to stay far away from home. They did the best they could.

And now Bess is gone. Thomas clenches his jaw as sheets of rain slide down the glass, distorting his reflected image. The weight of loss lodges heavily in his chest. If Thomas feels anything, it's shame and regret. Life has dealt him many blows throughout his fifty-plus years, and his face reveals all of them. He is alone. Divorced, no children, no parents, and no clear path forward.

"Hey, you doin' okay?" Cait asks softly as she threads her arm through his. He smiles, seeing her reflection in the glass next to his. His heaviness lightens a bit.

Cait is Bess's daughter and the only person who knows the deepest parts of Thomas. She knows him better than his brother does. Sure, Andy knows how Thomas has struggled with relationships, direction, and alcohol, but he doesn't know how Thomas feels. Andy is successful, brilliant, stable, and as solid as the Glacier Park mountains he loves. Thomas is sensitive and creative. He and Andy couldn't be more different.

Cait, like Thomas, is sensitive. She's had her struggles with alcohol, but stopped drinking in her thirties, thanks to the encouragement of a special uncle. Years ago, Cait dragged Thomas to an AA meeting when he was close to rock bottom. There is never really a rock bottom. Thomas discovered he could always go a little lower. Cait refused to let him push her away. Thomas had always been a mean drunk, and he hurled angry epithets at Cait about the holier-than-thou AA people. Cait stood her ground, and Thomas sulked through a meeting. Even though he wasn't ready to embrace sobriety, something got through to him. Maybe it was how much Cait cared, and, even in a fog of alcohol, he didn't want to disappoint her. She told him that after the meeting, he was on his own. He could destroy his life or get sober. His choice. It took Thomas years to accept the truth of Cait's words. He has been sober for almost a year now. It's long enough to know the benefits of sobriety, but too short a time not to crave the blessed relief alcohol afforded him. Old habits die hard.

"Cait, I've been thinking." He rests his hand on her arm, looped through his. "I want to buy this place—the condo. My dream of being a rock star doesn't seem important anymore. In fact, it feels stupid. Getting sober has changed a lot of things, and I owe that to you. Maybe if I move here and settle down, I'll have a second chance to do things right. Or at least better." Thomas looks to see what her reaction might be.

"I love that idea, Tom. It would be nice to have you close by. And don't you think Mom would be happy her condo is staying in the family?"

"Yeah, I imagine she would."

"Talk to the guys about your idea. If they're on board, I say go for it. I don't think anyone else in the family is planning to live here."

Cait takes Thomas's hand and leads him back to the family. Everyone is sitting by the fireplace. Hundreds of people showed up that day to celebrate the life of Bess Parker, an extraordinary woman, therapist, and friend to every stray human or animal that crossed her path. She'd lived in the small town of Niantic for most of her life and knew almost everyone.

Even in the rain, it has been a beautiful day filled with laughter and tears. Thomas is exhausted and craves a drink. Bess meant a lot to him. He needs time to figure out what the hell he is going to do. It took him years to recover from his mother's death and the mind fuck Maura put him through. He isn't sure how he will handle this latest blow.

Thomas settles himself on the couch next to his brother. Wanting a drink reminds him of how Maura encouraged his drinking. His father wanted what was best for Thomas, and Maura rewarded the exact opposite. He was stupid not to see that. From Thomas's perspective, the history between James and Maura is sketchy. He knows they dated in college, and as near as Thomas can figure, Maura vowed vengeance when his father married Caroline. According to his father, Maura tormented him for decades, but James kept it a secret because what father wants his sons to know that kind of thing? The longer it went on, the worse it got—for everyone. Thomas didn't realize that Maura was a bitter, manipulative woman using him to punish his father, until it was too late.

"Hey, Tom. You're awful quiet," Andy observes. "You okay?"

He wishes people would stop asking him that. "Yeah. Lost in thought. Tired." Thomas stands. "Goodnight, everyone. I need some sleep. See you tomorrow."

The next day, the plan is to sort through the contents of the condo while the family is together. Bess kept everything exactly as it was before James died. Most of it will need to be cleared out. Thomas feels sad that the meaningful things in a person's life can be discarded so easily after they're gone. Maybe that's why he appreciates music. It's immortal. A composer can be dead for hundreds of years, yet the music lives on.

Thomas finds his brother in the den, awake bright and early, sitting at their father's old desk.

"Hey, Andy, I brought you coffee. The first cup of the day is always the best." He sets the mug down in front of him.

Andy looks up. "Thanks. You know, I have so many memories of Dad sitting at this desk. I think Bess felt the same way, because she kept it exactly how he left it. I went through his desk after he died, and now, four years later, it's still the same. His lucky dimes and a stick of petrified Black Jack gum, are still in their place. I half expect Dad to walk in any second." Andy gently shuts the drawer.

Thomas pulls a chair over and sits with his brother. Matt and Cait will arrive soon. It will be a long day of sifting through possessions and memories. This is a rare quiet moment for the brothers to be together. Andy lives in Montana, and Thomas has lived all over the map, including Gainesville, Los Angeles, Austin, and Nashville. He's always been a wanderer, never settling down for long.

"Yeah, seeing you sitting in his chair made me do a double-take. The older you get, the more you look like Dad." Thomas blows on the hot coffee and takes a cautious sip. The warm mug feels comforting in his hands. "Andy, I've been thinking. I want to move here. Buy the condo. I mentioned it to Cait last night, and she encouraged me to check in with you and Matt. It's about time I grew up and stopped running away. What do you think?"

Andy turns the office chair to face his brother. "I like the idea, Tom. Niantic is a great place to settle. I found my place in Montana, and there's a lot of good that comes from putting down roots." Andy smiles. "Cait is nearby, and you two seem close. Makes me wish we were closer...in proximity, but also as brothers."

"Me too. There's time. We aren't dead yet." Thomas doesn't want to get into talking about family bonds, or lack of them. It's still a sore subject for him. "I'll check with Matt and see what kind of deal I can work out. I'll clean out my stuff in Nashville and move my instruments and equipment here. Maybe I'll make this my music room. But you'll have to fight me for Dad's desk." Thomas stands and slaps Andy on the back.

"Oh crap, I was going to strap the desk on my back and cram it in the overhead on the plane." Andy laughs and reaches out to hug his brother. "I think we can work something out." They embrace each other for several minutes, reluctant to let the rare moment pass.

"Andy, have you checked the closet? I'll trade you what's behind door number one for the desk. I think there's something in there you might want."

Andy walks over to it, pulling open the white bifold door. "Is that Dad's kilt?" Andy exclaims. Leaning back in the chair, Thomas crosses his arms over his chest, enjoying his brother's excitement.

When their father died, they thought briefly about burying him in his kilt. But Bess was against it. She couldn't bear parting with it or the memories it held. Andy pulls the black garment bag out of the closet and lays it on the bed. The unzipped bag exposes the perfectly cared-for Ogilvie plaid kilt in shades of green, orange, and blue. Bess loved seeing James in his "regalia," as she called it. Now it's Andy's turn to carry on the Highlander tradition.

"I think it will fit you, Andy. You have Dad's build and height."

At a robust six feet tall, with wild ginger hair and eyes the color of a Montana sky, Andrew James Ogilvie looks like his father. Thomas Malcolm Ogilvie, on the other hand, resembles his mother, with finely chiseled features, a slim five-foot-ten frame, thick, unruly dark auburn hair that just touches his shoulders, and gentle hazel eyes.

"I'm glad Bess held on to it," Thomas says. "Huh, I wonder where Gran's brooch is? It would be nice to keep that in the family."

Andy, exploring the contents of the garment bag, nods in agreement. Thomas scans the former guest room that his father used as an office. When James retired from teaching high school chemistry, he opened It's About Time, his clock repair shop on Main Street in Niantic. He loved old clocks and would immerse himself for hours in the mechanisms until they kept perfect time. Ten years ago, James retired from that as well. Everything from the shop that was worth keeping was moved into this room. The antique library table that once sat in the shop window has been dusted and cared for in the years since James's death. Clocks, tools, springs, wheels, and the ever-present 3-

IN-ONE oil sit just as he left them. A walnut bookcase sits in the corner, jammed with books, clocks, and keepsakes his father couldn't part with.

"Andy, we should go through the bookcase. There might be things we want to keep. Oh, and there's one other thing I would like to keep here at the condo, provided I can stay. Remember that special anniversary clock that stopped at the end of Dad's funeral ceremony? Bess put it on the mantle and never wound it again. It kinda feels like it belongs here. What do you think?"

Andy pulls his father's Jacobite shirt on over his head, smoothing it across his chest. There are centuries of history in every piece of Scottish highlander dress, and Andy senses all of them. He looks up at Thomas, eyes shiny with emotion.

"Did you find his kilt pin?" Thomas asks.

"Yeah, I found the pin in the sporran. Everything is here. It has to be over sixty years old. He and Bess took good care of it. I'll be proud to wear it. What did you ask me earlier? Sorry, I got sidetracked."

"I was wondering if we could leave Dad's special anniversary clock on the mantle where Bess put it after the funeral. It feels like it belongs here. Providing I stay."

"Absolutely. I agree. Just make sure it stays in the family if you ever leave here. Okay?"

"Of course. I promise."

Cait and Matt ring the doorbell and charge into the condo, heading straight to the kitchen.

"Hey, guys. We came bearing brunch!" Matt announces. Thomas strolls into the kitchen, greeting Matt and Cait.

"Where's Andy?" asks Matt.

"He's trying on Dad's kilt." Thomas opens a brown paper bag and inhales the yeasty aroma of fresh bagels. Cait unpacks the containers of cream cheese and smoked salmon. "This is a feast. Thank you, guys. I'm starving. I'll make more coffee." They bustle around the kitchen getting brunch on the table when Andy makes his entrance, fully outfitted in Ogilvie tartan.

"What do you think? Can I pass as a Highlander?" Andy poses with arms outstretched, turning around slowly.

"Shit man, I can almost hear bagpipes playing 'Scotland the Brave'" Matt raves.

"Andy, you look amazing. I have chills," Cait gushes.

"Thank you, Cait! Oh, wow, you brought food." Andy reaches into the bag and selects a fresh bagel. He slices it neatly and waits his turn at the toaster.

"Andy, Thomas was asking about the brooch. We'll find it," Matt says between cream cheesy bites. "I'm sure it's in Mom's room somewhere. We want you to keep it in the Ogilvie family. Who knows, you might have a use for it someday." Matt playfully punches Thomas's arm.

"Ouch. Great! Two big brothers picking on me." Thomas smiles and rubs his arm dramatically. "I don't know about that, but it would be nice to keep it in the family. Andy's son might have a use for it someday. You should hold onto it Andy." Thomas refills his mug with hot coffee.

"I have more business to bring up, guys. Matt, I mentioned this to Cait and Andy already. I would like to live here. Buy the place, rent the place, whatever we can figure out. Do you know if anyone else in the family is interested in living here? Kids, maybe?"

"I'll ask around, Tom. I don't want to make a snap decision and start a rebellion in the family, but I think your claim is safe. The estate was left to the four of us, equal shares. I'll get it appraised and make an appointment with our attorney to see what we can figure out that's fair. Sound good?"

"Sounds great. Thanks."

"In the meantime, stay as long as you like. Cait likes having you around." Matt nods toward Cait. "Right, sis?"

"Actually, I do. Don't mind my smartass brother, Tom. Stay as long as you want."

"Thanks, guys." Thomas feels better today; less mournful now that he has a plan.

One day at a time.

2

The Long Game of Love and War

When Thomas was sixteen, his brother Andy graduated from high school, and went away to college. The house felt empty. James struggled after Caroline died, which made it difficult for him to be emotionally available. Maura saw it as an opportunity to spend more time with Thomas. She listened to him, and they drank together. Sometimes Maura would encourage him to ask a couple of friends over, and they would party until they passed out on the floor. Thomas's father didn't seem to notice. James was not only aching from the devastating loss of his wife, but also, unknown to Thomas, the punishment Maura was heaping on him. His father saw everything, but didn't have the energy to do much about it. Thomas felt neglected by everyone except Maura.

In high school, Thomas put together a rock band. He composed music and played keyboards. The band became so popular that he considered quitting school to go on tour and maybe get a dream record deal. That was when his father fully engaged and put his foot down.

"Absolutely not, Thomas! You will stay in school. Play all the music you want, but school is required as long as you live in this house."

"Yeah, well, maybe I don't want to live in this house." Thomas shouted and slammed the door to his room so hard it rattled the windows.

There were volatile fights, and Maura always aligned with Thomas against his father. Her plan was to diminish James's parental role and ensure Thomas was loyal only to her. The result was family warfare. Maura called James an old fuddy-duddy. James accused Maura of interfering. Thomas slammed his door. The fights were loud, frequent, and fractious. Maura was Thomas's ally, and he wasn't willing to give her up. Maura bought him beer, played fast and loose with the rules, and told him not to take life seriously. She led Thomas to believe that being wild and free was part of growing up. She assured him he was different from Andy, who had never had a fun day in his life.

Thomas's band, The Rabble Rousers, was a cross between punk, heavy metal, and grunge. They followed all anti-establishment artists and considered their brand to be protest music. They protested just about everything, or at least everything their parents would let them get away with. They wrote music together, and when fans requested their original songs, it thrilled them. Even though the band was underage, they played in bars under their parents' watchful eyes. Bar owners didn't look too closely if they brought in the crowds. It was an education in the raunchier side of life that high school boys don't always get.

When Thomas looks back on those times, he has mixed feelings. It was fun, but most of what he remembers is in an alcoholic haze. He regrets how angry he was at his father. Thomas blamed him for everything he could, including his mother's absence and death. Maura did all she could to stoke that fire, telling Thomas stories to provoke him and keep him under her control. He needed acceptance, and Maura was there to provide it. No matter what Thomas did, Maura supported him. If he'd jumped off a bridge, she would have said it was a nice dive. Now Thomas knows that everything Maura did had nothing to do with him. It was all about piling as much shit on his father as possible.

After high school, Thomas wanted to go to Berklee College of Music in Boston. His father wanted him to have a more well-rounded education, suggesting UMass. Maura made a few alternative suggestions, which carried weight with Thomas. She poo-pooed UMass in favor of the University of Florida in Gainesville. It was a good school, but more importantly, it was far away from Connecticut. Thomas wanted to be beyond his father's control, and Maura agreed. He enrolled in a UF music program.

"Auntie Maura, I'm so happy to see you!" Thomas threw his arms around her. It was a beautiful spring day on the UF campus. Maura often visited Florida. She had been widowed for the second time, inherited a bunch of cash, and she was bored. She could always generate a little drama with Thomas to amuse herself. Maybe she could provoke a blowup between father and son, or talk Thomas into dropping out of school to tour Europe with her. That would piss James off for sure. Maura had a lot of experience in the pissing-people-off department. She was quite successful in coming between Caroline and James. If it weren't for Caroline's cancer, Maura might have manipulated them into a divorce, which would have been very satisfying. Eventually, cancer eliminated Caroline, and Maura had big plans for James and their happily ever after. She was infuriated when James refused to go along with her plan to have him all to herself. That was when Maura sized up the situation and decided that Thomas would be her best bet for making James pay for being so uncooperative. Maura had been grooming Thomas to trust her since he was young. Eventually, the long game would pay off.

"Tommy boy! It's so good to see you! You look great." Maura hugged Thomas, concealing a blank expression over his shoulder, before turning on her thousand-watt smile just for his benefit. "How's school going? You're almost done." Four years of college seemed to fly by.

"Let's go get lunch, and you can fill me in on your plans. Then later I want to see those bats!" Maura had a natural talent for ingratiating herself. The bat house was a big attraction at UF. They housed about half a million bats, and, at twilight, people gathered to watch them fly out for their nightly meal of insects. It was quite a spectacle, and Maura knew all about it.

"Absolutely!" Thomas followed Maura to her car, and they drove to a local lunch place. After they ordered, they toasted to Thomas's graduation with a Swamp Head microbrew. The icy cold IPA hit the spot, and Maura ordered a couple more. Thomas didn't hold back with Maura because he had no reason to. He was certain she was an ally against his father and the world. What he didn't know was that the war with his father was perpetuated by Maura's lies. She'd convinced Thomas that his father had abused his mother, that he favored Andy, and that he was disappointed in his youngest son. Maura didn't care that Thomas lived with the hurt of those lies every day. Thomas pushed away the people who loved him and embraced a deceitful, conniving—but very convincing—viper.

"So, what are your plans after graduation?" Maura prodded as she dug into her Cobb salad.

"Well, I *have* been thinking about that," Thomas said as he bit into a juicy burger. "I like being here in Gainesville, and I was accepted into the graduate school here. So, there's that. An MFA in music production would give me options and look good on my resume. Of course, I could go home and take a break. You know, reconnoiter? If the guys are interested, we could take the band on the road. That might be fun."

"Wow. Yeah, that would be fun. Is that a possibility?" Maura ticked off options in her head like a heat-seeking missile locking in on a target. Which option would best suit her purpose of punishing James?

"We've been talking, but nothing's for sure yet. Maybe I could get a job at a recording studio. Session musician, production...you know? I want to be in music. That's definite."

"Have you talked to your father about your options?"

"A little. Dad wants me to go to grad school, but not here. He's been hinting that I should go to UMass and follow in Mom's footsteps. I don't know, though. I'd rather find my own way, and I kinda like it here."

"I completely agree with you. Do your own thing. It's your life, after all. This place has a lot going for it." Maura opposed anything James wanted for his son. James's love for UMass was enough reason for Maura to steer Thomas in another direction.

"Yeah, it does. For sure. So, you think I should stay in school here?"

"Well, my first choice would be to see your band go on the road so I could be your most rabid fan! But if that's not possible, I think grad school is a great choice. Very mature decision."

"Thanks, Maura. I agree. Very mature! Are you coming to graduation? Dad will be here."

"Absolutely! Your Dad and I are so proud of you. Here's a little something from me." Maura slid an envelope across the table. Thomas opened the graduation card and was stunned to see a check for ten thousand dollars tucked inside.

"Holy shit! This is amazing. It will help me so much, Auntie. Thank you." Thomas jumped up, throwing his arms around her. A sly smile spread across Maura's face.

"You're welcome. Anything I can do to help is my priority. Love you, Tommy-boy. Your mother was my best friend, and she would want me to be here for you." This visit was a slam dunk. Maura believed she had Thomas firmly in the palm of her hand.

15

After Thomas's graduation from UF, life was peaceful for a while. Maura trotted off to seduce another rich old man, spending half her time in Spain. James ran his clock shop. Andy was completing a graduate program in environmental studies at Yale and was applying for a ranger position with the National Park Service. Andy hinted that he had met someone he was serious about. He was on track for a storybook, happily-ever-after life. That was one son James didn't worry about. Thomas, on the other hand, caused James to sprout a few gray hairs.

When life is peaceful, it is the perfect moment for something unexpected to happen. Bess Parker, a local therapist, fell in front of the clock shop. James saw it happen and rushed outside to help. Neither Bess nor James was in the market for a relationship, but Cupid and his little arrows had designs on them. As their friendship blossomed, everyone knew love would follow. When Maura caught wind of this new woman in James's life, she was livid. It was Caroline all over again. Maura paced angrily around her luxurious Greenwich mansion, slamming doors and yelling so loudly she scared the gardener.

"What the hell, Jimbo? Why is this so difficult to get through your thick, Scottish skull?" Maura heaved a Lladro porcelain statue against the wall. The piece, called *The Kiss Couple*, shattered. Maura wasn't in the mood to see the irony of that. "Why can't he accept that *he* belongs to *me*? What is his problem?"

Maura failed to see that *she* was the problem. There would be payback for his betrayal, and it would be a bitch. All was fair in love and war.

Whenever Maura was angry at James, she called Thomas. It was comforting to have at least one Ogilvie in her pocket.

"Hey, Auntie. What's up?" Thomas usually referred to Maura as an auntie, although she wasn't related to anyone in the family. Thomas stayed in Gainesville the summer after graduation and relied on Maura to fill him in on family affairs.

"Thomas, I am so pissed! Argh," Maura growled, and Thomas heard a loud crash like a chair being kicked down stairs. "I shouldn't dump this on you, but I don't know who else to talk to." Maura huffed, paused, and launched into a diatribe about someone named Bess. "You would never believe it. That woman has your father so pussy-whipped that I hardly recognize him. Your father, the strong, stubborn Scotsman, is now totally spineless. He does whatever she says. It's nauseating."

"Wait. What are you talking about? Who's Bess?"

"That *woman* your father has been palling around with. She's a local in that pathetic town. They say they're just friends, but it seems like more to me."

"My father is dating someone?" Newsflash for Thomas.

"Yes! Try to keep up, will ya? I got back from Spain after my dear, sweet husband passed." Maura paused dramatically for grief-stricken effect. "Of course, I headed straight to your father's place looking for comfort. After the support I gave him, you'd think he could find it in his stone-cold heart to return the favor. But *no*. I looked forward to seeing him, but he was cold as ice. He lied to me! Can you believe that? He tried to keep that Bess woman a secret. Said she was just a friend. I've known him for thirty years, and he *lied* to me. What the hell? If he thinks he can kick me to the curb, he has another thing coming. It's all *her* influence, Thomas. We got along so well before *she* showed up. The witch has him completely under her thumb."

"Wow. He kicked you to the curb? Why?"

"First of all, I haven't seen him in over a year, and he has the nerve to keep me waiting. When he finally showed up, he was so drunk he could hardly stand. Nasty and belligerent. That's the way he was with your mother. Remember?"

Thomas doesn't remember. He remembers Maura telling him that, though.

"The next day, he could barely function. He did manage to snarl at me and push me off the couch onto the floor. I still have a bruise. Later, when he was feeling less hungover, things seemed to improve. Then he snuck outside to call that bitch and lied to me again. Can you believe it? The next morning, I did everything in my power to smooth things over. I even made breakfast. You'd think he would appreciate that, but no. It was so tense in that house that I had to leave. I didn't come back until late afternoon."

"That sounds terrible, Auntie. I'm so sorry."

"There's more. When I got back to the house, I was *told* that we were going to a friend's house for dinner. Not asked, mind you, but *told.* I thought, what the hell, I'll go and see what this is about. We drove to an old farmhouse, and there were three people there. *Bess,* and a couple of people who seemed nice, but I can't remember their names. Thomas, I bent over backward to be friendly. I even brought them a bottle of my favorite, very expensive Spanish wine. But those people were just awful to me. They weren't interested in what I thought or in knowing more about me. They just prattled on about stupid stuff that only *they* cared about. And your *father?* He hardly said a word. Just left me twisting in the wind with these people I didn't know."

"I'm so sorry. That's awful." Thomas didn't know what else to say.

"It *was* awful. I've never been so humiliated in my life. Your father and that Bess person exchanged knowing glances the whole time. I was the butt of some disgusting private joke. Finally, we left. I was so upset that I started crying when we got in the truck. Your father told me to knock it off, and then he slapped me! He has *never* done that before. I was stunned. But that isn't even the worst of it."

"Jeez, there's more?"

"Yeah." Maura whimpered and sniffed, finally blowing her nose before she continued complaining. "I stayed at your father's house for the week. My Greenwich house wasn't ready, and I had nowhere else to go. I have always felt welcome there, but this time I was walking on eggshells. I wanted to know what was going on, so I paid Bess a little visit."

Thomas was fully engaged in the story, sitting on the edge of his seat.

"I brought food as a peace offering, and we had a glass of wine. I just wanted to get to know her. At first, it was okay, but then we started talking about your parents. Thomas, I was horrified to hear the lies your father told her about your mother and me. He made me the bad guy, and he came off like a saint."

Full stop. The liar was Maura. She lived in a version of whatever reality worked best for her. Maura was quite adept at spinning fantastic stories, making her the hero or the victim. Her tales did not contain small lapses in memory, but an entire reworking of history. Thomas didn't know that, however.

"What lies?" Thomas roared. "What did she say?" Thomas wasn't on video chat, so he couldn't see Maura smirk. He took the bait and she'd successfully set her hook in him. The feeling of control made her euphoric.

"I won't get into that. It would hurt you, and they are lies, so no point repeating them. The next day, I left for Greenwich, but there were problems with the house. That's another story. So, in the morning, I headed back to your father's place. On the drive to Niantic, I decided to sell that big, old house in Greenwich and buy a beach house in Old Lyme. I was excited to share the good news with James. He wasn't home, which was odd. He's always home. Since I was already in the neighborhood, I went to Bess's condo. I wanted to smooth things over and get the name of a good realtor. Imagine my shock when your father answered the door. He was making pancakes for his *friend* Bess.

They both looked like they'd just rolled out of bed. It was like a knife in my heart, Thomas. I'm so hurt."

"Breakfast? My father slept at Bess's? A person I don't even know?" That was a gut punch.

"Yes. I thought we could have breakfast together and talk. I would find a way to adjust. I care about your father so much. I just want him to be happy."

That lie was a whopper. Four Pinocchios for Maura. The woman has no shame.

"So, I put on my big girl pants, smiled, and tried to get along with them." Maura tearfully described how rude they were to her and how they threw her out of the house, telling her not to come back.

Thomas missed most of that because he was still processing the news that his father was sleeping with someone. It had never occurred to Thomas that his father might be equally shocked to know about the women Thomas slept with. But that's different, of course. No kid ever wants to imagine their beloved parent having sex. Ever. Fathers were not supposed to be sleeping around.

"What did you do? Have you talked to Dad?"

"I tried. But your father is adamant that he wants me out of his life. Period. I've never seen him like this. And he changed the locks!"

After they hung up, Maura smiled. Thomas popped the top on a beer.

At about eight in the evening, when the shock had worn off, Thomas called his father. Voicemail. Jesus. What was going on? Thomas had always been able to get his father on the phone.

3

Maura's Revenge

Time marched on as usual. Bess and James continued to get closer, gradually approaching a cautious commitment. Thomas, under Maura's tutelage, was a simmering pressure cooker of raw emotion. Mostly resentment. The slightest provocation, fueled by alcohol, set him off. The Ogilvie family reunion triggered a breaking point. It isn't easy to predict a person's last straw, but it's easy to recognize it when it happens.

It was a glorious October weekend in Blowing Rock, North Carolina. Thomas had wonderful times growing up with his father's side of the family in North Carolina. He adored Auntie Mary, Uncle MJ, and his cousins. He kept a tight lid on his pressure cooker for them. He hadn't seen his father since he'd visited Connecticut last summer, which was when he finally got the chance to meet Bess, and she'd seemed okay. Since then, Maura had been filling his head with stories. When his father mentioned that Bess would be coming to the reunion, Thomas felt the little regulator on top of his pressure cooker start to jiggle. Then, when his father got him and Andy on a video call before heading to North Carolina, Thomas knew something was up.

"Guys, I want you to know that I love Bess. She's a good person. I want to know how you feel about me getting married?"

Was this really happening? Had Andy even met her? And Thomas hardly knew her at all.

"Well, Dad, if she makes you happy, then I say go for it," said the ever-reasonable and appropriate Andy.

"Whatever," said Thomas. The pressure increased inside him.

On the last night of the Ogilvie reunion, everyone gathered around the bonfire. It was the perfect moment for James to propose to Bess. The family loved it. Thomas walked away from the spectacle before he did something he would regret.

The next day, Bess and Mary were in the kitchen when they heard a ruckus outside by the fire pit. Mary, James's older sister, rushed out of the kitchen to see what was going on, muttering something about mixing Scotsmen and whiskey.

Thomas could not help himself. He had reached the limit of his tolerance. Maura had stoked a fire that was about to consume him. He listened to his father joking with Mary's husband, Graeme, speaking fondly of Andy's upcoming wedding and his affection for Bess. Thomas couldn't contain himself another minute.

He hadn't planned on punching his father in the face, but, nonetheless, he did. He was swept up in a wave of angry adrenaline and would have done more damage if Uncle MJ hadn't intervened. His father stood there, jaw clenched, seeing a son he loved but hardly recognized. Thomas spewed venom at his father. MJ restrained Thomas's body, but his mouth was in overdrive. He was going to say his piece after holding it in for too long.

"You fucking piece of shit!" Thomas struggled in MJ's tight grip. "I hate you. How can you act like Mr. Wonderful after all you've done to our family? You lying, two-faced bastard. Does Bess know who you are?" The venom continued until Mary marched over to them, hands on her hips. She directed Thomas to the kitchen, which was like being taken out behind the woodshed in the old days. Mary was having none of this. MJ frog walked Thomas in through the kitchen door.

"Sit down!" Mary wouldn't take no for an answer. "What is going on here, Thomas? You have had a bug up your tush all weekend."

Thomas, red-faced and sullen, glared at Auntie Mary and was silent. He knew better than to disrespect her.

"Something is going on between you and your father. What is it? Does this have anything to do with Bess?"

"Auntie, you only know one side of Dad. The side he wants you to see. You don't know how he hurt my mother, and the drunken fights. My mother was afraid to come home. Did you know he was arrested for domestic abuse? Did you? Did you know that?" Thomas shouted. "No? I didn't think so." Thomas spit words out like bullets, fury in his eyes. "Andy is his golden child, but what about me? He treats me like I am one big pain in his ass. Well, he ain't seen nothing yet."

"Thomas, your dad loves you. If you are treated like a pain in his arse, then maybe you need to look at why. Lest you forget, I grew up with your father, and I know him pretty well, yeah? Let's talk about this. Where did you hear he was arrested? I think I would know if that ever happened. I'm open to hearing what you have to say." Mary was doing her best to be reasonable and patient.

"Auntie Maura told me all about what was going on and why Mom stayed away."

"Oh, now I understand." Mary sighed, the picture coming into focus. "Thomas, your parents loved each other. I can attest to that. Your dad likes his whiskey from time to time, but he is no drunk. And violent?" Mary huffed. "Hon, if he was violent, he woulda flattened you a little while ago. I think you should talk to him. Get his side of the story. Yeah?"

Thomas was not in the mood to be reasonable. Too much water had flowed under the bridge Maura built, for Thomas to question the story he believed. He clenched his jaw, grabbed his duffle bag, and without another word, stomped to his car. The rest, as they say, is history. He released more pressure when he picked a fight in a Columbia, South Carolina, roadhouse, then cooled his jets in jail waiting for his father and uncle to bail him out. When he was free, Thomas thanked his father for the help, got in his car, and drove away without explanation. James was sure this episode with his son had Maura's fingerprints all over it. But what could he do about it?

Communication between Thomas and his father was limited after that. James wanted to reach out but held back, fearing he would alienate Thomas further. Maura left James and Bess alone, but it didn't mean she was forgiving or forgetting. She sold her estate in Greenwich and bought a house on the beach in Old Lyme. The flood insurance was astronomical, but she didn't care. It was worth it to have James in her sights. Maura was waiting for the perfect opportunity to light the fuse and blowup everything James cared about—his family, his sterling reputation, and, most of all, Bess. There was no limit to her vengeance or the joy she received from making James suffer. Maura made the wicked queen in *Snow White* look like a Girl Scout. James had seriously underestimated what she was capable of.

Maura sat on her porch, basking in the glow of revenge. She heard the doorbell and impatient pounding on her door. A loud male voice identified himself as a Connecticut State Marshal. *Shit, now what?* Thought Maura. It was probably about that little fender bender she was in. *Damn cameras are everywhere these days.* What came next was so unexpected that Maura laughed at the sheer absurdity of it.

"Maura Jenkins? I am State Marshal Alfred Manfredie." The guy was all business and would be a challenge for Maura to schmooze, but she liked challenges. The gorgeously tan, impeccably dressed Maura batted her eyelashes and asked to see some identification. She actually couldn't care less about ID but was stalling to see what he would do. How far could she push this guy? The officer pointed to his badge and showed her a photo ID hanging on a lanyard around his neck.

"Officer Manfredie...how nice to meet you. Please come in. To what do I owe this pleasure? I already donated to the Police Benevolent Fund. Would you like a glass of wine? I have a bottle open?" Maura smiled her most inviting smile.

"No, thank you, ma'am." The officer thrust papers in her direction. "Maura Jenkins, you are served with a restraining order. I will take custody of any firearms you own now, or you can turn them in at the police station tomorrow. Your choice. If you choose to bring them to the station, and fail to do so, there will be a warrant issued for your arrest. Do you understand?"

"Restraining order? Gun? What makes you think I own a gun?" Maura was confused and not smiling anymore. "What is this about?" Maura looked at the papers. The name James Ogilvie jumped out at her. She was outraged but impressed that James had the balls to push back. Let the games begin. Maura walked the short distance to the hall closet and pulled a locked box down from the shelf. She held it out to the man.

"Here ya go, officer. Don't hurt yourself." Maura narrowed her eyes and smirked.

"Open it, please." The marshal smiled.

Maura used her thumbprint to open the box, exposing a Glock 42, a sweet little pistol that she bought recently. It complemented the Sig Sauer P365 tucked in her nightstand. The P365 was staying her little secret for now. The marshal lifted the Glock out of the box, racked the slide back to check for a live round, then slipped it into an official evidence case. He handed her a receipt and told her to sign it. Then he left. Maura watched him walk away, angry bile rising in her throat. If she had a gun in her hand, she might have used it to see how fast smiley could move.

What happened after that could only come from the darkest recesses of Maura's twisted mind. Rage consumed her. How dare James get a restraining order! Who did he think he was?

Maura sat on her sun porch, sipping wine and thinking. The restraining order nonsense was an inconvenience, but she would make it work for her. The first step was to call Thomas and play the part of the poor victim who couldn't figure out what was going on.

"Why did your father do this to me?" she sobbed into the phone. Thomas was trained to defend her, and it was easy to infuriate him at the injustice done to his sweet auntie. "Thomas, I'm so afraid your father will tell you awful things about me. Please don't tell him I called you. He is going to blame me, and it's all lies. Please believe me," Maura begged between fake dry sobs. "There is something wrong with your father. I didn't tell you everything because I didn't want to hurt you. But it's time you knew."

Thomas listened as Maura listed the horrible things his father had allegedly done to her. She twisted reality into so many knots that Thomas would never untangle them. In truth, all James did was leave Maura for Caroline thirty years ago. Thomas had no idea that Maura was the perpetrator of the transgressions she blamed on his father. Using reverse psychology, Maura planted the suggestion for Thomas to call his father and blast him. James would be so afraid of losing his son that he would cave. That would put an end to this restraining order nonsense, and it would be business as usual for Maura.

The next step was for Maura to research attorneys in case she needed to go to court. She looked for one with perfect optics. Two out of three judges are men, middle-aged, or older. A statuesque and stunning lawyer by her side, Louboutin stiletto boots, and a few tears should be enough to soften up the old guy to give her a break. Maura hired Angeline Shapiro. She couldn't care less where she went to school or how good a lawyer she was. Angeline reeked of status and wealth. She was tall, blond, and strikingly beautiful, which was all Maura needed. When they met, Maura explained the situation in an Academy Award-winning performance. It was a variation of James, the bad guy, and Maura, the poor victim. Many women have had issues with men threatening and stalking them, Angeline being no exception. She commiserated fully and assured Maura they would nail this guy. They immediately went to work preparing their defense.

Meanwhile, unbeknownst to Maura and her expensive attorney, James finally decided to come clean with his sons. After Thomas blasted his father for the restraining order, James saw no other option. He summarized the decades of Maura's abuse, and described the threats and vandalism that led to the restraining order. James showed his sons photos of the house and played a recording of Maura admitting she wanted to destroy him. That was tough for Thomas to hear. He'd been groomed to side with Maura since he was a child. Maura told him his father would blame her, and he was. But his father also had proof. Thomas didn't know what to believe. He wanted to hear what Maura had to say about these accusations.

"Auntie, my father told us everything. He said you did all those things you blamed on him. You wanted to hurt him because he loved my mother. Is that true?"

"Tommy-boy, I told you he would blame me. Please believe me. You know me. You know I would never do anything to hurt your father. Or you!" Maura pleaded.

"Maura, he had proof. Police reports, photos, and the envelope you sent to Bess. Your fingerprints were on it. That would be impossible unless you sent it. But it was the recording that convinced me."

"Recording? What recording?" Maura demanded.

"He played a recording of you telling Bess that you want to destroy him. Why? What did he ever do to you? Have you been using me to hurt him?" What happened next shocked Thomas. The sweet auntie he had always known turned into a raging beast.

"How dare you question me! I told you he would blame me," Maura screamed like a banshee. "You're a stupid, no-talent drunk. You wouldn't know the truth if you fell over it. Your father deserved all he got and more."

For the first time in Thomas's life, Maura's true self was on display and impossible to excuse. Thomas had been used. Duped by this woman he didn't recognize. The pain of betrayal was excruciating.

They say that what goes around comes around. Maura was finding that to be true in real-time. She lost the leverage Thomas gave her with James and her defense against the restraining order. Never in her life had she failed to get her way.

How dare James stand up to her. Her rage turned into ice-cold revenge. She had to be smart about it though. Maura smiled. Payback was going to be fun. His legal bullshit would do him no good. Maura wasn't aware, however, that her ordeal was just beginning. The other shoe was about to drop, and it was a steel-toed Doc Marten that would leave a mark.

Before Maura could decide on her next move, she was issued an arrest warrant. Things were going from bad to worse. Her back was against the wall and her hand was forced. Getting arrested was the last straw. Because she was beautiful and this was her first run-in with the law, the police cut her some slack and gave her a couple of days to turn herself in. It was just enough time for her to get even.

The weekend after Halloween, Maura caught wind of a party being thrown by Bess's friend, Virginia. Maura wasn't invited, although she toyed with the idea of disguising herself in a costume and crashing it to cause trouble. That was a fun idea. She could make an irresistible dessert that would send everyone to the bathroom or worse. She might flatten all the tires on the cars in the driveway. Maybe she would detonate a couple of cherry bombs and watch people scatter. That would amuse her. But her vendetta was against Bess and James, and it had to be personal. She decided to use her deceased husband's Lincoln Navigator to scare the shit out of them. That would bring James back into line.

The night of the party, it was drizzling. Maura sat in her SUV and waited for James and Bess to leave the party. When Bess's Honda finally pulled out of the driveway, Maura followed them. She tailgated them, flipping on her high beams. Maura laughed, imagining what was going on inside Bess's car. After toying with them, she pulled up alongside their car, inching closer until she made contact. The Honda HR-V was no match for the behemoth Navigator. Maura only intended to scare them, but once opportunity presented itself, Maura couldn't resist. Believing that no one could identify her, she impulsively forced their car off the road and down an embankment. The sound of the crash thrilled her. Maura didn't think about what would happen to them as they careened down the embankment, nor did she care. She pressed down on the Navigator's accelerator and sped off down the road.

As she fled the scene of her assault, she missed a curve, and the huge vehicle slid off the wet road, rolling over several times and landing upside down. Maura finally got payback for all the punishment she'd dished out. James and Bess were banged up in their Honda, but considering what could have happened, they were lucky. Maura was not as fortunate. It took time for rescue units to discover her crushed vehicle looking like a turtle on its back. Maura was still belted securely in her seat, upside down and unconscious. She never recovered from the traumatic brain injury and lived the rest of her short life in a nursing home. No one wished that on Maura, but it was a relief for James and Bess to be free of her.

The course of events was too much for Thomas to process in one chunk. His feelings were confusing and overwhelming. Maura had always been there for him, even though there were strings attached. Thick, dark, ugly strings, as it turned out. The accident proved to

Thomas that the Maura he knew didn't exist. It was hard for him to hold on to the reality of a vengeful, sociopathic Maura. His psyche wanted to shield him from her wretchedness.

Thomas spent a lot of time alone in the months following the accident. The knowledge that his father wanted to protect him surprised him. His father wasn't who he thought he was either. He hated Maura for coming between his parents and hurting his family. He was ashamed it was so easy for her to deceive him. Thomas stopped trusting after that. The only good thing that came out of the Maura debacle was a fragile connection between father and son. They now understood how they had gotten so far off track.

One day, Thomas packed his bag and drove straight from Gainesville to Niantic. He needed to see Maura in the nursing home and face his father. James cried with relief when he saw his son.

"I am so sorry, Thomas. Please forgive me. I thought I was doing the right thing."

"Me too, Dad. I didn't know. I *really* didn't know. I feel so stupid and awful," Thomas confessed. "I need to see her," Thomas told his father, referring to Maura. "Will you go with me?"

"Yes, of course. I need to see her too. I've been putting it off. But with you here, the time is right."

Father and son forgave each other. Thomas saw Bess standing back, smiling with tears in her eyes. He walked the few steps to her, and she opened her arms to him.

"I'm so sorry," Thomas whispered in her ear. "I thought you would hate me."

Bess held him, asking for nothing and in no rush to let him go.

That week, Thomas and James talked late into the night. James told Thomas the story of Maura and what she had done. They both questioned their ability to trust people after what they had experienced. At age twenty-four, one chapter closed in the life of Thomas Ogilvie. How the next chapter unfolds will be up to him.

4

The Prodigal Son Returns

Thomas pulls his recently-purchased Jeep Wrangler into the reserved space in front of Bess's condominium and sits, collecting his thoughts. At fifty-three years old, it seems late to start over, but here he is. He hopes he's a late bloomer, with some blooming still to be had. He pulls the key out of the ignition and pushes the Jeep's door open. *Here's to second chances,* Thomas thinks.

The drive from Nashville, Tennessee to Niantic, Connecticut seemed to take forever. After cleaning out his apartment, he was eager to get to his new home. The crappy thrift store furniture he had inherited from the previous tenant was tossed. His meager possessions were packed in boxes and shipped to Connecticut. Important items he couldn't afford to lose were loaded into his Jeep with not an inch to spare. Not everyone can fit most of their life's belongings into the back of a car.

Route 81 was pleasant enough. He drove through Virginia's Blue Ridge Mountains and into rural southern Pennsylvania. He skirted New York City and got jammed up on Interstate 95 heading into Connecticut. After seventeen hours on the road, he is weary, but energized at the same time. He can't wait to start unpacking and get settled.

Thomas pulls a bulging duffle bag from the back of the Wrangler and heads to the front door. He imagines all the times his father did the same thing. When his father first moved in with Bess, they were both about the age Thomas is now. That thought brings a lump to Thomas's throat. He prays to God he will be as fortunate as they were. Not that he is looking for a relationship, mind you. All he wants is a chance at a good life rather than the shitty one he's had so far.

Cait promised to meet him when he arrived. He tosses the duffel onto the small front stoop and walks back to the Jeep for his keyboard. As he is lifting it out, Cait pulls in and parks next to him.

"Have you been waiting long?" Cait asks.

"Nope. I just got here. Your timing is perfect." Thomas gives Cait a hug, inhaling the floral scent of her freshly washed hair. "Thank you for meeting me."

"My pleasure." Cait retrieves take-out bags from the back of her car. "Come on. Let's get you fed and organized." Cait tosses the condo keys to him with a grin. "Welcome to Connecticut and the glorious world of homeownership! I left a list of plumbers, electricians, and handy people in the kitchen, just in case you have a need. You might want to consider signing up for a cheaper electricity supplier. The electric bill is in the kitchen. Sit down before you open it. If you have any questions or need help, I am your go-to girl." Cait grins. "I'm happy you're here, Tom."

Thomas smiles. Cait is indeed his go-to girl. That is something he needs to be careful with. It would be easy to let his affection for Cait cross the line. The last thing he wants to do is betray her trust or cause trouble with her husband, Bart. Cait has always believed in Thomas, and thanks to her he is alive and sober. After Maura's betrayal, after years of drunken wandering and feeling like he didn't belong anywhere, he's learning how to let people in. That means going to AA meetings and not hitting on Bart's wife. A warm friendship is all he wants—no flirty funny business here. Thomas unlocks the door and holds it open for Cait to enter. The air inside is stale. They find their way around boxes stacked in the foyer.

"Thanks for being here for the delivery, Cait. I wasn't sure how close to my arrival it would be."

"No problem. The boxes beat you here by a few days." Cait opens the French doors wide. Thomas inhales the scent of fresh salt air from Long Island Sound.

"Every time Mom and your father came home, they would open these doors first thing, even in the dead of winter. I truly believe my mother could not live without ocean air. Come on." Cait grabs Thomas's hand and pulls him out to the patio. "Let's eat before I get all maudlin." The take-out bag is plopped on the patio table. The delicious aroma of fish and chips reminds Thomas how hungry he is.

"Yo? Hello? Anyone home? Should I check the bedroom?" It's Bart. Thomas immediately stiffens.

"We're out on the patio. Come join us." There's a perceptible change in Cait's behavior. Thomas is very good at picking up on nuance, and he's positive that Cait's tense body language has a lot to say. Thomas stands up and reaches out to shake Bart's hand. Bart ignores it, preferring to use both hands to pop the top on a beer.

"Well, isn't this cozy? Did you get me lunch?" Bart's smile looks more like a baring of teeth, and Thomas senses Cait's discomfort. She offers her husband a peck on the cheek.

"Sorry, hon. I didn't know you would be stopping by. I'm happy to share with you."

"Well, somebody needs to chaperone you two." Bart guffaws and pulls out a chair between Cait and Thomas and takes a long pull of beer. Cait laughs nervously. Thomas looks down at his food, trying to decide if he wants to challenge Bart on his insulting innuendos or let them slide. He'll let them slide for now. He probably needs to get to know Bart better before he pops off at him.

"So, Tom. You got yourself a plum piece of real estate here. I can't believe my wife and her brother let it go so cheap. She must like you." Bart glares. Thomas feels challenged and pushed to the edge of his patience.

"This place was also left to me and my brother. I paid a fair price. What's your problem, Bart? Have I done something to offend you?" Thomas asks. "Are you trying to pick a fight?"

"Me? Hell no. Just joking around. Don't be so sensitive." Bart punches Thomas's arm a bit too hard and guzzles the rest of his beer. "You ready to go, sweetie?" Bart asks Cait. "We should give Tom some time to settle in, don't you think?"

"Sure. Of course. You must be tired, Thomas." Cait quickly packs up the remains of her lunch, and, without any eye contact, she and Bart, walk out the front door. From the patio, Thomas can hear Bart's booming, angry voice. Is he yelling at Cait? For what? She did nothing wrong. And why is Bart acting like this? Sure, he's a big, intimidating-looking guy, but he usually acts like a big teddy bear. Thomas has never seen him this angry and volatile and it's worrying him.

Thomas strides to the front door and steps out onto the stoop, making himself visible. Cait is in her car, and Bart is in her face, yelling. When Bart notices Thomas watching, he pulls back, waves, and walks casually to his own car. Thomas wonders if he should text Cait later to check in, but he's afraid it will cause more trouble for her.

The first thing Thomas does in his new home is get rid of the booze. He searches the entire condo. If anyone wants to drink in his home—and he is still debating that—they will have to bring it themselves. Beer in the refrigerator is too tempting. He needs more sober time before he will feel indifferent to a cold one. Andy already took their father's bottle of Talisker scotch for sentimental reasons. Thomas dumps the rest of the alcohol down the drain. Mission accomplished.

It has been a few days since he's arrived, and, instead of complete chaos, there is now controlled confusion. An improvement. Tonight, he is going to his first AA meeting in town at the church around the corner. He hasn't heard from Cait since she left his condo, but he hopes she will be there.

Thomas walks to the church and pokes his head in the side door, looking for a sign directing him to the meeting. He heads in the direction of voices. The door is open, and the pervasive aroma of coffee indicates he is in the right place. A man in his late fifties, wearing a flannel shirt over a well-worn Willy Nelson tee, approaches Thomas.

"Hello. I'm Sam. You here for the AA meeting?" He shakes Thomas's hand.

"Hi, Sam. Yes. Yes, I am. I'm Thomas."

"Welcome. Coffee is over there. Find a seat and we'll get started in a few minutes." Sam walks back to the group he was chatting with. Thomas gets a cup of coffee and picks a seat. It's interesting how people find their place in a circle. Close, but not too close. How it feels and what direction they face is important. Once people stake a claim, they usually go back to the same spot like they own it. Thomas has seen disagreements erupt at meetings when someone unknowingly takes a previously claimed chair. Thomas likes being near the door for a discreet escape, if necessary. He has been to enough AA meetings to know they are all different. The format is pretty much the same—it's the people that make the difference. If Thomas can click with them, he will feel comfortable staying. If not, he will find another meeting. He hopes Cait shows up. That would help him in the clicking department.

A few more people wander in. As Sam starts the meeting, Cait rushes in, breathless. Thomas hopes they will have a chance to talk. Several people state their first names and talk about their situations and challenges. When there is a pause, Thomas clears his throat and starts to speak.

"Hi. My name is Thomas. I'm an alcoholic." The group welcomes him. "I'm still not real comfortable saying that." Thomas clears his throat again. "I just moved here from Nashville. Been sober for about a year. A friend urged me to go to a meeting, years back." Thomas raises his eyebrows, glancing at Cait. "I'm sorry to say the whole concept just pissed me off. My comment was something along the lines of 'Fuck all you holier than thou AA assholes.'" Cait and quite a few others chuckle and nod yes. "In time I came around, and here I am. Thanks for listening."

When the meeting wraps up, Thomas runs after Cait, who is making a hasty getaway. He reaches for her elbow.

"Cait. Hold up. Can we talk?" Thomas asks. Cait looks at him with a mixture of affection and worry. "What's going on with Bart?"

Cait looks exhausted. "Tom, I have to go. I need to get home." Cait gently frees her arm from Thomas's grasp. He doesn't want to cause a scene, so he lets her go, following her and others out to the parking lot. When Cait gets to her car, Thomas tries again.

"Cait, something is going on. I'm worried about you. I've never seen Bart act like that before, and you look stressed to the max. If you need help, someone to talk to, please..." Thomas doesn't finish the sentence. Begging her to let him help sounds so needy.

"Thanks, Thomas. I don't know what's going on. A few months ago, Bart started to change. He has trouble remembering things, but if I remind him, he flies into a rage. You saw how paranoid he is. We never had trust issues until now. I don't know what's wrong with him, but something is. He won't see a doctor. I don't even know if a doctor is what he needs. Sometimes his anger is so out of control I get scared. He's like a different person." She sighs. "I have to get home. He knows I went to a meeting, and if I don't get back right away, he'll get agitated, and I can't face another fight. Promise we'll talk when I can."

"Okay. Let me know if I can help." Thomas stuffs his hands in his sweatshirt pocket and starts walking home. He watches Cait pull out of the parking lot and says a quick prayer that she will be okay. He's usually not a praying kind of guy. Maybe all the AA higher power stuff is rubbing off on him.

Over the next few weeks, Thomas goes to a few more meetings at the church, but Cait isn't there. He starts to recognize some of the regulars. Sam has a calm warmth that is appealing. Thomas asks him to be his sponsor, and Sam agrees. After the meeting, they go to Dunkin' for coffee and to get to know each other better. Turns out he's a retired professional guitar player with an extensive discography. Thomas is not the only musician hiding out in Niantic.

"Yeah, I worked with a lot of big names like the Allman's reunion tour, Derek Trucks, and Marshall Tucker. But the most fun I ever had was touring with Willy Nelson. Oh my god. I did that off and on for many years. The man never quits. He was always on the road. Course, back in the day weed was illegal, but we consumed mass quantities of the stuff anyway. It was my drug of choice. Got us in some hot water with the law from time to time. But it was a blast. At least I think it was. I was stoned a lot." Sam laughs.

"Wow, that sounds like a wild ride," Thomas says. "Just by coincidence, I'm a musician too. Mostly keyboards. I studied music in college and got a doctorate in music production. My mother was a Grammy winner, and I wanted to be just like her. I played in bands, produced music in L.A., and ended up in Nashville. Alcohol was a problem for me. Destroyed my marriage and wrecked my career. There was a lot of other stressful shit going on in my family too." Thomas shakes his head sadly, sips his coffee, and looks at Sam. "I thought alcohol helped me cope, but it only created more problems. I think if I had been sober, I might have been more successful at everything. But who knows." Thomas shrugs and rolls his eyes. "Sam, we should start a band."

Sam roars with laughter. 'I'm afraid my band days are long gone, but I wouldn't mind getting together to play some music with you. We could get a few guys together. It would be fun."

"Deal!" Thomas says.

Thomas misses playing music and is trying to figure out how to integrate it with his new life and sobriety. Talking with Sam stirred up memories of unrealized aspirations—and failures. His biggest regret is how he left things with his ex-wife, Lydia. It was a long time ago. They were in their twenties and both musicians. She played classical violin, and he was all rock. Thomas has never loved anyone as much as he loved Lydia. Now, as he works the AA Twelve Steps, he wants to find a way to make amends.

Thomas opens his laptop and searches for Lydia's contact information. It's been almost thirty years, so who knows if he can find her. Her maiden name, Brown, is so common it might be like finding a needle in a haystack. Then he searches for Lydia Brown Ogilvie. Bingo. He's surprised she kept his name. The address is in Florida, and there's a phone number.

"Hello?" a woman answers. She sounds the same as she did thirty years ago.

"Lydia?"

"Nope. Mom's at work. Can I take a message?"

"Uh...okay...would you tell her Thomas called? Please? I can give you my number."

"Dude, it's the twenty-first century. I have your number." Thomas hears a baby crying in the background. "Shit. I gotta go. I'll give Mom your message. What did you say your name was again?"

"Thomas. Okay. Thanks." Thomas disconnects, his heart pounding. He's never thought about Lydia having a child and possibly a grandchild. Maybe calling out of the blue was not such a good idea. Thomas opens the top drawer of his father's desk and finds paper and an envelope.

Dear Lydia,

I looked up your number and called a few minutes ago. I know it's been a long time and you have a life, so you might not want to hear from me. I don't want to cause any problems. I only want to apologize. I am deeply sorry I hurt you. I loved you more than I thought possible and I was a total asshole. My fault. I am so sorry.

I have been sober for over a year and attending AA meetings. I moved back home to Connecticut and am trying to be a better person. Second chances don't come often, and I need to grab this one. I know that getting sober is long overdue and it doesn't make everything okay, but I wish it did. Please tell me if there is anything I can do to make it up to you, even just a little. If you're willing, I'd like to talk with you. Please call me. If I don't hear from you, I will understand and not bother you again.

Sincerely, Thomas

Lydia weighs heavily on his mind. He recognizes his loss and has enormous regret. Thomas hopes the letter is the beginning of a conversation, but his expectations are low considering how they left things. He took her love for granted, drank too much, and cheated on her. When she threw him out of their apartment for the last time, he cursed at her and slammed the door. It's been a long time, and Lydia has moved on. He wants to make it up to her but wonders how to make amends. Obviously, he can't change what happened. He can apologize, but that doesn't seem like enough. What does he want? Redemption? Forgiveness? Another chance? Is he hoping she will be delighted he's finally sober? Or will she be angry? Is it too little, too late? All good questions with very few answers. Thomas walks to the mailbox, and, with only a millisecond of hesitation, he puts the envelope in the mail. Then he calls Sam.

"Thomas! How ya doing?"

"Well, I've been thinking."

"Uh oh." Sam chuckles. "Just kidding. Thinking is an important part of recovery."

"Do you have time to chat?"

"Of course. Go ahead."

Thomas briefly lays out his past with Lydia, how he impulsively called her, and all the questions he has about making amends.

"Okay, Thomas, so, first of all, apologies are not the same as making amends. But it's a hellova good start. You're right, she may not be as happy about your recovery as you are. Of course, you want her to forgive and let you off the hook. That's human. The question is, what happens if she doesn't? There's no telling how, or if, she'll respond. The questions you ask about your motivation are super important. Are you seeing a therapist?"

"God, no." The thought of sitting in a therapist's office makes Thomas squirm. "Isn't it enough to have a sponsor? Like you?"

"If that's all you can do, it has to be enough. But I get enormous support seeing a therapist familiar with addiction issues. It's not required, and everyone is different. Why people drink is complicated, Thomas. The more we know about ourselves, the stronger our recovery will be. Recovery isn't just about not drinkin'. Get what I mean?"

"Yeah. I get it. I'll think about it."

"Good. In the meantime, also think about what you could do for Lydia that might help make up for some of the damage."

"Okay. I will. Thanks, Sam."

Thomas disconnects and decides to walk on the beach. It always seemed to help Bess figure things out. Maybe it will help him too.

5

Home Sweet Home

It's culture shock coming to Niantic from L.A. via Nashville, but Thomas is adjusting to New England Yankee reserve. Cait is busy with Bart, so Thomas doesn't see her as much as he would like. Sam and Thomas get together to play music a few times a month. The rest of the time he putzes around the condo, unpacking and fixing the place up. His dad and Bess took good care of the condo, but it hasn't been updated in years. Plus, it isn't Thomas's style. He wants to make the place his own.

The dusty bedroom curtains came down days ago, so now there are only room-darkening shades on the windows. It's a better look for Thomas. No one would ever catch an old rocker with tie-back curtains in his "crib." Thomas smiles at the thought. The new black lacquer platform bed and matching nightstands he purchased are more his style. He will keep Bess's dresser, mainly because it makes him feel close to her. Sometimes he opens a drawer to touch the rough wood and imagine what she kept there. He misses her.

The old carpeting will get pulled up because it's beat to hell and aggravating his allergies. When he sees what is under the rug, he will be able to decide what to replace it with.

Thomas pulls on a pair of shorts and walks into the bathroom. It's odd seeing his reflection in the same mirror his father peered into for years. His beard is fuller than the stylish L.A. designer stubble he arrived with, and more like his dad's beard. Maybe he will keep it like that. He frowns at the strands of gray showing up in his shaggy, dark auburn hair. How can he be in his fifties and still feel like he is thirty? He's disappointed that he has accomplished so little of what he set out to do. Once, he was young, ambitious, and driven. He wanted everyone to know who he was. Getting a doctorate was no easy task. What good was it though? It didn't automatically bring him fame and fortune. It didn't prevent him from sabotaging his future with booze. Being sober is his biggest accomplishment to date. He will never be a twenty-something rock star again, but he hopes he can still do something with the years he has left.

He splashes water on his face. He'll think about that tomorrow. Right now, he needs coffee.

He slips on his 'Ohana beach sandals and puts twenty bucks in his pocket. He hasn't quite figured out how secure his neighborhood is, but it feels safe. This morning, he will leave the door unlocked while he walks to the Italian bakery on Main Street. He stuffs AirPods in his ears and selects a playlist of classic folk rock from his phone. Croce, James Taylor, Cat Stevens, and Willie Nelson put a spring in Thomas's step. When Willie Nelson starts singing "On the Road Again", a slow smile spreads across Thomas's face as he imagines Sam touring with the musical icon. He likes Sam.

On his way to Main Street, he remembers his dad taking him to the bakery when he was a kid. One year, a rare hurricane blew through. Power was out everywhere, but the bakery was one of the very few businesses with a generator. People could live without a lot of things, but morning coffee was not one of them. They were cranking out coffee and egg sandwiches for people clustered around the front door and lining up down the block. People in line compared notes about the hurricane. Standing shoulder-to-shoulder for coffee became a morning ritual and a way to get the latest news. It's a pleasant memory.

At six-thirty in the morning, Main Street has only a handful of locals going about their business. Sometimes Thomas gets the sense he is living on a Hallmark movie set. In a few hours, the director will yell "Action!" and the street will be jammed with tourists and beachgoers. Right now, it's quiet, with a slight breeze off the water. Thomas is happy he moved here. When he gets coffee, he will be even happier.

Inside the bakery, the aroma of coffee and baking bread welcomes him. An older gentleman is chatting with the counter person, holding a hot cup of coffee and a little bakery bag. He wears a tan work shirt with "Dan" embroidered over the pocket. Red suspenders hold up his baggy jeans. Thomas nods hello and, since he isn't in any hurry, gives the man space to finish his conversation.

"Hey. Sorry to hog the counter. Come on up and order."

Thomas steps up and orders a regular coffee and one of those terrific egg sandwiches he remembers.

"My name is Dan." The man puts his coffee down and reaches out his hand. "I'm a fixture next door at the auto supply shop. I come in here every day to chew the fat. You're not interrupting anything important."

"I'm Thomas Ogilvie. Just moved here from Nashville. Nice to meet you."

"Ogilvie? That name sounds familiar. You related to the clock shop guy?" Dan must be a Niantic lifer, because his father's shop closed years ago.

"Yup. That was my father. My stepmother, Bess Parker, passed away a few months ago, and I moved into their condo."

"I remember that. It was sad. Bess was a good one. We all hoped those two would get together sooner or later. Took them long enough. Welcome home, son!" Thomas hasn't been called son in ages. How old is this guy? "Glad to meet you. Stop in AutoZone anytime. I don't work much anymore, but I've been there so long I'm like a mascot. I'll make sure you get the hometown discount."

"Thanks. I'll do that." Thomas picks up his breakfast and decides to take it to the beach before the crowds show up. The walk is just long enough to get him huffing. The lush green park is calling to him as he goes through the tunnel under the railroad tracks and turns right. Thomas prefers the quiet of the park to the busy boardwalk. He walks through the empty playground and soon arrives at the benches on top of the bluff. The view of Long Island Sound is a perfect setting for breakfast. The egg sandwich is as good as he remembers. He takes his time sipping coffee, enjoying the quiet, deep in thought. Suddenly, he is nose-to-nose with a dog interested in his sandwich wrapper. A pink leash is attached to the dog, but no owner is at the other end. Breathless, a woman dashes up and grabs the leash.

"I am so, *so* sorry. Eleanor has a talent for getting away from me." The dog is probably twenty pounds soaking wet—and she *is* soaking wet. "Ellie, get down. Leave the poor man alone." The woman has a soft southern lilt in her voice. She pulls on the leash, and Ellie, having discovered the wrappers are empty of breakfast, jumps down and looks around for other trouble to get into.

"No problem. I like dogs." Thomas asks her if she wants to sit for a minute. Her cheeks are flushed, and she is breathing hard from running after Ellie. She is an attractive, artsy-looking woman, probably in her late forties. No wedding ring. Shoulder-length pale blond hair peaks out from under a big, floppy sunhat shading her eyes.

Thomas extends his hand, introducing himself.

"It's nice to meet you. My name is Sunshine. People call me Sunny." Sunny shakes his hand.

"That's an interesting name. Suits you."

"Yeah, well, my parents were hippies. What can I say? At least I'm not called Moon Unit."

Thomas laughs and nods.

"Oh, are you a Zappa fan? You seem to get my obscure reference."

"Well, no, but I'm a musician, so I pick up on a lot of musical references. Zappa's band, The Mothers of Invention, was unique and memorable."

"That's for sure. You have the look of a musician. I've been around enough of them to know. I lived a large part of my life in the music capital of the South. I would still be there, but my mother needs help, and I'm it. Only child." Sunny shrugs acceptance of her fate.

"I thought I detected a touch of the south in your accent. So, music capital—would that be Nashville?" Thomas cannot believe he is meeting a woman from Nashville on a Niantic bench.

"Sure is. Been there?" she asks.

"I just moved here from Nashville. I've lived all over but love Nashville."

"Whatever possessed you to leave?"

"Long story. My stepmother died, and her condo became available, so I took it. Let's just say I needed a change of scenery." Thomas sips his coffee. "What a coincidence! Unbelievable."

"It certainly is. I've met a kindred spirit! Now, when I mention The Country Boy Café, you'll be the only one to know what I'm talking about. It'll be our little secret." She smiles, "It is such a pleasure to meet you. Well, I've caught my breath. Thanks for sharing your bench. I will leave you in peace. Y'all have a great rest of your day." Sunny stands and takes off after Ellie, who is loose again. That was an interesting encounter. Thomas finishes his coffee and heads for home. Maybe he should get a dog.

Thomas moves furniture out of the bedroom, then pulls up a corner of the carpet. He's thrilled to see hardwood flooring. Jackpot. That motivates him to get the carpet up and out. He is sweating buckets as he surveys the room, realizing that if he is going to refinish the floor, he has to paint the walls first. He lugs the old carpet to the dumpster, holding his breath as he tosses it in.

The day flies by, and Thomas is satisfied with the work he's gotten done. He fills a tall glass with ice and sweet tea, then lands in Bess's recliner with paper and pen: *Number one, paint the room. Number two, get the floor refinished.* Then, since he is launching a job search, he needs to update his CV and have it ready. He looks good on paper. It's other stuff that could be a problem, like disorderly conduct. Maybe Sam will be a reference for him. He will approach production studios first. If that doesn't work out, he will contact colleges. He wouldn't mind teaching.

Thanks to his father and Bess, and, dare he say, Maura, his financial situation is secure if he is careful. But he will go stir crazy without something to do. At fifty-three, he still has lots of productive years ahead of him, and he needs a creative outlet for his mental health.

When the bedroom is finished, he evaluates the spare room, which he now calls "The Studio". He keeps his father's desk, library table, and bookcase. The full-size bed is shoved to the far corner, as far out of the way as possible. He would love to get rid of it to make more space in the room, but he can't. His brother made him promise he would have a place to stay when he visits. Unless he can find another arrangement, the bed stays.

Over the next couple of weeks, Thomas gives the room the full treatment. The refinished floor gleams, and the large area rug he picked up at Lowe's adds a nice touch. Thomas slides the library table into the big double closet. It's perfect for recording equipment, and the bi-fold doors close when he isn't using it. He needs an electrician to add an electrical circuit to the closet. This will be a sweet little home studio when it's finished. Guitars stand at attention next to amps. His new, fresh out of the box Yamaha Genos2 keyboard is set up by the windows. Thomas positions a new rolling chair at the desk. There is a stool for Sam and a Yamaha piano bench for Thomas. Sam is coming over to help him break the studio in.

"Knock knock," Sam announces through the screen door.

"Sam, come on in," Thomas calls out. He meets Sam as he comes inside, setting his guitar case down. They man-hug, thumping each other on the back.

"Okay. Let's see what you got." Thomas leads Sam to the spare room.

"Wow. You've been busy. Last time I was here, it looked like my grandmother's guest room." Sam laughs and explores the room, checking everything out.

"Yeah, well, it's getting there. If you've got ideas, I want to hear 'em."

"Great. I'm itching to play." Sam unzips the gig bag and pulls out a very well-loved Taylor acoustic guitar. What follows is several hours of music, stories, and laughter.

"Oh my god, Sam. It's fun playing with you. I've missed this so much."

"I agree. I hope your neighbors like music, 'cuz they're gonna be hearing a lot of it. We need a drummer and a bass player. I know a couple of guys that might be interested."

"I thought you said your band days were over," Thomas teases Sam.

"Yeah, well, that was before I remembered how much I love this. I only have a few restrictions. I *never* want to be a bar band again. That's a grind I do not miss. I am willing to play for fun and maybe for a few friends. Are you good with that? Or are you thinking of taking us on the road to open for The Rolling Stones?" Sam laughs hysterically. "Can you fucking believe those guys are still touring? Jagger must be eighty if he's a day."

"At least eighty. I'm good with all that. The last thing I want is a grind! And I'm steering clear of bars, at least for now. I just want to have some fun."

"Me too," agrees Sam.

Thomas's Second Chance

After Sam leaves, Thomas stands in the doorway of the studio and admires it. He puts on wireless headphones and sits at the keyboard. He pauses and, without thinking, the music from the rock opera he wrote for his Doctorate in Music Technology comes through his fingers, taking him back in time.

6

Thomas and Lydia, Past to Present

The keyboard becomes a time machine, propelling Thomas back thirty years to the University of Florida. He can almost smell the boggy earth around UF's Lake Alice, where alligators sunned themselves. Strains of UF's marching band drift across campus. Thomas's mouth waters, remembering the aroma of hot dogs being grilled on charcoal fires. Nothing ever tasted as good as dogs with the guys, washed down with beer. Lots of beer. No matter how many showers were taken, the tang of sweat hung in the humid air. And the heat. So much heat. Florida at its finest.

Thomas was finishing up a doctorate program, lugging his keyboard into the Baughman Center where his band was setting up. A small UF orchestra was joining them for the opening of a rock opera written, produced, and performed by Thomas.

The Baughman Center, a chapel steeped in nature, wasn't normally used for concerts, but Thomas begged and finally got permission. The soaring, clear glass windows and natural wood created a dramatic yet peaceful setting. After the performance, Thomas was going to be eligible for a doctorate and, hopefully, a faculty position at UF.

Thomas greeted his friends as they set up. Space was tight because of the orchestra, but they managed. Even though it was only a rehearsal, Thomas remembers being nervous.

"Hey, Tom. Did you bring Jack?" asked Kyle, the lead guitarist, as he plugged guitar pedals into the sound system.

"Are you kidding?" laughed Thomas. "I never leave home without him." He reached into his gig bag for the bottle of Jack Daniels Old No. 7 and passed it around. At the time, he didn't see that as a problem. It was simply part of the culture, and what rock musicians did to take the edge off.

Thomas's rock opera was a tongue-in-cheek comedy about being in the graduate program at UF. He didn't try to create something award-winning. He only wanted to have fun and complete the requirements so he could move on from school and make it big in the world. That was his plan.

At rehearsal, he noticed a barefoot girl—a violinist in the orchestra. Her long, dark, curly hair was free and wild. Her skin was the color of milk chocolate. She wore a black camisole with stylishly torn jeans that hugged a striking figure. But what made her stand out to Thomas was the all-business, unpretentious way she prepared to play. That was refreshing in the land of musical egos.

When the musicians were settled, Thomas stepped to the front of the stage. He indicated a few changes in the score and led the orchestra through their parts. Thomas smiles, remembering how good it sounded. The challenge was to coordinate his rock band with the classical musicians. The next night, they were going public to a sold-out crowd, so they had to get it right.

Thomas remembers how he thought his opera was a bit of Ben Folds clever storytelling, combined with the panache of The Who's rock opera, *Tommy*. It's embarrassing to recall how young and arrogant he was. He had no idea what hard lessons would come.

The rehearsal was chaotic at first, but after several attempts, they got the hang of it. When they got through the whole piece, start to finish, it was exhilarating, and they all whooped with joy. It was late when they finally wrapped up. Play always followed work in those days, and that night was no exception. The band was going to a bar to celebrate, and Thomas wanted that beautiful violinist to come along.

"Hey. Violin One, what'd ya think? Did you like it?" he asked, positive he had impressed her and would get a solid five-star review.

"It was good," she said, hardly looking at him.

"Just *good*?" Thomas was disappointed. "I put my heart and soul into it, and it was just *good*?"

"Yes. It was good. My name is Lydia, by the way. Please stop calling me Violin One."

"Hi, Lydia. I'm Thomas." He smiled his most disarming smile, thinking he was making progress.

"I know who you are, Thomas." Lydia carefully placed her violin in its case.

"Great. We're going to celebrate. Wanna join us?"

"What are we celebrating? Surviving rehearsal? Don't you think waiting until after the performance might be better?" Lydia snapped her case closed and finally looked at Thomas. She was so beautiful.

"There is never a 'what' or 'why' to celebrating. It's kind of a constant process." Thomas shrugged. "Please come? We won't be out late." He pulled out all the stops trying to charm Lydia into joining them. She was thoughtful and finally agreed to meet him at Fat's, a college hangout.

Thomas remembers how sparks started to fly. They ate pizza, drank beer, and talked non-stop until they were the last ones to leave. Walking through the parking lot, Thomas put his arm around her. It felt natural and good. That was when it dawned on him what *good* meant. Maybe not such a bad review, after all. When they got to her car, he turned Lydia around to face him.

"Thank you for coming tonight," Thomas said as he tucked strands of hair behind her ear. He moved in close, and there was a kiss. A profound kiss. A meaningful kiss. A kiss he had never experienced before. Electricity shot through his body, and he almost professed undying love in that moment. Lydia moved close to him, returning his kiss.

It was pure heaven. Thomas tried to talk her into going home with him, but she refused. Lydia gently moved away, saying she would see him tomorrow. She got in her car and drove away. Thomas remembers feeling like his feet weren't touching the ground.

Students hanging out listening to the rehearsal loved the rock opera, and raves spread throughout the campus. Because of the limited seating in the Baughman Center, the overflow crowd sat outside the building to hear the performance. *The Alligator* student news printed a glowing review, and the band got bookings all around Gainesville. Success was sweet. But what was even sweeter was the love that grew between Thomas and Lydia. Within months, they were living together. They planned to be married after Thomas got his degree. He knew Lydia was the one he had been waiting for his whole life.

Thomas and Lydia were married in the Baughman Center with friends and family in attendance. It was a simple affair followed by a picnic outside under tents and away from the alligators. Music was abundant, since this was a marriage of musicians. A string quartet comprised of Lydia's friends played classical music and Thomas's mother's pop originals. A jazz quartet filled in, and, later in the evening, Thomas's rocker friends revved up the party. By the time the reception wrapped up, Thomas was seriously drunk. The hardcore, tattoo-covered rockers thought nothing of it, but it was not what Lydia wanted or expected. Thomas tended to overindulge at times, but she'd never considered it a problem. They were young musicians and artists. Drinking and pot went with the territory. At least within reason. But this was their wedding day. Thomas stumbled around and finally passed out in the grass in front of the band. Lydia needed help getting him back to their apartment. She had prepared a romantic wedding night complete with a thoughtful gift and candlelight. Maybe romance was just a girl thing, but she was disappointed. Once they got Thomas in bed, he stayed unconscious. He didn't know Lydia watched him all night to make sure he was still breathing.

The next morning, they were scheduled to meet their families for brunch at a local spot specializing in real southern cooking, including their famous apple fritters. Thomas's hangover left him in no condition for fritters. Lydia called her parents and Thomas's father, James, to make excuses. You know, newlyweds need some alone time. Everyone understood and made plans to meet them later for a tour of the campus and dinner. Lydia gave Thomas a pass because it was their wedding, and who wouldn't celebrate that? Thomas feels ashamed remembering that it was the first of many times Lydia made excuses for him.

Thomas finishes playing the opera and pulls off his headphones. The room is dark. He stretches out on the guest bed, feeling sick to his stomach. The memories are relentless, coming at him in a torrent, pulling him under.

One month after the wedding, Thomas was called to meet with the head of the undergraduate music department. This was it—the break he was waiting for and counting on. A teaching gig would give the newlyweds a steady income and enable Thomas to pursue other musical interests. Thomas shaved, showered, and dressed in clothes he hoped looked professorial, minus elbow patches. Lydia kissed him goodbye and wished him luck.

When he arrived at Dean Frank's office, Thomas sat on the edge of a chair, thinking about all the things he wanted to do as an instructor at UF. The dean came out of his office and approached Thomas, shaking his hand. Thomas remembers the conversation like it was yesterday.

"Come on in, will you? Want water or coffee?"

"No, thanks. I'm good."

The dean pointed to a chair, and Thomas took a seat. "So, Mr. Ogilvie, I have reviewed your academic record. You were a solid student, and the piece you wrote and produced was excellent. You have a wicked sense of humor, which could come in handy teaching under-grads. As a teaching assistant, the students gave you great evals."

"Thanks, Dean Frank. Being at UF has been a wonderful experi-ence."

"I wanted to meet with you about your desire to join our faculty." *Here it comes,* thought Thomas. *My dream comes true.*

"Sadly, after much discussion, we have decided that you are not a good fit for our department. Perhaps you could reapply in a few years, and we could reconsider that decision."

"What?" This wasn't how the conversation was supposed to go. "Why? I don't understand."

"I will be honest with you. We all like you and believe you are a talented composer and producer. But we're concerned about your abil-ity to do the job because of your drinking. And yes, I know this is col-lege and there is a lot of partying going on. I'm not so old that I don't remember my college days. But we need someone who will show up, meet deadlines, and represent the school in a positive light. I'm so sorry."

Thomas felt flattened by an ice-cold tidal wave. He was speechless at the time, and even now, in his darkened guest room, the rejection still hurts.

"Thomas, I wish you and your new bride all the best." Dean Frank stood, and Thomas knew the meeting was over. Thomas shook the dean's hand and thanked him, although he wasn't sure for what. He silently and politely walked out of the office. Once he was out of the building, he remembers letting his rage erupt.

"FUUUUUUCK!" he screamed into the parking area, causing sev-eral people to turn and look.

"What are you looking at? Fuck off." He got in his car and peeled out of the parking lot. He was in shock. His plans were in ruins.

"Lydi? Where are you?" Thomas yelled, slamming the door and throwing his backpack on the floor with a loud thud.

"I'm right here. What happened?"

"The dean says I have a drinking problem, and they can't hire me. Really? Me? Sure, I like to party, but it's never interfered with my work. *Ever!*"Thomas stomped to the refrigerator and pulled out a beer, twisting it open and taking a long pull.

Lydia watched him pace the apartment, draining one beer and reaching for another. He was upset, and she could understand him wanting a drink, but in the back of her mind, she was concerned. What if the dean was right?

From there, Thomas completely blew up his life. He took his band on the road. It was the last hope to save his dream. Lydia stayed home, playing violin with the Gainesville Orchestra. The orchestra didn't pay much, and any money Thomas made went back into the band's tour. He believed that once they made it big, everything would be okay. Lydia got a part-time job teaching violin to make ends meet.

When Thomas was on the road, his marriage was not a primary concern. At first, he stayed in touch with Lydia. But, as time went on, exhausting travel, alcohol, and women, pushed Lydia into the background.

The band worked hard and got a recording contract with a small but respected label. They opened for big names in large venues. Thomas remembers how exciting it was. They embraced a rock and roll lifestyle of excess and disruption.

The band never hit the big time. Their album was a dud, and the band's reckless behavior was so unpredictable that no one wanted to work with them. The music industry is forgiving of bad boy behavior if you are filling arenas and selling millions of albums. Thomas's band wasn't. Playing bars in Texas for beers and very little cash was not the career they'd imagined. After a heated disagreement about the future, they each went their separate ways. The only thing Thomas could do was go home.

Lydia was still living in their little apartment in Gainesville. She'd had only sporadic contact with Thomas for a couple of years. Half the time, Lydia didn't know if he was alive or dead. One day, Thomas walked through their apartment door unannounced, like nothing had happened.

"What are you doing here?" Lydia asked him, hands on her hips. Thomas wasn't sure how to answer that question. It seemed obvious to him. He wanted Lydia to open her arms and give him a soft place to land. "How dare you waltz in here like nothing's happened. Who do you think you are? Some big deal rock star I'll chase after like a groupie? I haven't heard from you in months. I didn't know if you were alive," Lydia yelled.

"Lydi, you have no idea how hard it was being on the road, trying to get a goddamned break. I was doing it for us," Thomas shot back.

"For *us*? Really? You're a drunk and a cheat, Thomas. You don't give a shit about me or our marriage. What you did was for *you*, not *us*." Lydia stomped into the bedroom and slammed the door. Thomas could hear her crying. He slumped down in a chair, head in his hands. Thomas couldn't argue with her. What she said was true enough.

"Lydi? I'm sorry. Can we talk, please?" Thomas knocked softly on the bedroom door. He opened the door a crack. "Can I come in?"

Lydia relented and let him into the bedroom. They had a frank discussion that brought Thomas to his knees. He promised Lydia he would stop drinking and get a job. Whatever Lydia wanted from him he would do. He begged her to take him back. Lydia wanted to believe this time would be different. They stretched out on the bed and held each other. Thomas kissed her on her forehead, the salty tears on her cheek, and, finally, her soft, sweet lips. He made love to Lydia like it was the very first time. Lydia had a different experience. Being with Thomas didn't feel the same because she couldn't stop thinking about the women he'd slept with on the road. She hoped with everything in her heart that this time would be different. It wasn't.

He tried. Working as a session musician and teaching kids piano didn't pay much, but it was only temporary. Thomas still held on to his dream of making it big. He stopped drinking—for a while, anyway. The problem was that he kept falling off the wagon. Lydia would pick him up and bring him home. There would be more promises and more lapses. Lydia finally threw him out for the last time and divorced him. It was the darkest point in his life.

Thomas sits on the edge of the bed in the darkened studio, overcome with shame. In the past, this would be the time to drink himself into oblivion. Instead, he calls Sam.

"Sam, is there a counselor you recommend? I think I'm ready."

Sam tells him he will be right over. Thomas waits motionless in the dark until he hears Sam open the front door.

Thomas walks toward Sam. Sam opens his arms and holds Thomas. The compassion Sam offers cracks Thomas wide open. Sam has been where Thomas is and knows what to say—nothing. There are no words from him that will absolve Thomas of his sins. Thomas sinks into the couch by the fireplace. Sam keeps an eye on him as he turns on a light and gets bottles of water from the kitchen.

They are silent until Sam gently asks if Thomas wants to talk about it. Thomas *does* want to talk about it. All of it. He starts by telling Sam what happened with Lydia. He picks up his phone and opens photos.

"That's Lydia," he tells Sam, showing him a wedding picture. Thomas explains how he'd started playing the music from his doctoral project, and the memories overwhelmed him. "Of course, I remember everything that happened, but I've never felt it like that before. It doubled me over."

"Remember when I said recovery isn't just about not drinking? I'm betting you would've gotten drunk when those memories surfaced in the past. Am I right?"

"Yeah. Something like that."

"This time, you felt the feelings and called me. That takes courage. Courage and the determination to deal with the actions of your past. Have you heard from Lydia?"

"Nope. I'd be surprised if I do."

"Ya never know. Maybe she wants to chew you out one last time. Whatever you hope for with Lydia, I hope you get it."

"Yeah, me too. I'm tired of screwing up my life over and over. Lydia is only half of it. Considering everything that led up to Lydia leaving me, it's no wonder I'm an alcoholic. What time is it?"

"It's about eight-thirty. I have lots of time and good ears for listening. Take as much time as you need."

They sit in front of the fireplace where Bess and his father did so much of their talking. Thomas can almost feel their presence. He tells Sam the story of his life, weaving the pieces together, starting with his mother's Grammy Award and her death. Thomas chokes back angry tears as he tells Sam how Maura lied and used him to punish his father. Thomas wasn't sure who he would be now if the truth hadn't come out.

"You were a kid. You couldn't have known, Thomas. Hell, most adults wouldn't have known."

"Yeah. Maybe. After I found out who Maura was, I was confused. My life felt like a Jenga game. She pulled the last block out, and it crashed down around me. Everything I believed—the story I told about my life—was smoke in the wind. There was nothing left to hold me up. I felt so betrayed. I didn't know if I could trust anyone. Shit, I didn't even trust myself. Finding out about Maura was like losing my mother all over again."

"I'm so sorry."

"Yeah, me too. A lot of shit went down and when I confronted Maura, I saw who she really was."

"It sounds like your father did the best he could. So did you, Thomas." Sam comments.

"Yeah. I guess. I wasted so much time blaming him and pushing him away. Loving people and losing them, one way or another, was too much to bear. So, I pushed everyone away. Everyone except my drinking buddies." Thomas shakes his head.

"I understand."

"When I was young, Maura and I would drink together. I thought she was so cool and that my father was a jerk. When I look back, I realize she taught me how to use alcohol to numb my pain. The *pain* that she was inflicting."

"She sounds like a real piece of work."

"Oh yeah. And then some."

"I'm so sorry, Thomas."

"Yeah, looking back, I can understand why I drank."

"Yup, me too."

"Not that I'm making an excuse. I was still the one who popped all the tops."

"Yup. Also, true."

"In time, my father and I forgave each other, but I didn't see him much. I was bouncing around playing music and never letting anyone get too close. I wasn't going to make that mistake again. But somehow, Bess got through to me in her gentle way. She didn't judge or lecture. She accepted me as the mess I was, and gradually, I let her in. After my father died, I started to look at my life. What was I doing? I went to a few AA meetings but didn't take it seriously until about a year ago. Then Bess died, and my heart broke again. Thankfully, her daughter Cait was there to keep me from shutting down. I decided it was time for me to grow up. I moved back here. The rest you know."

"I wondered what your connection to Cait was. I'm glad she was there for you. And I'm here for you, too! You've just doubled your support."

"Thanks, Sam. I've never told that whole story to anyone before. I feel like I've offloaded a heavy burden." Thomas sighs.

"You have. Telling your story is important." Sam pulls a business card from his shirt pocket and hands it to Thomas. "Per your request. He's a good therapist. He understands trauma and addiction."

Thomas looks at the card. The thought of getting into therapy scares him. But after tonight, Thomas sees no other way.

"Thanks. I'll give him a call. Don't you have any nice lady therapists in your contacts?"

"Ha! So you can charm her into going easy on ya? No way." Sam laughs. "How ya doing? Better?"

"Yeah. I think so. Thanks for coming over, Sam."

"Hey, no problem. That's what bandmates are for." Sam stands to leave. "You got this, man."

"I hope so." Thomas says, almost like a prayer.

7

The Old Guys' Jam

fter that cathartic evening and a few therapy sessions, Thomas
feels like he is heading in the right direction. To make things
even better, Sam finds a couple of guys interested in playing
music with them. When Thomas runs into Sunny at the grocery store,
he asks if she would like to come over and hang out while they jam. It's
their first get-together, so Thomas warns Sunny not to expect too much.

"I would be delighted. When should I show up?"

"The guys are coming over around four. But come whenever you
like."

"Early bird special, eh? You old guys can't stay up past your curfew?" she chides.

"Very funny! I'm more concerned about my neighbor's curfew. I
imagine very few of them would like a rock concert at midnight."

"Invite 'em over. That should take care of any complaints." Sunny
smiles and walks off, waving as she clears the end cap display and gets
in an express checkout line.

When Thomas gets home, he loads beverages in the refrigerator
and piles the snacks on the dining room table. It's called bachelor party
planning. Martha Stewart would be horrified. Then he gets busy moving the living room furniture to create space for the session. The little
studio is too small for a band. Amps on wheels and his keyboard roll

out and plug into strategically located power strips. The final setup will wait for Sam and his friends to arrive. Drums will be set up first, and the other musicians will work around them. It will be interesting to see if his neighbors are music fans or if they call the cops. Maybe Sunny is right about asking them over. He hasn't formally met all of them yet. It would be a good opportunity to introduce himself before he annoys the hell out of them. Thomas slips on his sandals and knocks on the few doors around his condo, introducing himself and giving everyone a heads up about band practice. He invites them over, assuring them the music will wrap up early. He is hopeful they can pull this off if they keep sound levels reasonable and Rage Against the Machine off the setlist. Since this is turning into a party, he gives Cait a call.

"Cait, a few guys are coming over to play music. Want to join us? Bring Bart. It will be fun."

"Okay. I would love it. I'll see how Bart's feeling. I may come alone and leave early."

"We may all leave early. We're starting around four to keep the neighbors happy, and we're going to end early to avoid disturbing the peace. I don't want to aggravate the home owners association."

"Good plan. Sure. See you in a bit."

Sam arrives with a couple of guys in tow. Jim is a tall bass player with intense blue eyes. A Fedora hat is pulled down to his eyebrows, and his bushy beard gives him a ZZ Top kind of vibe. Perry is a drummer with bulging, tattoo-covered biceps. After introductions, they get busy setting up.

They set up Perry's drums in the corner away from walls shared with neighbors, and Jim plugs in next to him. Thomas's keyboard is on the opposite side of the room, facing the two of them. Sam plugs into his amp and settles himself on a stool. Tuning and volume adjustments are like a homing signal for interested bystanders outside. Just as they finish setting up, Sunny and her dog, Eleanor, arrive.

"Yoohoo. Am I in the right place for the concert?" Sunny calls out in her soft, southern drawl. Eleanor, loose again, jumps into Thomas's lap, probably because he smells like food, or maybe because that dog just likes him. Hearing the voice, Sam spins around and sees Sunny.

"Holy shit! Sunny Skize, is that you?"

"Sam! Lordy, how long has it been?" The two old friends embrace in an emotional hug that starts Eleanor hysterically barking. So much for being low-key and subdued. Of course, expecting any of this production to be quiet was probably a bridge too far.

"It's been years. Probably since we did that last Willie tour together. Jeez, was it that long ago? How have you been? You look great. How did you end up here?" Sam asks.

"Here in Niantic? Or here in this room?" Sunny prompts.

"Well...both? Either? I'm just so surprised and happy to see you."

"I ran into Thomas at the park and then again at the grocery store. He invited me. Why did I leave my beloved Nashville? Mom. She needs me. But I had no idea you were here, Sam. We have a lot of catching up to do."

"You bet we do!"

"Before you two stroll too far down memory lane, we got some music to play," says Perry to the beat of his kick drum.

"Hey, smart ass, do you know who this is? This is the great Sunny Skize, the best damn vocalist in all the south, maybe the country. This lady could sing the classified ads and has shared the mic with all the greats. Boys, we are in luck! We got ourselves a real talent here. Please sing for us, Sunny."

Perry punctuates Sam's soliloquy with a drum roll.

"I only came to listen to y'all, but you twisted my arm, Sam. I'll do it for old time's sake." Sunny points to Thomas's acoustic-electric guitar with a raised brow and tilt of her head, asking permission to play it. Thomas smiles and graciously hands her the guitar. She checks the tuning while Thomas adjusts the volume.

Just as Cait and Bart arrive, Sunny launches into a rendition of Dolly Parton's "Jolene", one of the most heart-wrenching songs ever written. It sounds so good that people walking through the front parking lot stop to see if Dolly is visiting. When she finishes, the small crowd around the front door applauds.

"One more song and then I will get out of your way. This is for my new friend Thomas from Tennessee."

"My Tennessee Mountain Home" isn't one of Dolly's more famous tunes, but Thomas thinks it should be, and Sunny's version gives him chills. When she finishes, a few more curious neighbors, like moths to a flame, gather by the open front door. Some poke their heads in to see what's going on. Some slip inside, finding a spot to stand in the crowded room. Thomas smiles wide at Sunny and hugs her, whispering in her ear how lucky he is that Ellie brought them together.

No one notices Cait looking dismayed. Sunny is news to her. Is she going to have to share Thomas with this musical out-of-towner? Cait isn't sure she likes that idea, but she has no grounds to object. She glances at Bart, chatting with a couple of bystanders and enjoying the music. After Thomas has his moment with Sunny, he greets Cait and Bart, showing them to folding chairs and inviting them to help themselves to refreshments. The boys are discussing what's next in the lineup, and Sam insists on staying in the country vibe with Willie Nelson's "On the Road Again". Sam has a great voice, keeping the semi-chaotic accompaniment in check.

Thomas's turn. He plays the intro to Phil Collins's hit "Against All Odds", his new theme song. The rest of the guys join in. Perry has perfect timing with the drum roll. When Thomas gets ready to belt out the bridge, Sunny moves in close, harmonizing with Thomas. Their eyes meet, and everyone in the room feels the jolt of chemistry. As he ramps up the lyrics, they read each other perfectly. This song means a lot to Thomas, and Sunny makes it even better. There is a lot of talent in Thomas's living room, and the crowd outside is growing. Thomas hopes that isn't a problem for his neighbors, but he's having too much fun to worry about it. At least the cops haven't been called.

Someone outside, right on cue, yells, "'Free Bird'!"

Sam cracks up. "There's one in every crowd. Ya think we can pull it off, guys?"

"We can try. Doesn't everybody know 'Free Bird'?" asks Perry, counting them in with his sticks. After a couple of false starts, they find their groove.

Thomas starts with a very recognizable piano intro. Jim comes in with the bass line, and Perry keeps the beat going. The crowd outside goes wild. Sam has played lead guitar on this so many times that he could do it in his sleep. Thomas sings the lead, smiling at Sunny. Cait can't quite interpret that look, and she wonders if it's an invitation to something other than music. Cait hates the jealous feeling she is having. She has no right to it, yet here it is.

Sam jumps in to harmonize with Thomas, and Sunny adds her voice to the mix. It's rough, but fun. Sam's electric guitar is smoking, and the musicians are riffing off each other. When they finally exhaust themselves, they end with a dramatic final chord. Ta-da! They hoot and holler along with the crowd. Thomas and Sunny hug joyously. The crowd outside is ecstatic, cheering and waving cell phone lights. Music moves people—and that is exactly why Thomas loves it.

"You sound pretty good for a bunch of old farts. Are you sure you've never played together before? Seriously, you guys could sell tickets," Sunny suggests.

"You *guys?* You're a part of the old farts now, Sunny! You can't wiggle out. No way, no how," Sam tells her.

Thomas looks around for Cait, but she must have left. He will call her later. They go outside to chat with the neighbors and soak up the applause. Playing music tonight has made Thomas happier than drinking ever did. He hopes they didn't cause too much of a disturbance at the condo complex, because he wants to do this again sometime soon.

Show's over. Thomas shuts the front door, and they order pizza delivery. There is an easy camaraderie between them that doesn't always happen between people who have just met. Long after the pizza is consumed, they hang around talking and telling stories. Thomas has found his people. By chance, there are no small-town musicians in this group. Each one has experienced a tough business that can chew a person up. They have tasted fame and failure, which makes the joy of finding each other sweet. Around ten o'clock, they pack up and help Thomas reclaim his living room. Everyone agrees they must do this again. There is a bond forming between them that can't be denied. They will play together again. That is certain.

Thomas carries the pizza boxes and soda cans to the recycling bin, wondering if it is too late to call Cait. He locks the front door and walks out the back French doors to the beach. It is a gorgeous, clear night filled with stars. He kicks off his sandals and wades into the cool, salty water, deciding to make the call. If she doesn't answer, he'll leave a message.

"Hey, Thomas." After Cait's surprise episode of irrational jealousy, she is happy to hear from him.

"Cait, is everything okay? I didn't get to say goodbye to you."

"Yes, all okay. As okay as things are now, anyway. Unfortunately, Bart got a bad headache, and 'Free Bird' did him in. Loud sounds bother him lately. We snuck out. Thank you for including us, though. It was amazing. I can't believe you have never played together before."

"What can I say? We're trained professionals." Thomas chuckles. "I'm sorry you had to leave. We would love to do it again. We're letting the dust settle, hoping there aren't any complaints or HOA repercussions. We intended to keep it quiet and low-key, but it's music. It has a life of its own, and once it gets going, there is always 'Free Bird'. What can I say?"

"Well, we thought it was wonderful. If the neighbors gets grumpy, you'll figure it out. So, who is Sunny? I don't remember seeing her before."

"She's someone I met randomly at the park. Her dog got loose and wanted my breakfast sandwich. I had no idea she was a famous vocalist. Sam is the one who knows her from his band days. She's quite a find."

"Yeah. She is. Quite a find," Cait agrees with less enthusiasm than Thomas. "Listen, I'm glad you called. I want to talk to you about something."

"Go ahead. Shoot."

"It's too much to get into tonight. Can you come over tomorrow?"

"Sure thing. I can come over after lunch. See you then." It will be nice to see Cait. He has missed her.

8

The Fight

Thomas has been in Cait's house many times, but this time it feels different. There is a heaviness hanging in the air, and the house is quiet as a tomb. Cait has dark circles under her eyes.

"You okay, Cait? How's Bart doing? I haven't seen you at any meetings lately."

"Yeah, I've kinda had my hands full here with Bart and the foundation. Thanks for coming over."

"No problem. The foundation?"

"Yes, remember? Metta Support, the foundation your father and my mother started with Maura's money?" Cait walks to the dining room, and Thomas follows her. The table is covered with papers and stacks of file folders.

"Yeah, it's coming back to me now. I was never a part of that."

"True. Would you like to be?" Cait asks.

"What do you mean? What are you asking me?"

"Sit. Can I get you anything? I have some cold Pellegrino."

"Yeah, sure. That sounds good." Thomas pulls out a dining room chair and sits.

Cait comes back from the kitchen with the sparkling water. She sits heavily, gently moving a stack of folders aside like she is fending off a landslide.

"Thomas, I need help." Long pause. Thomas can see Cait fighting back emotion. "After my mother died, someone had to run the foundation. None of us wanted to let it go, but you were in Nashville, Andy couldn't do it from Montana, and Matt had a full plate. So, guess what? Good old dependable Cait takes it on. It isn't hard, but with what's going on with Bart and the kids, I can't do it all. I need help." Cait repeats softly, "I need help."

"The kids? Are they okay?"

"Oh yeah. Thank God. It's just the usual stuff—jobs and activities and needing Mema to help out."

"That's a relief. Do you want me to stand in for you with the youngsters?"

"That's a sweet offer, but no. They are the highlight of my responsibilities. Although you are welcome to tag along anytime. You know how they love you." Cait smiles. "I *am* offering you a job. I need someone to run the foundation. That would be you, if you are willing."

"Oh."

"Hear me through before you say anything. Okay?"

"Okay." Thomas leans back in his chair, prepared to listen with an open mind. He loves Cait and would do anything to help her, but a job running the foundation? He's not sure about that.

"I want to keep it going and in the family. The work Metta does is so important for so many. I don't know what's going on with Bart, but lately, living with him has been hard. Can you understand my situation? Look at this." Cait waves her hand over the raft of paper. "It hangs over me every single day. I am so far behind, I will never catch up." Cait exhales like she has been holding her breath for a long time.

"You want me to run the whole foundation? Cait, I don't know how to do that." Thomas is sitting up straight now.

"Listen! Please? I will do it *with* you if you can take on the bulk of the work. I'll show you everything. It's managing the money, reviewing grant proposals, approving providers, and screening clients. The foundation will pay you. It isn't anything you can't learn. Trust me."

"Oh, well, I'm glad that's all it is," Thomas says sarcastically. "Seriously, I don't know the first thing about it. I'm a musician!" He needs a job, but isn't sure this is how he wants to spend his time. Although when he thinks about it, this was his father's baby. All the shit Maura put his dad through was turned into an amazing program. Doing this might be another way to make amends.

"I know. But I will show you everything. If you can play 'Free Bird', you can handle this. We can do it together. It will help me a lot. Will you think about it? Please?" He wouldn't mind working closely with Cait. She has always been there for him, and he wants to be there for her. "I know this is a big ask, Thomas."

"I want to help you, Cait. What if I say, maybe? I'm willing to give it a try. If it's too much, or I suck at it, promise me you will find someone else?"

"I promise! Cross my heart." Cait is so relieved that she throws her arms around Thomas. "Thank you so much. You have no idea how much I appreciate this." Thomas struggles to stand with Cait's arms wrapped around his neck, tears in her eyes.

"What the absolute *fuck*?" Bart roars into the dining room, sweeping carefully organized papers off the table onto the floor. "I leave the house for one minute and come back to see you two fooling around." Thomas and Cait jump apart like they have been scalded.

"Bart, honey, calm down." Cait looks afraid. "Nothing is going on here. I asked Thomas to come over so I could get some help with the foundation."

"Don't tell me to calm down. Fuck the foundation," Bart yells in Cait's face. "I'm sick of hearing about it." Thomas's instinct is to protect Cait. He gently intervenes, hoping to calm Bart down.

Bart shifts his anger to Thomas. "Fuck you, Tom. Cait is *my* wife. Get out of my house." Bart pushes Thomas hard. Thomas doesn't want to fight, but Bart comes after him again, and Thomas has no choice but to defend himself. Cait is screaming for them to stop. Bart is a big guy, which puts Thomas at a disadvantage. He tries to talk to

Bart, but nothing he says diffuses the situation. Thomas takes a couple of hard gut punches. He's had enough, so he pushes Bart with everything he has. Bart loses his balance, trips over a dining room chair, and falls back, hitting his head hard on the floor. Dazed, he lies on the floor not moving, eyes open.

Cait panics. Kneeling next to Bart, she begs him to speak to her. A small pool of blood spreads out from behind his head. Thomas grabs a kitchen towel, handing it to Cait to help stop the bleeding. "I'm calling 911, Cait."

She nods in agreement and holds Bart's hand, looking terrified. Bart blinks and moans softly.

"Don't move, honey. Help is on the way." Cait reassures her husband.

There is nothing to do but wait for the ambulance. Sirens scream up the street and then are silent. Thomas opens the door and lets the police and EMTs inside. The cops pull Thomas aside, asking him what happened. Thomas tells them about the fight. Cait refuses to let go of Bart's hand until the EMTs get him on the gurney and wheel him to the ambulance. Thomas wants to comfort her, but the cops are clear that they need to stay away from each other. They question Cait, who tells them the same story Thomas did.

"Officer, it was an accident. I'm not filing charges. Something is very wrong with my husband for him to act that way. Please, just let us get to the hospital. Please."

The police may need to question them again later, but for now, they are free to go to the hospital.

"Cait, I'll drive. Get whatever you need and let's go."

Cait gets her purse, keys, and cell phone, and they rush out of the house.

Thomas parks his Wrangler in the emergency room lot, and they run through the automatic doors. The woman at the check-in desk asks if she can help. Cait says that her husband, Bart Bradford, was just brought in by ambulance. She needs to see him.

"Please have a seat. I will let them know you're here."

Cait doesn't sit. She paces nervously.

"Mrs. Bradford?"

"Yes." Cait rushes to the desk.

"You can't go back there right now. Mr. Bradford is being examined. As soon as they know what's going on, they will let you go back to see your husband. He's going to be okay. Your husband is in good hands."

Cait walks back over to Thomas and finally sits down.

"She said everything is going to be okay. What the hell does she know? I bet she tells everyone that." Cait hugs her body tight in an attempt to hold herself together. Thomas says nothing because he knows that at a time like this, Cait doesn't want platitudes. She wants her husband to be okay. Anything short of that will not cut it.

While they wait, Thomas is trying to catch his breath, wincing. There's a sharp pain where Bart punched him, and he wonders if he bruised a rib. No biggie. He's been in plenty of bar fights, so this is nothing to worry about, but he wishes he had some Tylenol. He shifts in his seat and feels a sharp pain like being stabbed with a knife. Cait notices him flinch.

"What's going on with you?" Cait gestures toward Thomas's side.

"It's nothing. I'm fine, just sore."

"Thomas we are in the goddamn emergency room. Get checked out! I can't be worrying about both of you." Cait is on the ragged edge, so to reassure her, he agrees. In the exam room, Cait waits for the doctor with Thomas.

Thomas leaps in the air when the PA presses on his left side. The area is turning a lovely shade of purple. The PA tells him he probably has a contusion, but they will take an X-ray to be on the safe side. While he is waiting for that, Cait meets with Bart's doctor. He lets her know they are doing a CT scan to see if he has a concussion or a fracture. She can see him when he is back from radiology. They will let her know the results as soon as they have them.

72

Thomas is right about the bruised ribs. Nothing to do but let them heal. They give him a bolus of Tylenol, advising him to see his primary care doctor. He heads back to the waiting room and will stay until he knows Cait and Bart are okay. An hour later, Cait sits heavily next to him. Her face is blotchy from crying.

"What's going on? You've been crying. Is Bart...is he..." Thomas can't bring himself to complete the sentence.

"They think he has a brain tumor, Thomas. They sent him for an MRI. I hope it's something benign that they can remove, and Bart will be back to his normal annoying self." Cait takes Thomas's hand, squeezing it tight. "Thank you for staying."

"Of course. I wasn't going to leave you here until I knew you were okay. That is not the news I expected, but it would explain a lot. You know—the headaches, and irritability."

"Exactly," agrees Cait. The doctor approaches Cait with an update.

"Mrs. Bradford, right now your husband is sedated. We have admitted him. It looks like Bart has an aggressive brain cancer called glioblastoma. We will know more after we operate. I called in the best neurosurgeon Yale has, and we scheduled him for surgery first thing in the morning." The doctor looks grim.

"He'll be okay, though? You can treat it, right? Can I see him?" Cait asks.

"We'll know more tomorrow. You can see him, although he's pretty sleepy. Then I suggest you go home and get some rest. Tomorrow will be a long day."

The diagnosis is serious stuff. We go blindly through our days believing all is well, and then *bam*, everything changes in a second.

"I'll go see Bart. Then I need to go home and get some things and come back. I don't care what the doctor says, I'm staying with Bart. Will you wait for me and drive me home?"

"Yes, of course. I'll be right here."

Cait waits with Bart until they get him moved to a room. After Bart is settled, Cait and Thomas, walk to his Jeep. Cait is in shock. If the doctor is right, Bart might have a year to live, maybe less. After surgery, there will be radiation and chemo. It sounds like an awful last year of life. If he chooses not to go through with treatment, this disease will overtake him with the speed of a wildfire. Cait slumps in the passenger seat.

"Now everything makes sense. But, I never expected anything like this."

Thomas reaches over the console and holds Cait's hand. "I'm here for you guys. Whatever you need. And don't worry, I'll take over the foundation. I wish I could do more."

"Thank you, Tom. If it weren't for the fight, we wouldn't have known about this until something terrible happened. Although I can't think of anything more terrible. So many cancers are survivable. Not glioblastoma. I'm praying they're wrong and it's something he can recover from." They pull into her driveway and get out of the car. Inside, Thomas wraps his arms around Cait. She buries her face into his shoulder and sobs.

"I'm so scared, Tom."

"I can't imagine how tough this is for you. I would be scared too." He pulls away gently. "You get your things together, and I'll make us eggs. You need something in your stomach."

Thomas goes to the kitchen. Cait appreciates Thomas's care but hardly tastes the omelet he whips up. All she can think about is getting back to the hospital. She has to call her kids and tell them about their father. They will want to be there. Her mind spins with worry and lists of things to do.

"Thomas, here is a key to the house. If I need anything, I'll text you, okay?"

"Yeah, sure. What else can I do?"

"Please take all that damn paperwork home with you. See if you can make sense of it. Right now, my family is all I can think about."

"Absolutely. I got it. Don't worry about a thing. I'll take care of it." Thomas picks up Cait's bag. "Ready?"

"Yeah. Thanks."

Thomas puts her things in the back seat. He hugs Cait and asks her to keep him posted. He watches her pull out of the driveway.

As promised, Thomas carefully puts all the folders and loose papers in the two banker's boxes stacked next to the dining room table. He scrubs blood off the floor so Cait won't have to see it when she gets back. Then he cleans up the kitchen and looks around to see if there is anything else he can do before picking up the boxes and taking them to his Jeep. All that activity is not making his bruised ribs happy. Time for more Tylenol.

Early the next morning, Thomas stops at Dunkin', then drives straight to the hospital. Cait is happy to see him, especially carrying coffee. Bart is still in surgery and not expected to be in recovery for several more hours. Thomas chats with Cait about the foundation, telling her he brought all the files home, and they are now spread out all over his dining room table. She laughs at that.

"Welcome to my world," she says. "Did it make any sense to you?"

"Well, no, not yet. But I'll figure it out. How are the kids doing?"

"I talked to them last night. They are on the way and will be here soon. Tom, thank you so much for being here with me. It means a lot."

"You're welcome. That's what friends are for, yeah? Just tell me what you need and I'm on it."

Time crawls by. People come in and out of the waiting area. The big board on the wall lets everyone know who is in surgery and when they're moved to recovery. Bart has been in the operating room for over three hours. Matt, Cait's brother, arrives, and they walk to the cafeteria for something to do. They get sandwiches and drinks, and, as they sit nibbling, Cait fills Matt in on what they know so far.

"Don't Google glioblastoma, Cait. It will worry you to death. What does Google know, anyway? Bart's a tough dude," Matt says.

Cait looks at her brother and smiles sadly. She knows the truth about this situation, and it isn't good, but she appreciates her brother's positive thoughts. She's eager to get back to the waiting area, even though she knows the OR will text her with updates. Matt waits with Cait. Thomas takes off and promises to be back later to see how Bart is doing. Two hours later, Bart is moved to recovery.

The surgeon tells Cait that she removed as much of the tumor as possible. Preliminary pathology confirms it is glioblastoma. Bart is on anti-seizure medication and steroids to keep brain swelling to a minimum. When Thomas returns to the hospital, Sadie and Barrett, Cait's kids, are with Matt in the intensive care waiting area. Cait is with Bart.

"How's he doing? Any news?" Thomas asks.

"He's pretty good. Considering. He got through the surgery okay. Now we wait and see. He'll be in the hospital for a few days if recovery goes well."

"Then he goes home?"

Matt shrugs and shakes his head. "We don't know. It depends on how he does. He may go to rehab."

Thomas isn't sure what to wish for. The future depends on what Bart and Cait decide with the information they have. If radiation and chemo don't offer a cure, they will have to decide if a few more months of life, under those conditions, will be worth it. It is certain that whatever decision is made, Bart will probably not survive the year.

9

Sunny Skize

Thomas brings chicken from the grill into the kitchen as the front door opens. A white fluffy ball of fur runs inside, finds Thomas, skids to a stop, and drops a favorite toy at his feet. Ellie's entire back end is in motion at the sight of Thomas. He squats down, scratching behind her ears, and offers her a morsel of chicken.

"Don't tell your mom!" he admonishes the pup. Ellie barks agreement.

Sunny is next to walk through the door, carrying a basket of vegetables from her mother's garden, now tended by Sunny. The huge garden produces a bumper crop of cucumbers, tomatoes, peppers, squash, and assorted greens. There is so much produce that they give it away on a small table in front of the house on Route 1. Sunny lands the heavy basket on the kitchen counter before hugging Thomas and kissing his cheek.

"You are spoiling my dog. No wonder she likes you."

"I know. You're next." Thomas grins.

The scent of freshly picked basil and tomatoes on the vine accompanies Sunny into the kitchen. Her flirtatious cards are on the table along with the produce. The next move is up to him. Thomas is very aware of Sunny's interest in him. He likes her, but he isn't sure he's ready for a complicated relationship. Not that Sunny is a complication.

Hell no. She is delightful. He likes that she is always barefoot and the way her eyes crinkle when she laughs. The kitschy way she dresses in vintage bell-bottoms, tank tops, and flowing scarves works for her. But what really gets his blood pumping is her voice. When they sang Janice Joplin's "Piece of My Heart" together at the last jam session, Thomas suspected that, as much as he might resist, he's a goner. She wanted to show the old guys that she could rock with the best of them, and man, did she. Nope, Sunny is just fine. It's Thomas who's complicated. He knows from experience that getting into something is a lot easier than getting out of it. He doesn't want to start something that would hurt later.

"Grilled chicken?" Sunny asks as she carries fresh salad ingredients to the sink.

"Yep. You good with that?" Thomas asks.

"Honey, I like anything you want to cook." She has a few other thoughts about what they could cook up together, but, for now, keeps them to herself. Sunny washes the vegetables, thinking about Thomas. His talent is impressive, as is his sobriety. She gives him a lot of credit for that. She looks over at him as she puts the salad together. Even in his fifties, he still rocks jeans and a T-shirt with the best of them. His shaggy, auburn hair has just enough gray to testify to a life fully lived. Sunglasses, pushed up on top of his head, keep the hair out of his eyes while he cooks. In her opinion, there is nothing sexier than hair she can run her fingers through.

"What are you looking at?" Thomas teases.

"Your cute butt, of course," Sunny tells him with a laugh. "Do we know each other well enough for me to say that?"

"We do now, apparently." Thomas tosses a dish towel at her, not at all offended. Sunny fills two tall glasses with ice, adds a slice of lime, and pours tonic water up to the top.

"Cheers!" she says. Sunny has no issues with alcohol, but she respects Thomas's rule about not having it in his house.

The tail end of summer makes for cool, comfortable nights. Eating outside will be nice. They fill plates and take them out to the patio. Candlelight and a hint of fog on the water provide a romantic setting as the first few stars make themselves visible. Ellie sits patiently next to Thomas. She knows a soft touch when she sees one. Sunny walks her fingers across the table and touches Thomas's fingertips. He accepts the gesture, covering her hand with his.

"You want to walk on the beach?" he asks. "It's a beautiful night."

"It surely is. A beach walk sounds delightful. I'll get the leash, and Ellie can come too."

They hold hands and talk about Nashville, the band, Sam, and family. When they reach the foot of the bluff, they sit on the rocks.

"How's Bart doing?" Sunny asks.

"Not great. He's home from rehab and struggles to walk and talk, but manages. He's a little better every day. He started radiation treatments last week. The family has pulled together, and I'm doing what I can to help." Thomas exhales.

"You're a good man. Cait must be happy to have her family around."

"Yes, she is. I didn't appreciate my family when I was young, but I get it now." Thomas stands. "Ready?" He takes Sunny's hand as she lifts herself gracefully off the rock.

"Ready for what?" she flirts. Sunny looks up at him, and Thomas kisses her. "Thomas Ogilvie. Are you starting something?"

"I don't know. Am I?" Thomas throws a driftwood stick, and Ellie takes off after it. The sand is still warm on their bare feet. They run after Ellie as the pup dips in and out of the salty water, barking at the waves chasing her. Thomas is happy living in Niantic. The condo was the right move for him. Life is peaceful compared with the drama of his past. Being with this woman is a benefit he hadn't anticipated. Thomas takes Sunny's hand as they walk.

"I would not object to that," Sunny says.

"Object to what? Starting something?"

"Yes. You surprise me in many ways."

"How?" Thomas has a hard time imagining Sunny being surprised by anything. She seems so self-assured.

"Well, you're a rocker. What was that song? 'I'm a little bit country and you're a little bit rock and roll'? That's us."

"Ha! I remember that song. I think it was Donny and Marie Osmond, wasn't it?" Thomas laughs and shakes his head. "Haven't thought of that one in a very long time. Now it's stuck in my head, thank you very much. I think next time we jam we should pull that one out just to see the look on Sam's face." Sunny and Thomas laugh. Thomas drapes his arm over Sunny's shoulders as they stroll under the stars.

"You're different from the other rockers I knew. You aren't strutting around in tight pants, with groupies hanging all over ya like ornaments on a Christmas tree," Sunny observes.

"That's because I'm old. You shoulda seen me in my prime. Lots of groupies hung off this Christmas tree, as you so colorfully put it. I'll show you some of our promo shots. I might still have some old videos somewhere. Fortunately, I am not that kid anymore. Some memories make me cringe."

"Oh my god. I have got to see those videos! Be still, my heart." Sunny thinks for a moment. "But seriously, Thomas, for a hard rocker, you have a soft side."

"Oh shit, don't let anyone know that! My reputation will be ruined."

"Stop it!" Sunny gives him a gentle shove. "Stop deflecting. Accept the compliment. You've lived a lot of life. Good and bad. I wonder if you're ready for something...I don't know...something different?"

"Are you speaking musically?" Thomas asks, continuing to play dumb.

"I'm speaking of love." Sunny puts her arm around Thomas's waist and bumps her hip against him. "Sobriety changes things, don't ya think?"

"Oh, you're talking about *love!*" Thomas laughs. "Sorry. I'm teasing you. Sobriety does change a lot. Honestly, Sunny, I wish I knew what I was ready for. I've been alone for a long time. Sometimes I miss having a lovely woman, such as yourself, in my life. Can I be blunt?"

"Sure. Shoot."

"I don't think I'm relationship material. I'm not stupid. I see you flirting, and you so tempt me. But...it's complicated."

"Complicated? How so?" Sunny tilts her head, questioning.

"When I was in high school, we had a band called The Rabble Rousers. We thought we were the coolest thing on two wheels. We played up the bad boy rocker image—smoking, drinking, and getting away with whatever we could. My brother Andy was the golden child: smart and successful. I went out of my way to be different. *Way* out of my way." Thomas shakes his head sadly. "Thinking back, man, my father had his hands full. The band got popular and played in local dives. Our parents chaperoned because we were all underage."

"Sounds like normal teenage stuff to me." Sunny shrugs. "Keep going."

"One night, a woman took my hand and pulled me into the ladies' room. She locked the door and let's just say she opened up a whole world of pleasure. She was probably only twenty-five, but she seemed really old to me at the time. From there, I got as much as I could, as often as possible, with little regard for anyone. That is not something I'm proud of." Thomas pauses, waiting for Sunny's reaction.

Sunny shrugged. "That's life for a testosterone driven young male. Don't be too hard on yourself."

"Thanks for the vote of confidence." Thomas picks up a stone and skips it across the water.

"Then, when I met Lydia in college, I fell hard for her. That had never happened before. We moved in together right away and got married within the year."

"Interesting. What happened?"

"I fucked it up. Royally. The UF faculty didn't hire me, so I went on the road with my band. Becoming famous would show 'em. Drinking helped me forget what a failure I was. A couple of years later, the band broke up, so I went home to Lydia. I can't believe she took me back after the way I treated her. I stopped drinking and tried to be a good husband. We stayed together until she had to accept that I was not going to change. She deserved better and threw me out. I went downhill from there. It's a miracle I'm still alive. Cait was the one who tried to talk sense into me. She took me to an AA meeting about twenty years ago, but I thought it was a joke. It's not, by the way. What about you? What's your story?"

"I was married. A couple of times. Divorced the first one. We were both too young. I have a daughter, Celeste, from that marriage, and I wouldn't trade her for the world. She's brilliant. Not in the music business, thank God. Married and has a couple of kids that I adore. They live in Idaho, so I don't get to see 'em much. My second marriage was a shit show. He played mandolin in the Grand Ole Opry. I'd call it passionately dysfunctional. We were off again and on again more times than I could count."

"You divorced him?" asks Thomas.

"No." Sunny looks off down the beach, remembering. "He was killed in a terrible accident. A bunch of Opry guys were in a van heading to a gig when they went off the road. There were four guys. They all survived except for Jeff. I don't know if that accident saved us from a life of suffering or not. Depends on how you look at it. We would probably still be lovin' and fightin' if he had lived. Seems we couldn't stay away from each other." Sunny sighs. "Sorry. I didn't mean to throw a wet blanket on this beautiful evening." Sunny picks up a shell and puts it in her pocket.

"What about Sam? Were you two an item?"

"Oh yeah, but it was nothin'. You know how it is. It's lonely on the road, and things happen. It's delightful to reconnect, but there is nothing between us now except fond memories."

Thomas stops walking and turns Sunny around to face him, hands on her shoulders.

"If we do start something, Sunny, I want us to be clear about it from the beginning."

"Okay. I get that. Right now, it's a relief to talk about this. I've been flirtin' with you since Ellie jumped in your lap. Dogs know things. Of all the people in the park, she picked you. Singing with you at that first jam session took my breath away. I have been dropping hints ever since. Like you, I'm old enough to know the difference between lust and love. Lust is like a big ole slice of chocolate cake. It's delicious, but ya need more than that to survive. Love takes time to grow." She dips her chin and coyly looks up at Thomas. "Right now, I'm craving chocolate cake. I've been on a diet for too long."

"I hear ya, woman! Me too."

"If we're negotiating here, tell me what else we need to be clear about. Fill me in," Sunny asks.

"Good question." Thomas pauses to collect his thoughts. "I want you to know that I care about you. I've had enough hookups. That's not what I want. Beyond that, I'm not sure. If you're looking for a happily ever after, I'm not sure I'm that guy."

"I can live with that. Just so you know, if we start something, I want no bullshit. We are grown-ass adults, Thomas. If we like each other and want to spend time together, in bed or out, why shouldn't we? Not that I'm trying to seduce you. Well, maybe I am. Just a little." Sunny smiles seductively, raising her eyebrows. "I want us to be upfront about what we are doing. Casual is fine as long as we agree on it. If it turns into more, put it on the table. Deal?" They stand at the shoreline, saltwater licking their toes.

"Deal. There is way too much talking going on here." Thomas holds Sunny's face gently in his hands, kissing her like he has wanted to since they first met. Thomas slides his hands over her shoulders, down her arms, and pulls her against him.

"My word, Mr. Ogilvie, you are taking my breath away. Can we go home, please, before we are arrested for indecent exposure?"

"It's dark, who would know?"

"You suggesting skinny dipping? If you are, I'm game." Before Thomas can answer, Sunny strips off her jeans and pulls her tank top up over her head. "Well, Ogilvie, you coming or not?" Thomas strips, and together they splash into the dark water under a canopy of stars.

"It's freezing. Whose idea was this?" Thomas shivers.

"Mine!" Sunny laughs and splashes Thomas. They move out deeper until the water comes up to their chins.

"Come here, woman, and warm me up." Sunny shivers as Thomas pulls her close and kisses her salty lips. "You're as cold as I am. Let's go home." They wade out of the water, pick up their clothes, and run to the condo, naked and laughing.

"Thomas, you make me feel like a teenager again. I hope I don't catch my death from that dip."

Thomas wraps her in a beach towel and grabs another towel for himself. They curl up on the couch in front of the fireplace, sipping hot tea. After a few sips, Thomas takes Sunny's mug out of her hands and places it on the coffee table. He pulls her close, kissing her neck.

"I can't wait any longer," he whispers in her ear. "Come with me, I know another way to warm up." Thomas takes Sunny's hand and walks her to the bedroom. Standing next to the bed, Sunny boldly tugs Thomas's towel away from his hips before letting her towel drop to the floor. He slowly runs his hands over her body. Sunny closes her eyes and moans deep in her throat. Thomas lifts Sunny, laying her on his bed. Their lovemaking is intense, leaving them breathless.

There is sand everywhere, on the rug and between the sheets, but they don't care. Sunny is a petite thing, a bit over five feet with a slight build. She fits nicely against his body, tucked in under his arm. Her head rests on his chest, and she listens to his heart, wondering what it will tell her.

Suddenly, Ellie jumps up on the bed and starts barking. Sunny sits up. "Thomas, I have to get home. Shit. I can't leave Mama alone all night. If anything happens to her, I will never forgive myself." Sunny leaps out of bed, scrambling to find her clothes. Thomas watches her with a warm feeling in his chest. He doesn't know where this is going or how it will end, but for now, it's just what he needs.

Sunny dresses and comes back to the bedroom to kiss Thomas goodbye. "Don't get up. I'll lock the door and see you tomorrow when I come by to pick up equipment for the jam session. I'll text you. Come on, Ellie, let's check on Mama." She cradles the dog under her arm and starts to walk away, stops, and turns to Thomas.

"Thank you for tonight. It was scrumptious." She offers him a chef's kiss and leaves. Thomas rolls over, smiles, and pulls the sandy sheet around himself.

10

Shaking the Foundation

The foundation files are organized in neat stacks on Thomas's dining room table. He has become familiar with most of it. The legal jargon is as foreign to him as music theory would be to an attorney. He forces himself to stay with it until it makes a little sense or gives him a headache, whichever comes first. He likes reading about the work the foundation is doing. It's impressive how many people have been helped. His dad was a good man, and Thomas is grateful to know that after their many difficult years. He promised Cait he would take the foundation off her shoulders, and he is doing his best. The more time he spends with the piles of statements and documents, the clearer the big picture becomes; they need help. Finding and delegating to the right people may be his most worthwhile contribution. Cait is coming over so they can work on it. Fingers crossed she will like his plan. Thomas makes a pot of coffee and gets in the shower. As he is toweling off, he hears Cait at the front door.

"Tom?" She is one of only a few people to call him Tom, and he likes it.

"Come on in," he calls out. "I just got out of the shower. Coffee is ready. Help yourself."

Thomas lifts his jeans off the bedroom chair, watching sand sift out of the damp, rolled-up cuffs. After shaking them out, he pulls them on and selects a clean T-shirt from the laundry basket by the dresser.

"Cait. It is so good to see you." Thomas hugs her. Cait holds on to him for a long time, and Thomas inhales the familiar scent of her shampoo. She is his safe harbor. Cait sighs and finally lets him go, kicking off her shoes.

"Thanks, Tom. That hug and French roast are just what I need."

Thomas pours himself a mug of hot coffee, noticing last night's dishes in the sink. "Give me a minute, Cait. Be right there." He quickly slips the plates and glasses into the dishwasher and rinses the sink. He needs to get better at housekeeping. He joins Cait on the couch in front of the fireplace.

Cait dusts off the couch cushion. "What's with all the sand, Tom? Did you have an indoor beach party last night?"

"Oh, just an evening swim. I haven't had a chance to vacuum it up yet." *Or do the laundry,* Thomas thinks, remembering the sandy sheets.

"Well, that sounds nice. Give me a call next time. I would love to join you." Thomas smiles but says nothing. "I'm really glad you bought this place."

"Me too, Cait. And I'm glad we could get together today. Sam asked about you because you haven't been to a meeting in a while. I hope you're okay with me telling him about Bart."

"I've known Sam for a long time, you can tell him anything."

"Speaking of Bart, who's with him today?"

"Sadie. She's taking him to the radiation treatment and then hanging out. Bart doesn't need a babysitter—yet—but with time being short, we want to be with him as much as possible. His speech is improving. It frustrated him to no end when he couldn't express himself. He's still unsteady walking, but he stubbornly refuses to use a walker."

"What's the latest report? Any good news?"

"I wish. He has five more weeks of radiation and chemotherapy. His mood is pretty good, mostly, but there are bad days. How could there not be? We all know there is no cure. After this treatment cycle, we wait and see how he does. He can't drive or do much on his own, which is hard for an independent guy to accept. The treatment is wearing him out. At some point, he'll decide enough is enough. Then we'll call hospice. I'm preparing myself for that day." Thomas cradles Cait's hands in his.

"Your father used to hold my mother's hands just like that. It's very comforting." Cait smiles.

"I am so sorry all of this is happening, Cait. I wish there was more that could be done. Please don't hesitate to ask me for anything. Promise?"

"I promise. Helping with the foundation is enough for now. It's been a relief not to stare at those damn folders every day."

"Good. I hope that I can further relieve you of foundation worries. I've looked at everything and have some ideas." Thomas picks up their coffee mugs and leads Cait to the table. "Cait, I don't have to tell you that Metta Support has been neglected. I think after our parents set it up, they let it run itself. That was fine then, but now we need to take a more active approach. Are you aware of how the investments have grown? There are millions of dollars in the fund now. And that was without paying much attention to it." Thomas opens a folder containing financial statements and shows Cait. "I'm no investment expert, and I think we could use one, or at least more active involvement with the one we have. That is...hold on...I can find it..." Thomas searches through papers. "Bank of America. When was the last time anyone reviewed this account?"

"I have no idea. I assumed it was fine." Cait looks through the statements. "There is a lot of money here."

"Oh yeah. That's why I think my plan will work."

"You have a plan?"

"I do." Thomas is excited to tell her his ideas. There is a space in town that they can rent for an office. Then he proposes they hire an administrator to manage daily affairs. "You know, pay the bills, answer phones, set up appointments. That kind of stuff. If it's okay with everyone, I will oversee the daily decision-making. For a price, of course. A man has to live! We'll figure that out later. That means you, Matt, and Andy will only have to handle big decisions when they come up. Once we get everything going, I may have other suggestions, like opening a center. What do you think?" Thomas is on the edge of his chair, waiting for Cait's response.

"A center? But Tom, we want to keep this in the family. Remember?"

"Absolutely. It will stay in the family. You, me, Matt, and Andy will remain trustees, with all decision-making power. But we'll have help from people who know more than we do about running a foundation. Having a center means people know where to go for help. It would keep everything in one centralized location. But that is for the future. For now, having an office means we no longer have all this stuff piled on the table dogging us."

"Well, it would be a relief to have an office and help. That's for sure. Tell me about the office. Can we go see it?"

"You'll be so surprised, Cait. We can see it today after Sunny picks up the stuff for the jam session. I can't wait to see the look on your face. I have a theory that when things easily fall into place, they're meant to be. This is *so* meant to be."

"That's kind of cryptic. Can't you tell me anything about it?"

"I want you to be surprised, so no spoilers. It's on Main Street and has been empty for a little while. We can do any remodeling we want. I'm thinking it might make sense to buy the building, but one step at a time."

They pour over the files, shoulder to shoulder, happily planning the future, when the front door opens.

"Sugar, you still have a whole beach-load of sand on the floor here. Keeping it as a souvenir, or what?" Sunny stops short seeing Cait at the table. "I'm so sorry. I didn't mean to barge in here like a house afire, disruptin' your business."

Thomas stands and welcomes Sunny with a quick kiss. "No problem. Cait, you remember Sunny?"

Cait nods that she does, indeed, remember Sunny. Once again, that uncomfortable, possessive feeling surfaces in Cait. She tries to be friendly, but her smile is forced. She and Thomas were having such a good time together—she hates that the "country girl" has intruded and spoiled the moment. Cait stands.

"You two have things to do." Cait's tone is acerbic. "I'll just get out of your way." Thomas would have to be unconscious not to sense the climate change from tropical to glacial.

"Cait, please stay. I want to show you the office, remember?" Thomas implores, trying to figure out what the problem is. Sunny senses the cool reception and is confused about why.

"Don't let me interrupt. You two carry on. I just came to pick up equipment for the jam session later." Sunny heads to the studio. Cait observes how Sunny makes herself at home in Thomas's condo. Apparently, she has spent time here. *Damn it, this place was my mother's. That woman can't just sashay in here like she owns it,* Cait says to herself. But that's not true. The condo belongs to Thomas now, and Cait has no say in what he does.

Thomas follows Sunny into the studio, handing her the guitar and gig bag filled with cords.

"Hey?" Sunny wraps her fingers around Thomas's arm. "What's going on?" she whispers. "I feel like I crashed a party."

Thomas shrugs. "I don't know, but I feel it too. I'll talk to her later."

"Okay. Hey, again." Thomas looks up from the amp he is pushing across the room, and Sunny kisses him. "I couldn't resist." Thomas smiles and kisses her back. "We'd better get going. I still have lots to get done with Cait."

90

"Yes, I'm sure you do." Sunny raises an eyebrow and gives Thomas a side-eye. She has no desire to get pulled into a drama and hopes whatever is going on gets sorted out. Thomas wheels the amp out through the living room and helps Sunny load everything into her Prius.

"I can bring the rest of the stuff. What time are we starting?" Thomas asks.

"I told Sam around five. I got the garage cleaned up, and it should be a great space to practice. No close neighbors, but lots of room in the driveway in case we attract a crowd. My mother is excited to hear the band. I think it will be good for her. She hasn't been doing well lately."

"Jeez, I'm sorry to hear that. Find out what her favorite song is. We'll play it."

"She would love that."

Thomas finishes getting everything in the back of the Prius, and under the shade of the hatchback, he kisses Sunny. "I'll see you later."

"You bet ya will." Sunny laughs.

Cait watches them chatting in the parking lot with a sinking feeling in her stomach that makes no rational sense. It's easy to see something growing between Thomas and Sunny. They have every right to that. Cait should be encouraging Thomas. But that is the last thing she wants to do. Instead, she wants to ban Sunny from the condo and send her packing back to Kentucky, or wherever the heck she's from. Cait stares blankly at the bank statement she is tightly gripping. *What's going on? She loves her husband—and God knows he needs her now—but she's also jealous, and that doesn't make sense. Sure, she and Thomas are close, but they've always been completely appropriate with each other.* Maybe she's jealous that Thomas can canoodle while she has to be the adult in the room. Maybe. But Cait doesn't think so. If she were to be painfully honest with herself, she's attracted to Thomas, which is confusing. Admitting that, even if only to herself, makes her feel guilty. Cait is lucky to have Bart and the kids. Maybe she is attracted to that bad boy rocker image Thomas has going on. It's probably nothing. Yet, she can't deny feeling bereft as she watches Thomas kiss Sunny before he comes back inside.

"Okay, where were we?" Thomas asks.

Cait scowls.

"What's wrong, Cait?"

"I'm annoyed at the interruption. There are a lot of things I would rather be doing today. Can we focus, please?" Cait snaps.

"Sure." Thomas is confused. He's getting that caught-between-two-women vibe that he hates. Sam said relationships are complicated, and he wasn't kidding. "Cait?" Thomas carefully moves papers aside and reaches for Cait's hand. She snatches it away.

"What's going on? Are you mad at me? Is it about Sunny? Help me here." One thing Thomas has learned is to ask questions.

"I'm tired, I have a lot going on, and I just want to get this crap sorted out, okay? That's why I came here today. Remember?"

"Okay. If you say so." Thomas pauses to figure out which direction to go in. He decides to stay with the business for now. "Well, if you agree with my plan, we can move that along. Are you sure that's all that's going on?"

"Thomas!" Cait barks. "Give it a rest, okay? God. Your plan is fine, let's just get it done." Cait knows she is being prickly, and she hates that. "Can we see the office now?"

"Yeah. Sure. Let's go." Thomas wishes she would tell him what's upsetting her. He knows damn well it isn't about being tired. She was fine until Sunny arrived. There has to be a connection. He's been around enough women and isn't stupid. They take Thomas's Wrangler to the rental space, pulling up in front of the building after a short and very quiet ride.

"This is it." Thomas looks at Cait for her reaction.

"Wait. Isn't this where your father's clock shop used to be?" Cait's mood suddenly lifts, and Thomas grins.

"Yup. It's amazing that it's available. Timing is perfect. Fate. Full circle and all that stuff. I put a deposit on it, but we can get out of it if we have to." Thomas climbs out of the Jeep and stands at the door waiting for Cait. He unlocks it, and they walk back in time. Cait covers her mouth, holding back emotion. Thomas puts his arm around her shoulders.

"Hey. What's going on here? Are those happy tears or something else?" Thomas asks gently.

"I don't know what they are, Tom. My emotions are all over the place. I'm sorry I snapped at you. Walking through the door, I pictured my mother being here with your father, in this very place. Now here we are, helping each other, just like they did. I swear I can feel them watching us. It's like they planned this."

Cait reaches into her pocket for a tissue as they explore the empty space. She runs her hand over the rough brick wall where James anchored shelves for clocks. The back room still has the antique walnut cabinet where James stored supplies. Thomas opens all the drawers, feeling into the back corners for anything left behind.

"I feel something." Thomas bends over, peering into the dark drawer. "It looks like a photograph is stuck in a crack." He works it free and shows it to Cait.

"It's them! Our parents when they got married." Cait's eyes are wide as she looks at Thomas. "It's a sign, Tom! They *are* here. We need to buy this place. I don't want to ever let it go."

"I agree. Finding the picture clinches that idea. I'll get on it right away. You know what else I'm thinking?" Thomas asks.

"I have no idea, but I'm all ears."

"Let's put that old library table back in the front window. We can put the anniversary clock on it. Dad had it in the window every day he was here. Seems right to continue that tradition. Then, we frame this picture and put that there too, along with a plaque honoring my father and your mother. What do you think?"

"Yes! Yes! Yes! That's perfect," Cait says, bouncing up and down, clutching the picture to her chest. "This is the first good thing that's happened to me in a long time. See? I knew you could figure this out.

Thank you. You're brilliant! I love you." Cait throws her arms around Thomas's neck and kisses him squarely on the mouth. The words *I love you* hang in the air like a helium balloon. The sweetness of their lips touching so unexpectedly freezes the moment until Cait turns away.

"I'm sorry, Tom. I got carried away. Please forgive me." Cait covers her face with her hands. She now knows for sure that something is going on with her. If the kiss was totally innocent, she would not feel so guilty.

"Nothing to forgive, Cait. No problem. We're just excited," Thomas says, suspecting that is not the whole truth. The kiss surprised both of them. Thomas felt a charge of electricity run through him like the first time he kissed Lydia. They fumble nervously, looking away, desperately seeking something else to focus on.

"Those windows really need washing. My gosh, look at the time. I have to get back and relieve Sadie," Cait says, desperate to make an exit.

"Yeah. You go relieve Sadie. I'll get this real estate deal going," Thomas suggests as he locks the door. Cait jumps out of the Jeep as soon as they get to the condo parking lot.

"Thanks, Tom. You've been a big help. Keep me posted." Then she's gone.

11

Thanksgiving

New England's explosion of colorful leaves is on the winter side of its peak. The aroma of pumpkin spice and mulled cider fills the air. The Halloween costume parade on Niantic's Main Street, the first one since the foundation office opened, finds Thomas handing out treats. He has a lot to be thankful for this holiday season and wants to get everyone together for Thanksgiving. Cait loves the idea and offers her house. Matt is on board. Thomas calls Andy in Montana to invite him. Cait fills the kids in on the plan. A full house gives them something fun to look forward to.

Buying the old clock shop building was easy. Thomas and Cait worked hard renovating the office space. Everything was scrubbed clean, the bathroom updated, and the floors refinished. Area rugs, comfy furniture, and office equipment completed the space.

Thomas organized files in cherry cabinets that he picked up at a thrift shop. Amy, the admin he hired, is working out beautifully. She's young, but has organizational chops. She was an admin at Pfizer and left to have a baby. This job is perfect for her. Fewer hours, less stress, and she can bring baby Cally when she needs to. Thomas hasn't spent much time with babies, but he's been enjoying this little one. When Amy ducks out to run errands, he picks Cally up and walks her around the office, showing her things and telling her stories.

Working in an office is something Thomas never imagined for himself. But *this* office, doing *this* job, suits him. Sometimes he leans back in his chair, closes his eyes, and swears he smells 3-IN-ONE oil, the scent he associates with his father's shop. He and Sunny are in a comfortable rhythm. They see each other a few times a week, plus band get-togethers. She can't leave her mother overnight, so they never wake up together, but Thomas is okay with that. Thomas likes Sunny and appreciates the gentle, low-demand relationship. Bleu, Sunny's mother, is eighty-five years old and mentally sharp, but health issues are slowing her down. Thomas likes hearing her stories about adventures at Woodstock and living in Haight-Ashbury, the hippie enclave in San Francisco. Bleu was a hippie before hippies were a thing. Having lost three parents, Thomas is sensitive to the pain of losing a mother at any age. Cait and Sunny want one more Christmas with the people they love.

The kisses are electric. Thomas's hands explore Cait's soft skin, and he is overwhelmed by a surge of desire. Cait whispers his name. Thomas's heart pounds. Their naked bodies press against each other. Thomas inhales sharply and opens his eyes. He stretches out his arm, sliding his hand over the cool and empty bed. It's three in the morning. Even though it's a dream, he feels like he's betraying a trust. Ever since Cait impulsively kissed Thomas in the old clock shop, he has had this recurring dream. As much as he tries, and as much as he likes Sunny, he cannot get that kiss out of his mind.

Sunny's arrival in his life was a complete surprise. She's attractive and fun, and singing together is pure magic. They have a lot of chemistry musically and in the bedroom. But that one kiss from Cait sent him reeling. He rolls over in the dark and tells himself that he's lucky to be with Sunny. Pining for Cait while Bart is dying is unacceptable.

Sleep evades Thomas. Finally, around four in the morning, he gets out of bed and starts a pot of coffee. Outside the French doors, the beach is dusted with early November snow. He carries a Nashville mug of coffee through the dark condo to the studio. He settles himself at the keyboard, hands poised on the keys, eyes closed, waiting. A melody starts far off, like someone humming a block away. Gradually, the melody comes closer, until he hears it clearly. His fingers move, and the music flows. Words find their places in the melody. When the music in his head stops, he pulls off the headphones and gets more coffee. He knows the melody will stay with him, but the words need to be written down.

The gas fireplace comes to life, casting a warm glow in the room. First light is dawning in the indigo sky. Thomas sits on the couch, feet resting on the coffee table, notebook in hand. Good songs that last the test of time come from truth, shared humanity, and a depth of emotion. This song has that. Thomas quickly writes down the words, crossing out and rearranging phrases as he hums the melody. It's a song of enduring love over space, time, and circumstance. There is redemption, promise, and hope in each verse. The dream stays with him as he writes "Cait's Song."

I don't know how it happened, or when.
I can't say, "Yes, it was that moment" when things changed between us.
It happened like the start of a gentle rain.
You saved me, your love was warm rain on parched ground.

Thomas hears the bridge in his head sounding like raindrops. Then the chorus.

Lived a life of shame
No one else to blame.
Walking in the rain,
Heart of my heart,

Show me the way.

It's rough but holds promise. He plays the melody over and over, listening for words and feeling, feelings. He likes it. It's coming.

Bradley Airport is packed with Thanksgiving travelers. Thomas circles arrivals, driving around the airport until he gets a text from Andy that they are at baggage claim. Thomas finds a place in the line of cars waiting for passengers. Andy waves vigorously, and he and his wife Emily wheel their bags to the Jeep. The brothers hug each other tightly.

"Hey, what about me? Don't I get a hug?" Emily teases.

"Welcome to a real New England Thanksgiving. Climb in before the cops think we're terrorists and shoo us away."

They drive home, talking about the flight, family, and Thanksgiving plans. It's the Tuesday before the holiday, and they have lots to do. Thomas fills them in on Bart's condition and tells them Sunny can't wait to meet them.

"Before we get home, can I show you the office, or are you exhausted?" Flying from Montana is never easy and can involve a couple of layovers.

"We are tired, but I'm game if you are, Em," says Andy.

"Let's do it. I've heard about the clock shop and would love to see it. And I'm looking forward to seeing more of Connecticut, too," Emily says.

"That's great, Em. After Thanksgiving, we'll have time for the grand tour. There's lots to see. It's different from Montana. Right, Andy?"

"Yup. I told Emily about The Seaport and Mystic Pizza. Let's plan on a day in Mystic."

"Great idea. We can watch that movie tonight to get in the mood." Thomas pulls into a parking spot on Main Street in front of the foundation office. "We're here."

Amy looks up from her computer. Cally is on her lap, trying to grab the keyboard. She waves hello to Thomas, who introduces everyone. After wandering around the space, the brothers end up at the front window display. Andy gently rests his hand on the anniversary clock, remembering how it stopped at his father's funeral.

"You know, I half expected the clock would start again after bringing it here. I guess we could try winding it," Thomas says. Andy shakes his head no.

"Best to leave that to Dad, don't ya think?"

"Maybe you're right. If it starts up again, I'll let you know."

"This place is perfect, Thomas—all of it. I'm impressed with what you have done, but also with you. I think Connecticut suits you. You look better than I have ever seen you.

"Thanks. I think it does, too. I stopped chasing the dream of fame and fortune and started living a simple life. Took me a while to figure out what was important. Drinking myself to death was not it. Did I tell you I'm in therapy?" Thomas rolls his eyes. "Who would have thought? Recovery is hard, but worth it. Being here near Cait's family, going to AA meetings, and having a purpose feels good. Did I tell you about our band?"

The brothers continue catching up. This is the brotherly connection Thomas has always wanted. Bess was right. The love is there if he can let it in. Most people are doing the best they can with what they have. Others—well, evil *does* exist. Thomas knows about that firsthand.

He parks the Wrangler outside the condo's front door. Thomas helps Emily with her bag.

"*Mi casa es su casa.* Help yourself to whatever you need. Shower, nap, food. I was thinking of ordering take-out for supper. If you have the energy, we can watch that movie. Tomorrow we will go over to

Cait's and help set up. At last count, we have about twenty adults and a small flock of kids."

Andy looks around, peeking into Thomas's bedroom. "Wow, Tom. You've really done some work here. The floors look fantastic. What's going on in the spare room?"

"It's now my studio. But I kept your bed, as promised."

Thomas tucks a few of the amps and guitars into the closet. Andy helps pull the bed out of the corner, and Emily collapses on it, sighing.

"Sheets are clean, towels are on the desk. I'm going to an AA meeting and will be back in about an hour or so to figure out dinner. You guys good?"

"Yup, we're good. You go do your thing."

Thanksgiving is a bright, crisp November day with a touch of frost. Emily carries her freshly baked pumpkin and pecan pies to the car, tucking them in carefully. Andy carries the casserole dish of candied sweet potatoes.

Cait's house is warm and smells delicious. There is happy chaos as people arrive, bringing food. Lots of food. Drinks are passed around. Someone hands Thomas a beer. He looks at it and quickly passes it off to Andy like it's a hot coal. Cait brings him a can of seltzer. Most people know he's sober, but not everyone. Children race around, and the family splits off into small groups, staying away from the busy kitchen unless needed. Sunny knocks on the door.

"Are we in the right place for a party? It smells delicious in here." She has her mother on one arm and cradles a wiggly Jello mold in the other. Sam follows them, wearing a pilgrim hat and bearing a flower arrangement for the table.

Thomas gives Sunny a quick kiss as he relieves her of the Jello. The guests keep on coming. Everyone brings their favorite dish. Thanksgiving is one holiday where no one wants innovation. Everyone wants the food they have enjoyed since childhood, including cranberry sauce from a can.

"Sam, thank you for the flower arrangement! It's beautiful. Put it right here on the table. I am so happy you could join us." Cait hurries back to the kitchen. Elderly Uncle Fred sits with Bleu and Bart in comfortable chairs away from kitchen traffic patterns. They sip bourbon and laugh at Bleu's colorful stories.

In due time, the turkey is carved and platters are reverently placed on the table. Parents make plates for the children at the kids' table. Adults reminisce about the day they graduated to the adult table. It was a rite of passage, although they admit the kids' table was more fun. Bowls of vibrant red cranberry sauce are placed at intervals along the white linen. Cold Irish butter sits next to baskets of warm Parker House rolls and squares of cornbread. Fragrant gravy stays warm in a crock pot on the buffet table, crowded with side dishes. When everyone has a full plate and a seat at the table, Bart stands.

"Thank you all for coming to Thanksgiving dinner. It is a joy and a blessing." Bart bows his head, gripping a cane in his left hand to keep him steady. His words come slowly but are strong. "Lord, thank you for this day, this delicious food, and for the love of family and friends. None of us know what the future holds, especially me, so we are grateful for this moment together." Bart's voice cracks with emotion. He pauses and looks at Cait. "I know this situation isn't easy for you, Cait. Not easy for me either. But I want you to know how much I love you and how grateful I am that you are the one I spent my life with." Bart raises his glass. "Cheers."

Everyone lifts a glass. "Cheers!"

"Can we eat now? Before I faint from hunger," Matt complains, poking his brother-in-law. No one needs encouragement. After dinner, some wander off to the den to watch football. Others hang out at the table, chatting as they digest. Sadie and Barrett take the kids outside to burn off some energy. Bart, Bleu, and Fred nod off by the fireplace, while volunteers mobilize for cleanup. Cait thoughtfully provided stacks of take-out containers for Thanksgiving leftovers. With a batch of dishes in the dishwasher and food put away, desserts are set out on the buffet table. Before long, the aroma of freshly brewed coffee lures people back to the table.

Guests try a sliver of this and a bite of that. Bart is running out of energy, so Cait brings him a slice of pumpkin pie and sits with him in the living room. Sunny sits close to Thomas at the table, teasing him with a fork full of mince apple pie.

"Come on, sugar. It's good. Try it. Here comes the airplane, open the hangar." Thomas opens his mouth and takes the bite of pie, topped off with a kiss to sweeten the deal. Then, just to keep the play even, Thomas picks up a can of whipped cream and asks Sunny if she would like to try that. Their laughter bubbles up from the table.

From the other side of the room, Cait observes their fun with disdain. Sunny is likable, but Cait is unable to tolerate her. She feels like she is losing Thomas. That's crazy, because they see each other all the time. She hasn't lost him at all. But Cait fears Sunny has taken over a special place in Thomas's life that Cait wants for herself. She pushes the thought away and brings her attention back to her husband.

After dessert, no one can eat another bite. Containers are filled with leftovers to take home, and the rest is jammed into the refrigerator. Matt stands at the sink, elbow-deep in sudsy dishwater, scrubbing pans. Andy dries, stacking pots on the counter to be put away.

"Hey Thomas, how did you get out of kitchen duty?" Matt calls out.

"I'm the entertainment. Gotta keep my hands dry." Thomas holds up his hands, wiggles his fingers, and grins. He pulls the guitars out of the closet, handing one to Sam.

"Now for the musical portion of the holiday," Thomas announces. Everyone cheers and gathers around the trio.

"We tried to pick songs that reflect the meaning of Thanksgiving. You know—love, gratitude, and family. My pick is James Taylor's "Shower the People". It's a reminder to let people know you love them. So, I'm tellin' ya'll—I love you." Thomas starts the song while Sam and Sunny harmonize. Thomas's heart is as full as his belly. Family members join in singing the chorus. Cait sees Thomas and Sunny singing together and wonders if they've said "I love you" to each other. It sure looks like Sunny has that lovin' feeling. Cait, unable to watch the spectacle for another second, flees to the kitchen.

"Lean On Me" is Sam's Thanksgiving selection. Sam's gravelly, resonant voice fills the room, and people sing along.

"Okay, enough of that, boys. We need some country music!" Sunny announces. Thomas hands her his guitar, and she launches into John Denver's "Country Roads".

"Come on, ya'll. Sing with me! One more time!" Sunny encourages. Everyone sings along. It's a foot-stomping, hand-clapping good time. Cait, despite her feelings toward Sunny, can't resist joining in. Thomas sees her slip back into the room and smiles at her.

"And for our grand finale, please join us in our funky rendition of James Taylor's 'How Sweet It Is'. Happy Thanksgiving." Sam starts them off, and before long, everyone is singing. Andy and Emily dance. Thomas looks at Cait as he sings. Sunny tries to catch his eye, but Thomas doesn't notice. It's innocent, of course. Thomas has a lot to thank Cait for. Suddenly, the roles are reversed, and Sunny is feeling low on the totem pole. It's not a place she tolerates well.

Sam thanks everyone for singing along. The room fills with requests for more. Thomas and Sam keep the mob happy while Sunny makes her way to where Cait is standing.

"Hey. What's going on with you?" Sunny can be blunt.

"Not a thing. Why?" Cait makes a face like she smells something noxious.

"Okay, good. Just checking in. I see the way you look at Thomas. I want to remind you that you are a married woman, and Thomas is mine."

"Believe me, I remember that every single day." Cait slowly turns to look at Sunny, eyebrow raised. "Excuse me. I have things to do. Being a married woman and all."

Cait walks straight to Thomas in defiance of Sunny. She and Andy hug him and gush over the music. They rarely get to see him perform, so this is a treat. Emily joins them, putting one arm around her husband's waist and the other around Cait. Sunny is the outsider, and she doesn't much care for it. She makes a beeline for Sam, pulling him into the group, her arm around him. She narrows her eyes at Thomas, not smiling. He sees the look and cocks his head, wondering what's going on. Sunny whispers something in Sam's ear, and they laugh. Oh, the games people play.

It's time to take Bleu home. Thomas goes to the den to retrieve their coats. Sunny follows him and pulls him aside, whispers in his ear, and kisses him seductively. Cait doesn't miss the display, which she imagines is for her benefit. Sunny is letting Cait know that she will defend her territory. It's so stupid and unnecessary. There is absolutely nothing going on between her and Thomas.

Bart is exhausted. Cait gets him settled in bed for the night. That leaves Cait, Thomas, Andy, and Emily chatting by the fireplace, nibbling on leftovers. It's a relief for Cait to have Sunny out of the picture. At least for the moment. Cait sits next to Thomas on the couch, her hand resting on the cushion, palm down. Thomas rests his hand next to hers, unable to bridge the tiny gap between them.

12

Love Me, Love Me Not

After visiting Connecticut, Andy and Emily fly back to Montana. Because of houseguests, Sunny and Thomas had no private time over Thanksgiving. Thomas isn't aware that Sunny's knickers are in a twist. At band practice, Sunny flirts with Sam, which is a sure sign that something is amiss. When Thomas tries to get close to her, she turns away. He is too old for these games, and this is a confusing new side to Sunny.

Later that night, as they lay in bed, Thomas finds out what's on Sunny's mind. She asks the age-old question posed by millions of men and women throughout the ages: "Where is this relationship going?" Thomas is surprised because Sunny has made so few demands. The first thought in Thomas's head is something a band buddy said years ago: *Are we on a train? Do we have to be going somewhere?* Thomas bites his tongue. Sunny is serious, and a comedic approach will piss her off even more. Best to tread lightly and get more information.

"Where do you want it to go?" Thomas asks. Sunny tells him she feels stuck. What they have is okay, but she wonders why Thomas never shares how he feels and why they never talk about the future.

"Are we friends, partners, lovers, or what?"

If they were anywhere but in bed, Thomas imagines Sunny would have her arms crossed, tapping her foot. Thomas takes a breath. "Well, all of the above. I think?" It's a question more than an answer.

Sunny rolls her eyes, sits cross-legged, wrapped in the sheet, and looks intensely at him. Thomas sees stormy Skize coming that could flatten him like the gales of a nor'easter. Sunny tends to be blunt, which is appreciated, unless it's coming at you.

"See. That's *exactly* what I'm talking about. You deflect all the time. Pinning you down is like trying to sack fog. How do you feel? Am I just one of the guys? I do *not* want to be wastin' my time loving you, Thomas Ogilvie, if you're not interested. Tell me the truth. We promised we would always tell the truth. Remember?"

Well, that makes her earlier mood clear. Thomas wonders where this is coming from. Suddenly, this low-demand relationship is all about meaning and future plans. When Andy left for Montana, Thomas felt the loss. The closer he gets to Andy, the more he misses him. He's aware that keeping people at arm's length has protected him from that uncomfortable feeling of emptiness when they leave. And sooner or later, everyone leaves. Deflection keeps things from getting too serious. Loosely bonded has always been safe.

"Sunny, you're right. I'm sorry. I thought we were getting along fine, but I hear what you're saying." Thomas tries to explain why he is slow to commit, but it sounds like whiny excuses. He pivots to sobriety and AA, telling Sunny that he needs to go slow because he is still in recovery. It's true, but not the whole story.

"What about Cait? What's going on there?" Sunny demands. Thomas, startled, braces himself.

"Cait? What are you talking about?" Thomas asks.

"I see how close you two are. Thanksgiving, I had to remind her to keep her distance."

"You did what?" Thomas barks. "What did you say to her?" he demands.

"Calm down, will ya? Jeez. All I did was remind her she is a married woman. I'm reminding you, too. See how you rush to her defense? I'm not stupid. You two are close—big whoop. Lots of people are close. I have no problem with that. But, Thomas, you and I got to a certain point, and we stopped getting close. We sing, hang out, and sleep together. Period. I wonder if your feelings for Cait are responsible for that."

Thomas doesn't know what to say. He is irritated about being confronted with a truth he hasn't even admitted to himself.

"Is that what the little performance with you and Sam was about? Sidling up to Sam. Whispering in his ear. Were you trying to make me jealous?"

"You're deflecting again. If I was trying to make you jealous, it didn't work, did it?" Sunny rebuts. "Ya know why? Because you don't give a shit about us." The words slap Thomas.

"What? That's not true. Sunny, you mean a lot to me."

"Wow. I mean a lot to you. Uh-huh. Listen, I have no interest in convincing you to love me, Thomas. It's too much work. You will or you won't, but time's a-wastin'. I will not be Miss-right-now forever." Sunny stretches out next to Thomas, her hand resting on his belly, feeling the rise and fall of his breathing. "I love you, Thomas Ogilvie. You need to level with me. Maybe level with yourself, too, while you're at it."

There it is. The three little words that have the power to change lives. He wishes he could tell Sunny what she wants to hear, but he can't.

"I know," Thomas says.

"I know, you know." Sunny rolls out of bed, gets dressed, and leaves without a goodbye.

Thomas buries his head in the pillow and thinks there is probably a song to be written about this. But not right now. *Bess, I wish you were here to tell me what to do.*

Thomas takes his dilemma to therapy, but those solutions take a long time. "How do you feel, Thomas? What do *you* want to do?" If he had those answers, he wouldn't need a therapist, for God's sake. Is the man stupid? What Thomas needs is practical, down-home advice.

"Sam? You got time for coffee?"

Sam and Thomas slide into a booth at Dunkin' with hot coffee and a couple of crullers. Thomas fills him in on what happened with Sunny.

"Well, Thomas, I am not the best person to give love advice."

Hearing the word love, Thomas frowns. "Yeah, but you know her. Give me your take on this situation," Thomas pleads. "You're a man. Give me *man* advice."

"Well, Sunny is a spitfire. She doesn't take shit or prisoners, as the saying goes. She calls 'em as she sees 'em."

"That's for sure. I admire that about her. Except now, when I'm on the receiving end."

Sam smiles and shakes his head in agreement. "Yup. Been there a time or two myself. Listen, instead of trying to figure out how to handle her, I suggest you consider how you feel. What do you want? I don't mean just about Sunny. Look at the big picture, Thomas. How do you want to be in your life?"

Thomas groans. "Now you sound like my therapist." Thomas bites into the cruller, sweet and light in his mouth.

"I'm flattered. I'll consider hanging out a shingle. Won't take insurance, though. Cash only. No refunds." Sam chuckles. "I could be wrong, but I think you already know what to do. You just don't like that option." Sam slides out of the booth. "Come on. Let's walk."

They walk down Main Street to Hole-In-The-Wall Beach and then up the hill into McCook Park.

"I wish Bess was here. She always knew what to do."

"So, ask her. All the wisdom and love Bess gave you is still there." Sam pokes a finger at Thomas's heart. "Just ask."

"Okay, I will."

"Not later, now. Let's sit." They find a bench and gaze out at calm water dotted with the white sails of a dozen small boats. Before long, Thomas has an answer.

"If I can't give her what she wants, she needs to know. I like being with her. She is fun and sexy, and the music is amazing. But it's selfish to hang on to her if we want different things. I have to tell her how I feel, and let her decide what she wants to do, like mature adults. There's a risk that she will dump me, and I hate that option."

"There you go. I knew you had the answer. So now I can add my two cents. I know Sunny. She has a big heart, and she loves you. And her mother is dying. That's a lot for a person to handle. It might explain why she wants more from you now. The floor is about to give way, and she wants to know you'll catch her. Or not, I don't know. Whatever you do, Thomas, be kind. Okay?"

Thomas helps Sunny and Bleu as much as he can during the ever-shortening time they have left. The relationship talk is on hold for now because Thomas thinks that being kind means not throwing more at Sunny. She uses his shoulder to lean on, and he is happy to be there for her. He runs errands and plays music for Bleu. Sunny and Thomas sing the American spiritual, "Down to the River to Pray", Bleu's favorite song. He imagines seeing her down at that river, praying, on her way to whatever afterlife there is.

Thomas desperately wishes he could give Sunny the forever love she wants. If there ever was a time, it's now. Thomas loves Sunny, but not the way she wants him to. He knows Sunny won't settle for friendship and dreads the coming conversation. It causes Thomas to wonder what being kind really means. Is being kind to her now going to feel cruel later? If it were him, he would want to know the truth. But she isn't him, and relationships are complicated.

Bleu's funeral is small and simple as she requested. Sam, Thomas, Sunny, and a half dozen people who were close to Bleu are invited to Temple Emanu-El for a service. The urn containing Bleu's ashes sits next to the *yahrzeit* candle on a special table. Everyone gathers around the urn. Sunny, wearing a long black dress, silently steps forward to light the candle that honors the dead. It will be kept burning until it extinguishes itself, like life. Sunny recites the *Kel Maleh Rachamim*, a plea for Bleu's soul to be granted rest. Thomas holds Sunny's hand as the Rabbi speaks eloquently about life, death, and what a blessing Bleu Skize was to all who knew her. The ceremony is deeply moving in its simplicity. Sunny lifts the urn off the table, tucking it safely in the crook of her arm. She picks up the candle and asks Thomas to carry it.

"Come on, Mama. Time to go home," Sunny whispers.

Christmas this year will not be a joyous celebration. Bleu is gone, and Bart is barely hanging on in hospice. Sunny and Cait are not speaking, so Christmas together will not be possible. Thomas doesn't have the heart to leave Sunny alone this Christmas, even if she is Jewish. On Christmas Eve, he stops at Cait's house to distribute presents. Thomas is loaded down like Santa Claus.

"Ho, ho, ho. Santa Thomas is in the house!"

Cait hugs him. Thomas checks in with Bart, who is lying in a hospital bed they've set up in the living room. He offers Bart his gift. Bart blinks as Thomas unwraps a pair of colorful Christmas socks with little bells attached to the toes. Thomas helps Cait put the socks on Bart's feet. They poke out from under the bedsheet like festive decorations. Bart manages a lopsided smile.

"Nice Christmas outfit, hon," Cait tells Bart, kissing him on the forehead. "How's Sunny doing? I am so sorry about her mother. She seemed like an interesting lady."

"She was, for sure. Sunny is doing the best she can. It's tough, especially this time of year. It helps that she's busy, with lawyers, probate, and sorting through her mother's things. You know how it is." Thomas pauses, looking down. "So do I."

"That's true. You've been very kind to them." Cait looks at Bart. The brain tumor is vicious. Bart can no longer talk or walk and needs constant care. Cait hired a day nurse to help. "Hospice is amazing. The social worker comes and talks with Bart. I'm not sure how much he understands, but he seems engaged. I get to talk with her too, which helps."

"Thankfully, we all have each other. Let me know what you need. Anything. Understand?" Thomas covers Cait's hand with his. She self-consciously pulls it away, tucking it in her sweatshirt pocket.

"I know. Thank you, Tom. You've helped us so much already. It means a lot." Thomas wonders if she knows how much it means to him. He passes out presents. Sadie and her family get Christmas socks, including little Gracie. Barrett and his family get matching Christmas T-shirts.

"I went all out this year, you guys!" Thomas announces. "Here, Cait. Open your present." Thomas hands Cait a package wrapped in Santa paper. She carefully tears open the package, revealing a beautiful box embossed with the name Lochcarron of Scotland. Cait runs her hand over the raised letters.

"Open it. Come on!" Thomas urges. Cait lifts the top off the box, and inside, wrapped in white and gold tissue, is a Shetland wool throw handmade in Scotland. "It's Ogilvie tartan. You can wrap it around you and know that Dad, your mom, and I are all here with you."

"Thank you. It's beautiful. I love it." Cait wraps the soft wool around her shoulders and gives Thomas a quick hug.

"There is something else in there." Cait searches the tissue and tucked inside is a CD.

"I wrote a song I want you to have. I know CDs are passe, but I wanted you to be able to hold it in your hands. Listen to it before you decide to share it, okay?"

"That sounds very mysterious. Okay. I will do that. Can you send me a digital link so I can listen on my phone?"

"Sure. Let me know what you think. I'm a little self-conscious about it."

"Now I'm intrigued."

Christmas at Sunny's is bittersweet. The house is in disarray as Sunny sorts through her mother's things. They got a small Christmas tree, the last one on the lot still hanging on to a few needles. Sunny opens her mother's box of ornaments.

"Even though my mother grew up Jewish, we always managed to squeeze in every holiday possible. You know, Christmas trees, flags for Flag Day, Easter baskets, fireworks, whatever was traditional. Mama said that her God would never kick her out of heaven because she celebrated life."

Sunny smiles and starts going through the ornaments, telling Thomas about them. "To keep things even, we would put this Star of David on the top. I made it when I was in fourth grade."

"It's nice your mother kept it. I like it." Thomas reaches up to set the paper mâché star at the top of the tree, and then he pulls an oddly shaped, strangely wrapped gift out from underneath the tree.

"Merry Christmas, Sunny."

"What is it?"

"Open it. I hope you like it."

Sunny tears into the paper, eyes wide. It's an instrument case. She opens it carefully, and inside is a restored vintage mandolin.

"Oh my god, Thomas. This is gorgeous. A Kentucky Standard! I had one of these eons ago." She throws her arms around Thomas, kissing him passionately.

"She is gorgeous, and the sound is perfect. I'm trying to imagine who owned her before me."

"I'm glad you like it. It had your name written all over it. Play me something."

"You will recognize this one." Sunny plays the introduction to Rod Stewart's "Maggie May", a classic featuring mandolin. Thomas tries out his best Stewart impression, singing along with Sunny's music. He finds it oddly prophetic that Rod opens the song by telling Maggie he has something to say. What Thomas needs to say has been gnawing at him. When they finish playing, they pick up Chinese food for dinner and watch a Christmas movie.

"Please stay with me tonight," Sunny says. They have never spent the night in this house before. Thomas is reluctant to agree because he knows they have to talk. After that, he doubts she'll want him in her bed.

"I can't, Sunny." That is as far as he goes. No excuses or stories. He just can't stay.

"Okay." Sunny frowns. "I don't know if this is the right time to mention this, but what the heck." Thomas braces himself. "I'm selling Mama's house and heading back to Nashville. As soon as I clean this place out, it will get listed. I am planning to be back home in Tennessee by February. I don't need a whole New England winter to contend with." Sunny takes Thomas's hand. "Please come with me? We could have a good life in Nashville. Maybe get gigs with the Opry, just for fun."

Thomas holds his breath. It's now or never. Sometimes you can't pick your moment, it picks you. "Sunny, I wish I could...but...I can't. I'm sorry. My life is here now."

Sunny pulls her hand away, surprised. "No? I don't understand. I thought you loved Nashville."

"Sunny, I'm happy here. I don't want to go back to Tennessee. For the first time in my life, I feel settled. I didn't think it would happen here in Niantic, but it did. Bess's condo, my dad's old shop, Sam...it's home."

"You left Cait off the list."

"Okay, and Cait. But it isn't what you think it is."

Sunny frowns and shakes her head in disagreement. "Okay, have it your way, if you insist. I would be willing to stay here if..." Sunny pauses.

"If what?" Thomas asks.

"If...you wanted me to." Sunny looks down at her hands and sighs. "You don't, though, do you?"

"Oh my god, Sunny, I would love for you to stay, but I can't ask you to do that. You have to be where you're happy. If I asked you to stay, it wouldn't be fair. Besides..."

"Besides what?" Sunny demands. Ellie senses the increasing tension and jumps up on the couch, landing between them. "No, don't tell me," Sunny says. "I already know. You don't love me. You had fun, and that was enough." The words hit Thomas right in his core. His youth was spent having fun, not caring about anyone's feelings. Lydia called him selfish. This time with Sunny was different. Everything he did was because he cares.

"Sunny, you are my most valued friend. I love being with you. You're important to me."

"Friend? Is that what I am? What the hell, Thomas? After all this time and everything you did for me and Mama, that's the best you can do. *Friend?* You never said the words, but I felt loved. Goddamnit. *I feel loved.* How dare you lie to me? This is about Cait, isn't it?"

Thomas wonders what he can say to fix the unfixable. Sunny stands over him, hands on her hips.

"I am not a liar, Sunny. Cait has nothing to do with this. I can't give you what you want," Thomas admits.

"Oh, really? What is it you think I want?" Sunny asks with fire in her eyes.

"Well, for starters, a life together in Nashville. I'm not stupid. You want a forever love and a happily ever after. You deserve that. I love you. I do. But not like that. We want different things. It's no one's fault. It's complicated." There it is, finally out in the open.

"Complicated? Thomas, I love you. That is not complicated. You are the one who has complicated this. How long have you known?"

Thomas sighs and looks away. This feels so awful. He knew at some point it would come to this, but he still isn't prepared.

"Oh my god. All this time? While you were singing to my mama? Comforting me? You *knew*?"

"I'm sorry, Sunny. I couldn't talk about this while your mother was dying. I *wanted* to be here with you. You're ignoring the part about how I care. Doesn't that count for something?"

"Actually, no, it doesn't count for shit. You better go. Oh, and take this with you." She thrusts the mandolin at him.

"I'm sorry, Sunny." Thomas gathers his things and leaves without another word spoken between them.

13

A Dark Cloud Descends

Thomas's heart aches when he gets home from Sunny's on Christmas night. Her angry rejection hit him hard, and didn't give him a chance to explain. *Shouldn't kindness get some sort of acknowledgment? Everything I did was because I care about Sunny. How can she not see that? Maybe she does see it, but it isn't enough.*

Thoughts spinning, he bundles up and goes for a run on the beach. The frozen sand crunches under his feet. Cold air bites into his lungs. After several loops, breathing heavily, he collapses on the rocks by the bluff. *Dad, if you're there, I need your help,* he whispers like he's praying on sacred ground. There is no response. A black, leaden cloud descends on Thomas. *If I sit on the rocks long enough, maybe I'll freeze to death and be done with all of this,* he thinks. *What's the point of even trying? Being a selfish drunk or doing the right thing offers the same result: pain.*

His despondence isn't just about Sunny. When she shouted that he used her, it kicked him in the gut. That was how he'd treated Lydia and the long line of women in his youth. He took what he wanted, not giving a damn about them. He is different now—kinder and more thoughtful. Or is he kidding himself? Maybe getting sober and going to therapy doesn't change anything. Once an asshole, always an asshole. When he and Sunny walked the beach that first time, he thought they were clear about what getting involved would mean. That twitchy little feeling, down deep inside, telling him to *watch out,* was easy to ignore. His desires got the best of him and led to suffering for them both. Inevitable suffering is why he never let himself care about anyone after his divorce from Lydia. If he got too close, he would drink himself into oblivion and move on.

The next day, Sunny isn't answering his calls. He won't call Cait and risk clinging to her. He can't show his face at an AA meeting because Sunny probably cried on Sam's shoulder. That means the band is over. Lydia never called him. His dark cloud gets blacker. He has no one. Alone and burdened with self-loathing, he seeks solace from a friend who never lets him down. Jack Daniels.

Thomas pulls a baseball cap down to shade his eyes. Oakley sunglasses make him look like an incognito celebrity as he rushes through Niantic, head down. Hopefully, no one will notice him slipping into the package store on Main Street—everyone's business is front-page news in a small town. Thomas does not want Sam or Cait to find out what he's doing. Buying a bottle of bourbon is impulsive and not without consequences. Back at home, the unopened bottle of Jack Daniel's Old No. 7 sits on the coffee table taunting him.

"Come on, my old friend. I've missed you. Let's hang out. I always understand," the bourbon seems to say.

Thomas feels torn to shreds. He wants the bourbon but knows he will feel worse about himself later. How much is he willing to risk for a bit of relief? He picks up Sunny's mandolin and plays an old bluegrass standard by The Soggy Bottom Boys called "I Am a Man of Constant Sorrow". Ain't that the truth. The song evolves into "Maggie May". Misery, thy name is Thomas. Decision made. *Crack* is the sound of a new bottle of bourbon being opened. *Crack* is the sound of Thomas breaking his promise to stay sober. All he wants is a sip to relieve his pain. No one will be the wiser. He lifts the bottle to his mouth and drinks.

"God, Jack. I have missed you." Thomas feels himself relax as the numbing effect of alcohol spreads through his body. After a few gulps, Thomas stops thinking about Sam, AA, Lydia, and Sunny. Cait is safely tucked away in the back of his mind, not nagging him anymore. No regrets. No self-judgment. No more anything. Just the way he likes it.

Days pass, and empty bottles of bourbon line up on the coffee table. The package store delivers, and Thomas takes full advantage of the convenience. Pizza boxes litter the floor. It's him and Jack on the couch watching mindless television, strumming the mandolin, and passing out. His head is foggy. He isn't sure what day or time it is. Someone is pounding on the door. *Fuck them,* he thinks, and he shuffles to the bathroom to relieve himself. His face in the mirror shocks him. Bloodshot, sunken eyes accuse him of mistakes he has long tried to bury.

"Thomas, 'ol boy, you need to get your shit together," he tells his reflection. Stumbling out of the bathroom, he comes face to face with Cait.

"Holy Mother of God...you scared the crap out of me. Why are you here? How did you get in?"

Cait leads him to the living room where coffee and an egg sandwich wait for him.

"You gave me a key, remember? Thomas, I have been worried sick about you. You went completely off the grid. Not answering calls, absent from the office, and missing meetings. It's been a week. Now I see why. Please tell me what's going on. Besides the obvious," Cait pleads.

"Thanks for the coffee." Thomas bends over, his pounding head in his hands. "I feel like shit."

"Yeah? Well, you don't look much better. Tell me what's going on."

Thomas tells Cait what happened with Sunny on Christmas Day.

"She's going back to Nashville. She wanted me to go with her, but I couldn't, so she threw me out. End of story."

"I'm sorry, Tom. That hurts. There's more to the story, though, isn't there?" Gotta hand it to Cait, she is perceptive.

"Of course. Isn't there always?" Thomas snaps. "It would never work out with Sunny. It's bad enough I've kept that truth from her. It would be worse if I went to Nashville and then told her I didn't love her. Man, that sounds so cold." He shakes his head. "What I mean is, I care about her, but not in the way she needs. *I did not use her,*" Thomas shouts defensively. "I tried to help and do the right thing when her mother was dying. That's all. See how that worked out?"

"What are you talking about?" Cait asks.

Thomas sighs. "The truth is, I like Sunny. A lot. But I don't love her like I love..." Thomas catches himself. He absolutely cannot reveal his feelings for Cait right now. "*Loved* Lydia. Saying 'Sorry, your mother is dying and I don't love you' was out of the question. But I knew I had to tell her sometime. The how and when were tricky. When Nashville came up, it was the right moment. When she first told me she loved me, ya know what I said?"

"No. What?"

"I said, *I know.* I'm such an asshole." Thomas, elbows on thighs, rests his head in his hands again. He pulls his fingers through knots of hair much like his father used to do. "That would have been a good time to come clean, but I didn't. I couldn't. Circumstances felt wrong. Timing was off. I think she knew the truth, at least in that moment, but then her mother declined. I wanted to make that easier for her. I should've told her as soon as I knew. It would have saved us both a lot of grief."

"I understand. You made a choice, and it wasn't a bad one, Tom."

"Looking back, I think I had the stupid idea that if I was good to Sunny, it would make up for how I treated Lydia. Being sober changed how I saw things. Sam asked me to be kind, and I was. Maybe too kind." Thomas straightens and looks at Cait. "I should have trusted her to handle the truth. This went on too long and gave her the wrong impression. She felt loved, and the truth hurt her. So...I came home, retreated into self-hatred, and washed it down with bourbon."

"Did that help?"

"At first. Now it's one more thing I feel bad about."

"Tom, breakups happen, and they hurt like hell. I feel for you there. You reached for the thing that always made you feel better. It happens to the best of us. The first time I fell off the wagon, I thought everyone would hate me. They didn't. Sunny may leave, but I'm here. Sam and the meetings are still here. The family loves you. Recovery is rarely a straight line, so you start again. That's all. Or you can wallow in self-pity and drink yourself to death. Always an option." Thomas is thoughtful as he listens to Cait. "You did the best you could. I can't fault you for that. Did you intend to hurt Sunny?"

"No, of course not."

"Maybe you can tell Sunny that. She may not want to see your face, especially the way you look now," Cait wrinkles her nose. "But give her time. What's the worst that can happen?"

"Yeah, you're probably right."

"Okay, now I am going to get bossy because I care about you. Here comes some tough love. Get yourself cleaned up. I'm taking you home for a good meal. A man cannot survive on cold pizza. Then we are going to a meeting. Together. I will not say anything about what happened. But you'll feel better if you talk about it. A meeting is the best place to unburden yourself. It will surprise you how much people understand and care. Sam isn't going to reject you. You don't have to be perfect to be loved."

Thomas looks at Cait, trying to understand the strange concept of acceptance she speaks of. He finishes the coffee and takes a bite of the egg sandwich.

"You can always say no, and I'll go."

"I'm going to take a shower and get dressed." Thomas walks away and then turns back to Cait. "You are bossy. Thank you, Cait."

Head down, Thomas holds Cait's hand for moral support. His trajectory through recovery has been smooth sailing until now. Going into an AA meeting, facing Sam, and admitting what he's done scares the crap out of him. They walk through the parking lot toward the church entrance.

"How ya doing?" Cait asks.

"Honestly? I'm terrified. Can a person be kicked out of AA?" he asks

"I suppose anything is possible, but if this gets you kicked out, it isn't much of a support group. It'll be okay, I know it." It's reassuring to know that Cait, sober for twenty-plus years, at one time thought she could manage one drink, too. "I learned from my mistakes. So will you." Cait reassures him.

They enter the community room filled with people. Thomas avoids Sam and takes a seat in the back with Cait. Thomas hasn't decided if he will say anything. Maybe he will sit quietly, get his act together, and move on. No one has to know anything. Except for Cait, of course, and his conscience.

A member recites the Serenity Prayer aloud, and the meeting opens to anyone who wants to speak. A few people ask for support. A new person talks endlessly about her struggles. No one rushes her or judges her. Cait squeezes his hand. Thomas looks at her, and she smiles in encouragement.

"Do what you want, but you will feel better if you come clean," Cait whispers in his ear. "Promise." Thomas takes a deep breath and exhales slowly. He stands, his heart pounding out of his chest.

"My name is Thomas." A long pause follows as he summons up the courage to continue. "I am an alcoholic. An alcoholic who thinks he knows more than anyone else. An alcoholic who convinced himself he could handle one drink." Heads nod, and there is a murmur of agreement in the group. Thomas's eyes sweep the room, searching for allies. "I had a rough Christmas. Someone that I care about dumped me. I tried to be a good friend, but it didn't work out." Thomas quickly glances at Sam, expecting daggers of disapproval heading his way, but Sam has his hands folded, nodding, understanding. Thomas thinks he's probably having an alcoholic hallucination. He can't imagine Sam will ever trust him again.

"I didn't mean to hurt her. The remorse I felt broke the dam, and every shameful thing I ever did was in my face. It was like watching a horror movie, and I was the monster. I judged myself. Hated myself. I couldn't stand the feeling, and all I could think of was having a drink to make it go away. After all the times I managed to stay sober, this time I caved. I got drunk and stayed drunk until Cait showed up. Now I'm here. Thanks for listening." Thomas sits down.

No one looks horrified, runs from the room, or kicks him out. Thomas feels a tiny bit relieved, as Cait promised. Shared stories and the vulnerability of admitting relapses are part of what binds the group together. It is an unfamiliar and startling experience for Thomas. To his awareness, no one has ever accepted him after screwing up. These people, who have slipped, fallen, and gotten back up, understand and accept him. Speaking with Sam is his next step. If Sam can forgive him, then he might survive. After the meeting breaks up, Thomas lingers with Cait at the coffee urn. Sam approaches them.

"Hey, I'm craving a cruller. What about you guys?" Sam asks.

"Sounds delicious, but I need to get home to Bart. You two enjoy," Cait says, and she slips away.

After sliding into a booth at the coffee shop, Sam gives Thomas time to collect his thoughts. They inhale the sweetness of pastries and the aroma of fresh-brewed coffee. The door opens and bangs shut as people come and go.

"I don't know where to start," Thomas tells Sam. "I was afraid you would hate me."

"Life isn't easy. A friend reminds me all the time that life is complicated. I will never fault you for doing the best you can, Thomas."

"Did Sunny tell you what happened?"

"She gave me her version, yes. Thomas, I don't know what you're thinking, but you were good to Sunny. You cared about her and helped her through a tough time. If you swore undying love and lied about your intentions, I would have to kick your ass. You didn't do that. How she feels is her business to work through. I asked you to be kind, and you were."

"Yeah. Maybe too kind. I don't know. Breaking up with Sunny, her throwing me out, was painful. The only thing I wanted after that was to be numb. I don't know what would have happened if Cait hadn't shown up. I feel like such a fuck-up, especially after I tried to do everything right. I'm sorry, Sam. You must be so disappointed in me."

"Me? Hell no. You don't need my approval. Besides, I've been where you are. Many times. You came to a meeting, and that took guts. How you feel about yourself is what's important. None of us is perfect, Thomas. Even when we are doing all the right things, people can get hurt. Are you still seeing that therapist?"

"Yeah."

"Good. How was the meeting for you?"

"Surprising. I expected to be thrown out. But people understood."

"Yup. That's the gift of a meeting. Some of those folks have experienced far worse. We don't go to a meeting to show off how wonderful we are. We go for support when we feel lower than snake spit. It's a humbling experience."

"I was afraid to face you, Sam. I thought you would be angry."

"Thomas, I will always be honest with you, and sometimes you might not like that. But I will never judge you. I have had too many failures of my own to judge anyone. If you are ever tempted to solve your problems with Jack, call me, knock on my door, or chase me down the street. Seriously. I mean it. We will talk it through. Then, if you want to drink, I won't stop you. Got it?"

"Yeah, I got it," Thomas agrees. "Thanks, Sam."

14

Alpha to Omega

With her shopping list between her teeth, Cait juggles her purse, keys, reusable shopping bags, and phone. She manages to lock the car without dropping anything, then spins around to dash into CVS pharmacy. Head down, scrolling through text messages, she crashes into a woman exiting the store.

"Oh, I'm so sorry—I should have..." She looks up. "Sunny?"

"Yep. In the flesh. Hello, Cait." It is a freeze-frame moment. Cars stop moving down the street. People stand mid-stride on one foot like inanimate storks. Birds hover in mid-air, and the world is quiet. Of course, none of that happens, but it feels like that for the two women locked in an awkward moment. Considering the ultimatum Sunny gave Cait last Thanksgiving, this encounter isn't one they would seek out. Sunny's lips are pursed in a hard line. They do that little dance people do, trying to move past each other until Cait waves a white flag.

"Sunny, do you have a minute to talk?" Sunny agrees. They sit on a bench near the CVS entrance. Cait takes a deep breath. "I'm sorry about your mother, and sorry we got off on the wrong foot. Tom told me you are going back to Nashville. I'm sure you will be missed around here." *But not by me*, Cait says to herself.

"True. That's my home. I was only here to tend to Mama. Did Thomas tell you I asked him to go with me?"

"Um, yeah, I did hear that." Cait is cautious, unsure of where Sunny is going with this line of questioning.

"You probably know that he refused. Do you know why?" Sunny prods. More questions.

"He told me this is home now. I'm glad he feels comfortable here. I feel like I am being interrogated, Sunny. What's going on?"

"There is a bigger reason he's staying."

"There is?" Cait asks.

"He's staying because of you. He loves you. Apparently, I was only a *friend* and placeholder." If this were a soap opera, there would be ominous organ music playing.

"He said that?"

"Not in those words. But it's obvious. You can't tell me you didn't know. I picked up on it loud and clear. Why do you think I told you to back off?"

"That's crazy."

"Is it? Do you love him?"

"Of course, I love him. I've known him for over twenty years. But I'm not *in love* with him. What are you suggesting?"

Sunny shakes her head like she can't believe how obtuse Cait is. "Honey, you are either a master of denial or a liar."

"I have to go." Cait gathers her things and rushes into the pharmacy. In a quiet corner by the household supplies, she stops to think. Her husband is close to death, and she would never betray him. Not now, not ever. But Sunny's words echo—*Thomas loves you.* Cait is close to Thomas because she helped him with alcoholism. Having that in common makes them AA boot camp buddies. It can't possibly mean more than that. Can it?

"Excuse me. *Excuse me, please.*" An elderly woman nudges Cait with a shopping cart, snapping her attention back to CVS.

"I'm sorry. Lost in thought." Cait laughs nervously and steps aside.

"I can see that." The woman trundles past, tossing toilet paper and paper towels in her cart. Cait needs time to process Sunny's information. Forgetting why she was even in CVS she rushes out of the store and into her car. Cait has to be with Bart right now. Just because she has affection for Thomas doesn't mean she has done anything wrong. He has been great with the foundation and helping her during Bart's illness. There is no reason to feel guilty.

Bart is no longer conscious, and hospice is keeping him comfortable. When Cait gets home, the house is quiet except for Sadie's voice reading to Bart and soft classical music playing in the background. Cait's phone buzzes. Thomas. She lets it go to voicemail.

"Hungry, Sadie? I can make us some lunch while you read."

"Sure. Did you get my prescription?"

"Oh, crap. I forgot it. I'm sorry. Not sure where my mind is these days." Cait sighs. Sadie hugs her mother.

"It's okay. I'll get it later. Mom, the hospice nurse was here. She said Dad is getting close." Sadie's voice cracks with emotion. "We need to let people know." Cait pulls Sadie back into a tight embrace.

"I'll take care of that. You go back to reading. Is a tuna sandwich, okay? I don't think we have much else. Grocery shopping hasn't been high on my list lately."

After lunch, Sadie leaves to pick up supplies. Cait sits with Bart, holding his hand. His face is slack and expressionless. Cait wants him to give her a sign that he's aware she is with him, heart and soul.

"I wish this wasn't happening to you, honey. You don't deserve this kind of ending. I always imagined us riding into the sunset on your Harley, at a ripe old age. You were a good husband. Most days." Cait chuckles softly. "Truth be told, sometimes you were a real pain in the butt. Despite that, I always did, and always will, love you. I hope you know that. Being married a long time, we know marriage is hard. Love got us through it. I'm sorry I wasn't more patient with you. I wish we had taken that trip to Greece you desperately wanted. We probably could have afforded it. I don't know why I was so resistant." Cait pauses, dabbing at a tear on her cheek. "Remember that huge anniversary party we had? Oh my god, it was so much fun. We danced...and danced..." Emotion chokes off Cait's words. "I love you, babe. You know that, don't you?" Cait grips Bart's hand and rests her head on his bony shoulder.

Thomas follows Sadie through the kitchen door, arms loaded with bags of groceries. He gives Cait a peck on the cheek. That has always felt normal to Cait, until now. After what Sunny told her, nothing feels normal around Thomas anymore. Every small kindness is suspect. Bart was extremely jealous of Thomas, and Cait thought it was the brain tumor making him paranoid. Maybe it wasn't. Damn it, Sunny.

"What's with all the groceries?" Cait asks.

"I ran into Sadie at the grocery store. She told me your pantry is bare, so we did a little shopping. I'm cooking for you tonight. I hope you like spaghetti. It's my only specialty." Thomas retrieves more bags from the car. "We also picked up fruit, sandwich stuff, coffee, and toilet paper. Can't have too much TP!" He unpacks the bags, and Sadie puts everything away. Cait stands in the middle of the activity, feeling grateful, confused, and unsure how to respond. Three words, *Thomas loves you,* stick in her head.

Thomas sits next to Bart's hospital bed, talking softly. Cait can't hear what he's saying, but is touched by the sweetness between two men who went at each other with fists. Thomas is a kind person. That's all it is. Sunny must be wrong.

"Hey, old man. I'm cooking tonight. I know you usually cook, but I'm giving you the night off. Bart? I'm sorry about the fight. I want you to know that nothing was, or is, going on between me and Cait. She loves you, man, so don't worry about it." Thomas pauses, considering what else needs to be said. "For a long time, I didn't see the point of family. But you and Cait, your kids, showed me I was wrong. Family is a place where people care. I needed to learn that, and I'm grateful. Bart, when you're gone, not that I'm rushing ya, I promise to do all I can to help your family. Whatever they need. Yeah? Okay. Good. Well, I have to get busy in the kitchen. Your wife is a slave driver. But you know that." Thomas pats Bart's hand, sits quietly for a moment, then goes to the kitchen.

"I have to let people know what's going on," Cait says softly and closes herself in the den.

"Sadie, what's going on? What's your mother talking about?" Thomas asks as he gathers meatball ingredients together.

"The hospice nurse said Dad could go any time now. Mom is letting people know." Sadie blinks away tears.

"Oh, Sadie, I am so sorry." Thomas opens his arms, and Sadie clings to him. There are so many mixed feelings. It's painful seeing Bart helpless as a baby, but no one is ready to say goodbye. There is never enough time with the people we love. Thomas looks sadly at the closed door to the den.

They make enough spaghetti and meatballs to feed a small army. Sadie tosses a salad and slices garlic bread. Cait finally emerges from the den, eyes red and swollen, clutching a wad of tissues in her hand. Thomas approaches her.

"I'm so sorry, Cait. Sadie told me what the nurse said."

"Thanks, Tom. People are coming." Cait avoids eye contact. "Thanks for cooking." Thomas tries to hug her, but Cait excuses herself and moves past him.

For the next few days, the family camps out around Bart's hospital bed. They take turns leaving to shower, change clothes, or pick up food to keep them going. Thomas makes a huge pot of chicken soup. Sadie makes brownies. Matt stocks the refrigerator with drinks. Friends and neighbors drop off an array of baked goods. Bart's friends from grammar school, his fishing buddy, guys he golfed with, and Sam come to reminisce and say goodbye. Everyone who cares about Bart is welcomed and fed.

On a frosty January night, surrounded by his family, Bart takes his last breath. Cait sleeps in a recliner next to Bart, never leaving his side. The sound of his labored breathing lets her know he is still with her. Then it's quiet. Bart is gone. Cait crumples forward onto his body, sobbing. The family, roused from restless sleep, gathers around. No one knows what to say. There are no words that could help. Sadie makes coffee, knowing no one is going back to sleep. Cait holds Bart's cool hand. They say that when you die, your life passes before your eyes. For Cait, a new widow, it also seems to be true. Memories of life with her husband flood her brain like a Technicolor movie.

"I love you, sweetheart. Godspeed to wherever it is you're going. Let me know you get there safely, okay?" Cait blots an endless stream of tears. She blesses herself with the sign of the cross, the way she was taught in Catholic school. "Lord, please bless Bart and take good care of him. He's a good man but terrible with directions, so show him the way. And while you're at it, we're hurting here, me and my family. We could use your blessings too. Amen."

There is a chorus of quiet amens. Sadie and Barrett hold their mother, clinging to their family, now reduced by one. Matt calls hospice to let them know Bart is gone. The hospice nurse arrives quickly, comforting the family and officially pronouncing Bart's death. Thanks to hospice, the details were decided weeks ago. Hospice contacts the funeral home, and within hours, they arrive to take Bart's body away. Cait sits pale and motionless on the couch. Sadie helps her into the bedroom, tucking her in bed and then curling up against her. Thomas peeks into the room, and his heart aches seeing mother and daughter together in pain. Gently, he closes the door.

February is a gray, dismal month followed by a raw and unusually snowy March. By April, everyone is ready for spring. Daffodils and tulips poke up out of the ground and burst into colorful blooms. Spring is a time for hope and new beginnings. Bart's death sits heavily on Cait's heart, but spring inspires her to move forward a bit at a time. She sorts through Bart's things and plans a memorial. Grief isn't something that can be rushed. When its grip loosens, moving forward feels not only possible, but necessary.

Bart was very clear about what he wanted after his death. Cremation for sure. No wake or funeral. He couldn't imagine people staring at his lifeless body. Not that he would care at that point, but still, in his mind, it was creepy. He wanted a big party with food, stories, photos, and music.

Cait rents the VFW hall and gets to work with the help of Matt and Thomas. Being busy is a relief. Thomas's band practices Bart's favorite tunes. Chester's restaurant is hired to provide smoky barbeque with all the fixings.

The memorial is a cheerful event punctuated with moments of sadness. Friends and family laugh, share stories, and eat heartily. Cait sets a place for Bart at the front of the room. An open beer bottle sits on the table, and his favorite jean jacket is draped over the chair, leaving the impression that he'll be right back. People sit at the table, chatting as if Bart is present and engaged. And maybe he is.

Friends step up to a mic between songs and tell stories. They are sweet, poignant, and often funny. His buddy tells the story of when they went trout fishing. They were new to fly fishing and not very adept. That's an understatement from the sound of it. In grand style, Bart whipped his line over his head and hooked his flannel shirt lying on the bank. The attached shirt flew over his head and slapped the water, scattering trout in all directions. They laughed long and hard.

At the end of the night, everyone pitches in to clean up. Leftovers are packed up. Cait tucks a stack of sympathy cards in her bag. She takes a deep breath, accepting that a chapter in her life is officially closed, but never forgotten.

"Hey. You ready to go home?" Matt asks. "We thought we would come over and help you eat leftovers. Unless you want to be alone?" He side-hugs his sister.

"That sounds good to me. I would love the company."

Thomas finishes helping the band pack up and loads equipment into his Wrangler. Matt and Cait load their cars with projection equipment and leftovers. Thomas and Matt check the hall to make sure they have everything.

"Meet you at the house? Yes?" Thomas asks.

"Yup. See you in a minute," Matt says. Thomas expects that the excitement of the party will wear off before long, and it will hit Cait that Bart is truly gone.

When they get to Cait's, Sadie is waiting for them and starts warming the leftovers. Thomas wanders into the kitchen.

"Hey, kid. How are you doing?" Thomas reaches out to Sadie and wraps her in his arms.

"Okay, I guess. It's tough. Do you still miss your parents?"

"Yup. Every single day. It gets easier, though. I miss your Gramma Bess, too."

Sadie steps back and looks up at Thomas. "I'm glad you are here, Thomas. I know Mom is glad too."

"I would not want to be anywhere else." Truer words were never spoken.

15

Tying Up Loose Ends

By June, Cait is ready to let go of some of Bart's things. Sadie and Barrett help their mother sort through clothing and a basement full of tools and parts from Bart's various projects. His classic Harley-Davidson Super Glide motorcycle has been covered and stored in the back of the garage for so long that it was almost forgotten. Bart couldn't bear parting with it, even though he hadn't ridden it in years. Thirty years ago, he bought it in pieces, cheap. Every spare minute was spent restoring the bike until it was perfect. The family decides to sell it to a Harley enthusiast. They vet the buyer like he is adopting a child. Bart would like knowing the new owner loves the bike as much as he did.

Cait keeps Bart's favorite Nirvana CDs, his jean jacket, and the worn Nirvana T-shirt from a show they went to in New York City. They were still newlyweds, and Cait remembers how excited Bart was to go. He wanted to ride the Harley into the city, but the idea terrified Cait. I-95 on a motorcycle? Never. She wanted to get there in one piece without bugs in her hair, so she insisted on taking the train. When they arrived at the Coliseum, Bart spent thirty minutes waiting in line at the merch table to buy that T-shirt. It became a talisman against the blues hitting Bart at random times. Cait knew something was going on when Bart put that shirt on.

Widowhood is an adjustment, and Cait recoils at that label. The kids and Matt are close by, looking out for her. Thomas and Cait spend a lot of time together. They share a bowl of popcorn while watching movies at his condo. They go to the beach, out to eat, and hike the hills. He is always invited to Sunday dinners with the family. Cait often shows up at band practice, suggesting songs to play. Thomas maintains a respectful distance, waiting for a sign that she is ready to love again.

The band, now called The Old Guys, is performing at East Lyme Day in July. Throngs of people descend on Niantic to stroll the main drag lined with food trucks and vendors. A stage is set up that hosts a variety of local musicians throughout the day. The Old Guys are last to play in the evening before the fireworks. Hanging out with the band reminds Cait of being a teenager waiting outside stage doors hoping for a peek at her idol. The Old Guys play a few originals and classic rock hits that get people singing and dancing. Cait moves through the happy crowd, handing out flyers she created to promote the band. They close out the set with requests and end with "Free Bird", of course.

While packing up equipment, they chat with people and sign flyers. This is not how Thomas saw his music career going, but he feels content. His desire to play arenas has faded along with his youth. After the equipment is stashed in their cars, Thomas and Cait stroll Main Street, before joining spectators to watch fireworks explode over the beach. Cait is happy and holds Thomas's hand as they walk back to the car. She has fewer moments of sadness as time goes on. Neither comments on how effortlessly their warm hands connect. When they get to the condo, Thomas asks Cait to come in. Animated chatter fills the kitchen as they find food to snack on.

"What is this green fuzzy thing, pray tell?" Cait makes a yucky face illuminated by the refrigerator light.

"That's my science experiment. Leave it be."

Kitchen cooperation and teasing are reminiscent of how Cait's mother, Bess, and Thomas's father, James, began an epic love affair in that very kitchen many years ago. Possibly, history is repeating itself. Thomas wonders how Cait feels about him. Cait wonders what kissing him would be like. They make sandwiches and carry them to the patio.

"You lit a candle?" Cait notices the light flickering on the table.

"Hell no. I'm a guy. It's one of those battery candles that turns on and shuts off automatically."

"You are such a *guy*. Although it's pretty nice." Cait finishes her sandwich and washes it down with iced tea. A guy for sure. She likes him that way.

"Want to walk?" Thomas asks. "Okay." Thomas takes Cait's hand and they walk along the water line, chatting about the festival.

"Did you notice that woman in front of the band?" Cait says. "I thought she was going to ask Sam to sign her boob. Good lord. I don't know how you guys deal with all that adoration." Cait rolls her eyes.

"Yeah. It's tough, but we manage." Thomas laughs.

Cait slips off her sandals, gathers up the skirt of her sundress, and wades into the gentle surf.

"It's warm." She splashes Thomas, challenging him to get his feet wet, which could also be code for something else. He trots into the water, splashing Cait and soaking his shorts. This reminds him of the night he and Sunny walked the beach over a year ago. So much has changed. The circumstances are similar, but he has very different feelings. With Sunny, he was attracted but reluctant to get into something that might be hard to get out of. With Cait, he is all in. She plunges into the water, clothes and all. He dives in after her. Cait is a fast swimmer, even when dressed. He swims after her, then they wade back to the beach.

"Well, that was refreshing." Cait grins. "You're a good sport."

"Thanks."

Dripping wet, they walk back to the condo. Inside, Thomas hands Cait a beach towel from the pile by the door.

"Hang on. I'll get something for you to put on." When he returns, Cait is wearing the towel. Her soggy clothes lie in a sandy pile on the floor.

"Sorry. I made a puddle."

Thomas's heart is beating fast. In the old days, he would be making his move, coming in close for a kiss, and tugging on the towel. But this is Cait. He respects her too much to rush into casual sex. If anything happens between them, she will have to make the first move.

"Don't worry about it. It's just water. Here, you can put this on." He hands Cait one of his flannel shirts and takes her wet clothes to the dryer. Cait goes to the bathroom to change. Thomas turns on the fireplace, and Cait joins him on the couch.

"The shirt looks better on you than it does on me. I think you should keep it." His heart is beating fast. A man's shirt is so damn sexy on a woman.

"It was a fantastic day, Tom. I had so much fun. I hate for it to end. Do I get a percentage if you guys get gigs from my flyers?" Cait laughs. Thomas loves her laugh. "Hey, there was so much going on, I never talked to you about that song you gave me for Christmas. I love it and listen to it over and over."

"I'm glad you like it. A dream woke me up, and I couldn't go back to sleep, so I wrote that song."

"What was your dream about? Do you remember?"

"It isn't one I will forget. But I would rather not share." Thomas's cheeks flush pink.

"Well, it must have been some dream because the song is beautiful. Thank you. Did you really write it for me?"

"Oh man, now I'm embarrassed."

"Why?" Cait asks.

"I don't know." Thomas shrugs. "I feel exposed, I guess. It wasn't so much a song for you as one about how I felt. I'm sorry. I shouldn't have given it to you. It was a weak moment."

"I'm glad you gave it to me. I like it even more now." Cait smiles.

"Listening to it now, it sounds like a corny romantic comedy where the guy serenades the girl, and they fall in love and live happily ever after. If only relationships were that simple. Right?" Thomas says.

"Not corny at all. When I was young, falling in love was pretty simple. Sexual attraction took over, and wham bam, I was in a relationship. They didn't last, though. Then I met Bart, and it was different. It felt substantial and real. Now, being older, having kids, and losing my husband, it's more complicated emotionally." Cait sighs and shyly arranges the flannel shirt tail to cover her thighs. "The lyrics say I saved your life. How?"

"You cared about what happened to me. I didn't think anyone cared if I lived or died. I know now that wasn't true, but it felt that way. You dragged me to AA and warned me of what I was doing to myself. Without you, I wouldn't be here now. I might be in a Nashville bar, passed out. Or dead," Thomas confesses. Cait is thoughtful.

"Interesting. I do care about you." Cait pauses. "I have to tell you something, Tom. Before Sunny left for Nashville, I ran into her. Literally. I was running into CVS, and she was coming out. It wasn't a moment I was prepared for. I told her how sorry I was about her mother. We sat on a bench and had a little chat. She told me you didn't go to Nashville with her because you're in love with me. Is that true?"

He didn't see that question coming. "Jeez. I'm so sorry she said that to you. I was hoping, at some point, I could tell you myself."

"So, it's true?"

"Yes. It's true. I said nothing about my feelings to anyone. I barely acknowledged them to myself. She picked up on it, though, and wouldn't let it go. I've loved you for a long time. At first, I thought it was simply affection because of your kindness. But since moving here, and knowing you better, I know it's more than that. There was nothing

I could do about it, because...well, for obvious reasons. So, I kept it to myself."

"Interesting. I love you, too," Cait announces without a moment's hesitation. They are so close that Thomas can feel the heat radiating from her body.

"I'm glad to know that. I wasn't sure."

"I wasn't sure either, Tom. I guess we should thank Sunny for breaking the news, eh?" Cait laughs nervously, wondering what happens next. Thomas kisses her softly.

"I wondered what kissing you would be like," Cait whispers. "It's nice." She boldly kisses him back...lingering...tasting and exploring sensations like she is studying a unique specimen. Cait holds Thomas at arm's length, breathless.

"At first, I thought I only had feelings for you because we've known each other forever and gone through a lot. That's true, but there's more. When Bart was being so awful, you protected me. Remember when he was yelling at me in your parking lot, and you came out on your porch? You were my knight in shining armor. That's how I saw you. I'll never forget that. I wanted you to take me away somewhere safe, so I didn't have to deal with anything. Then, when we found out about Bart's illness, I felt so guilty. What kind of wife was I? I tucked my feelings away so I wouldn't have to deal with them. Then Sunny blabbed. Until then, my feelings were my secret. Now, I'm confused. What about Bart and the kids? Are there rules about this kind of thing? Do I have to spend the rest of my life without you to respect my marriage to Bart? I don't know."

"Ya know, Cait, you went through a lot. I can't imagine what it was like for you. It's understandable, to me anyway, why you wanted an escape. I never doubted you loved Bart. You never did anything to be ashamed of. Neither did I."

Cait smiles, reaching for Thomas. He holds her, gently kissing her forehead. Cait looks up at him and Thomas kisses her passionately. It is everything he dreamt it would be.

"Cait? We need to stop, or something could happen that we might regret."

"I don't want to stop."

Thomas can hardly believe this is happening. They had a wonderful day, and now this. He leads her to his bedroom. They lay on the bed. Thomas brushes wet hair away from Cait's face and kisses her softly. Her skin tastes of sea salt.

"Cait? Are you sure about this? If I keep kissing you ..." Her kiss interrupts his words.

"I'm sure." Cait slides her hands under his T-shirt, feeling the warmth of his chest and his heart beating. Thomas slowly moves his hand up Cait's thigh, slipping under the flannel shirt. He unbuttons the shirt and slides it off her shoulders, tossing it on the floor. Thomas feels the heat of her skin against his body. Moonlight bathes them in a soft glow. Is he asleep? Is this a dream?

"I love you, Tom," Cait whispers in his ear.

"I love you, Cait." She's real. It's happening.

"This feels so weird." Cait, wearing Thomas's shirt, makes morning coffee.

"Really? Why?"

"It's a déjà vu thing. I don't know if you are aware, but it's like we're repeating history. My mother told me that your father made pancakes in this very kitchen. This is where they fell in love. Now here we are. Don't you think that's weird? I'm not sure how I feel about that. Do you think they're watching?"

"Jeez, I hope not." Thomas chuckles. "If it's any reassurance, I don't make pancakes."

"Good to know."

Thomas wraps his arms around Cait and kisses the top of her head. "But I make a mean omelet."

Cait stiffens. A crystal-clear memory slams into Cait's mind. The only omelet Thomas ever made for her was the night of the fight, after Bart went to the hospital. The memory jolts Cait into reality. This is all wrong. She can't be doing this. What would her kids say?

"I have to go." Cait rushes to the bedroom and puts on her wrinkled sundress. Thomas's shirt is discarded in a crumpled pile on the floor.

"Cait—" Thomas goes after her as she picks up her purse and rushes to the front door. He tugs at her arm to slow her down.

"What's the matter? What's going on? Talk to me. Please."

"I have to go home." Cait leaves. Thomas watches her get in her car and drive away. He was worried this would happen. Second thoughts, guilt, whatever you want to call it. Maybe it was too soon.

Cait tosses her keys on the kitchen counter, looking around her home. She regrets getting rid of so many of Bart's things. She must keep his memory alive. Collapsing into the living room chair Bart spent so much time in, she runs her hand over the worn fabric, hoping to feel his presence.

"Bart. Talk to me. I'm so sorry." Cait closes her eyes and rocks.

"Cait?" Startled, Cait sits up. For a second, she thought Bart was talking to her, but it was her brother Matt. "Are you okay?"

"Hey Matt. I must have fallen asleep. What brings you by?"

"It's Sunday dinner time. I came to help. Nothing is cooking. Are you sure you're okay?"

"Yeah, I'm fine. Tired. That's what I am. I blanked on Sunday dinner. It will be take-out, okay?"

"Sure. We can figure that out when the kids get here. Can I get you anything? Tea?"

"No thanks. I need to get in the shower." Cait is embarrassed to be caught in yesterday's wrinkled sundress. She rushes up the stairs to the master bedroom. Matt has to be wondering what's going on. No wonder he keeps asking if she is okay. Her hair dried in a mass of salty blond curls. She looks like she has been out all night. Oh my god, what must Matt think? Steam from the shower fills the bathroom as Cait scrubs her body. Wrapped in a towel, she picks out a T-shirt and a pair of shorts. After combing knots from her wet hair, she brushes her teeth, hoping to erase the taste of Thomas. She had sex last night. Beautiful, glorious, exciting, passionate sex. How will she explain this to the kids? Maybe she won't have to. It's just one time. Right?

The family is sitting around the living room studying take-out menus when Cait emerges.

"Mom, you are glowing!" Sadie hugs her mother.

"I am? I just got out of the shower. The water was hot." Do they know? Will Thomas say anything? *Oh my god. Thomas! He usually comes to Sunday dinner.* Cait dashes to the den and shuts the door. The call to Thomas goes to voicemail. Shit. What if he is on his way? Oh man, that would be so awkward.

"Hey, Tom. It's Cait. But you know that...caller ID and everything," she rambles nervously. "Um, I'll text you." He's more likely to see a text.

No Sunday dinner. Talk soon. Send.

In other words, stay away, Tom. Cait composes herself, takes a calming breath, and emerges from the den. The family has decided on sushi from The Spice Club. The minutes tick by slowly. The more time that passes, the more likely it is that Tom got the message. Cait starts to relax a little.

"Mom, what's up? You're acting weird." Barrett observes.

"Me? Jeez, why is everyone asking if I'm okay? I'm not acting weird," Cait chirps. *Oh man, that was weird.* Sadie looks at her funny, like she is trying to read her. They know something is going on. *Chill, Cait. Mind your own business. Pretend everything is normal and you didn't just sleep with Thomas. Oh, dear god, what have I done?*

16

Two Steps Forward, One Step Back

Cait walks inside a large Victorian house at the Pine Grove Spiritualist Camp. There is an eerie atmosphere in the meeting room. Heavy, dark wood trims the doors and windows. The floor has a patina of ancient varnish and layers of wax. Lace curtains, dusty with age, hang at the tall windows. Mismatched chairs create a lopsided circle in the center of the room. A table lamp and a single candle shed just enough light to soften the gloom. If there are spirits of the dead, this is the perfect place for them to hang out. Cait takes a seat to the right of Reverend Janet. The room is buzzing with conversation until Janet rings a small brass bell. Then silence.

"Welcome, everyone. It is wonderful to see you. How many of you are new to a message circle?"

Cait shyly raises her hand and is relieved to see several other newbies.

"Well, that's wonderful. Welcome. Before we start, let's fill you in on the rules and what to expect. When we begin, I ask you to be quiet, unless spirit speaks directly to you. Okay?" Everyone nods in agreement. "I let spirit lead. If I say a name that is familiar to you, raise your hand. I won't go in order, but hope to get a message to everyone tonight. Ready?" People settle themselves in their chairs. Some open notebooks, preparing to record their message. The room is quiet except for the hum of a fan feebly trying to circulate warm, humid air. Cait holds Bart's Nirvana T-shirt on her lap.

After sleeping with Thomas, Cait was wracked with guilt. She desperately wants to know if Bart is okay with her moving forward in her life. She has talked with him and asked him for a sign, but so far, nothing has come through. Will he give her his blessing? Or not speak to her ever again through eternity? That's a heartbreaking thought. Cait knows very little about talking to dead people except what she saw in the movie *The Sixth Sense*. People say it's woo-woo stuff, like carnival fortune tellers taking advantage of vulnerable people. *Well, welcome to the club, Cait. You are now one of those vulnerable people wanting to hear from your dead husband.* Unsure how to approach this, she did what anyone would do—a Google search. There were some very famous and well-respected mediums in the world, like James Van Praagh, John Edward, and the late, great, Sylvia Browne. Cait went to the library to do more research. The librarian, noticing her selections, suggested she visit the Pine Grove Spiritualist Camp in Niantic.

When she got home from the library, Cait looked it up. It was established in the 1800s, the heyday of the Spiritualist Movement. All that was left of the original camp was the rustic temple building and the old Victorian mansion that houses guest mediums and message circles. Cait clicked on the program schedule and saw that there was a message circle scheduled for Wednesday night. She bookmarked that page. The library books told stories about how mediums have helped people find peace after loss. That's what Cait wants. Peace. Encouraged that this spiritual stuff was helpful, Cait made a reservation to attend the message circle. She doesn't know if Bart will speak to her, but she has nothing, except the thirty-five-dollar donation, to lose. Reverend Janet, with over thirty years of experience in the Spiritualist Church, is hosting.

There is a hush as Janet starts the readings, and Cait brings her attention back to the circle.

"Albert is here," Reverend Janet announces. An older gentleman on the other side of the circle raises his hand. "Ah, good. He says he is your brother. Is that correct?" The man nods yes. "He passed away some years ago. He wants you to know he is well and looking out for your grandson."

The gentleman smiles and thanks Spirit for the message. Janet takes a deep breath like she is letting go of Albert, and she sits with her eyes closed while the group waits expectantly. After a few brief messages, Cait wonders if coming was a mistake. It's probably a waste of time. So far, the messages have seemed as vague as newspaper horoscopes.

"Okay, I am hearing music." Janet hums the melody she is hearing. "I'm hearing 'Hello...hello...hello'," Janet sings. It's the bridge from Nirvana's "Smells Like Teen Spirit". Bart would play that song over and over until Cait begged him to stop.

"Oh my god, that's my husband, Bart," Cait whispers, raising her hand. The hair stands up on the back of her neck, and chills run down her arms.

"He wants you to know he feels much better. He misses you and the kids. Was there something important to him in the garage? He's pointing."

"Yes, the Harley he had for years. We just sold it."

"He seems good with that. He's smiling. One last thing, and then I have to move along. He wants you to be happy and not spend your precious life grieving him. Those are his exact words. Okay, moving on." Reverend Janet lets go of Bart and delivers the next message.

Cait shivers. That had to be Bart. She feels it in her body. There's no way Janet could pull those specific details out of thin air. Only the family and a handful of close friends know about Nirvana and the Harley in the garage. *This means, oh my god, there is something after we die. We may not be here anymore, but we are somewhere.* Cait doesn't know what to make of this new information. She is so busy thinking that she misses the rest of the messages. The best part is that Bart wants her to be happy. That message is the answer she was seeking. It's such a relief.

After the last message is delivered, people thank Reverend Janet and file out of the room, chatting. Cait's legs feel like rubber and she has yet to get out of her seat.

"How are you doing?" Janet asks. "I saw the impact the message had. I hope it wasn't my singing." Janet smiles, resting her hand on Cait's shoulder.

"Oh no. Your singing was not a problem. I have never experienced anything like that message before. My husband died in January." Cait shows Janet the T-shirt she is clutching. "This was his favorite shirt. That song? He played it all the time. The message meant everything to me. You have no idea. I didn't expect much from this experience, but I'm in shock. That was Bart. No doubt about it. I have so many questions."

"I am happy to help. As you noticed, not every message comes through with the intensity yours did. He really wanted you to know it was him, without a doubt. If you ever want to sit for a private reading, let me know. I think it might be interesting."

"I'll consider that. Thank you." Cait stands, her legs wobbly, hoping she can make it to her car. She picks up Janet's business card, flyers, and a schedule on her way out. Once in the driver's seat, she takes time to process what happened. This is far beyond the reality she is familiar with. No one told her about any of this in Catholic school. She has to tell Thomas. She turns on her phone and sends a text message.

It's me. Can I come over?

Cait parks in front of the condo. As she gets out of the car, Thomas zooms into the parking lot and parks next to her.

"Cait. I'm happy to see you." Thomas has been worried she might not want to see him. "I was going to call you when I got home."

Cait is smiling—always a good sign. Her eyes are sparkling. Inside, Thomas goes to the kitchen, reaching into the refrigerator for a can of seltzer.

"Can I get you anything?"

"No, thanks. Come, sit. Hurry. I can't wait to tell you about the most amazing thing that happened. Please don't think I'm weird."

Thomas pops the top on the soda can, trying to imagine what would ever make him think that.

"Sit, please." Cait pats the couch cushion. Thomas sits. "First, I want to say I'm sorry I ran out the other morning. When you mentioned making an omelet, it brought back a memory of the night Bart went to the hospital after the fight. Sleeping with you was wonderful. I felt good. It was a relief to finally know, for sure, how we feel, and to hold nothing back. Then the omelet memory made me feel like I cheated on Bart. I was on cloud nine and came crashing back to earth. I worried about what the kids would say. When I got home, I was so distracted, I forgot about Sunday dinner." Cait is talking fast, trying to get all her thoughts out.

"When Matt walked in, he scared the crap out of me. I was still in that wrinkled sundress, not showered, and my hair was a mess. That's why we ordered take-out, and that's why I sent you that weird text. I was so afraid you would show up and say something about us. The kids knew something was going on. Barrett told me I was acting weird. The thought of sitting across the table from you, after...after...what we did, made me self-conscious. What if they figured it out? I felt guilty like I'd betrayed the trust of my family. Logically, I know that's not true, but it felt that way." Cait pauses to catch her breath. She was getting to the good part of the story.

"After all that, I needed to hear from Bart. I know that sounds insane. He's gone. But I was curious about talking to people who have passed, you know, like in that movie? I did some research online and went to the library. The librarian told me about The Pine Grove Spiritualist Camp. Have you heard of it?"

Thomas shakes his head no. Cait excitedly tells Thomas about her experience at the message circle.

"*It had to be Bart!* I was shaking. He said he misses us, me, and the kids. And, now this is the important part, he wants me to be happy and not spend my life grieving. Can you believe that? Wow. I'm so relieved. What do you think?"

That is a really good question. Thomas isn't sure what to think, but he feels let down. He is happy for Cait if mediums are helpful for her. He has no idea if she heard from Bart, but Thomas has just listened to Cait talk non-stop about him. He has a niggling feeling in his gut that Cait isn't ready to move on quite yet. He can't ignore it. So, while Cait is elated, Thomas is disappointed.

"I think it's great you feel better and believe you heard from Bart."

"I don't *believe* I did—I *did* hear from him," Cait tells Thomas. "Aren't you happy? It means we can be together. Of course, it will take a while before the family will be ready to know. I want to keep this between the two of us for now." Cait is excited as she snuggles up against Thomas on the couch. "You look so serious, Tom. What's wrong? I thought you would be happy."

"Cait, I love you. Saturday night was a dream come true." Thomas takes a slow breath. "Look at me." Cait faces him, frowning, her head tilted, questioning. "I hate saying it, but I think we jumped the gun. Bart is still a big part of your life. Thinking about him, worrying about how he would feel, and then going to this medium person? That's proof. I don't want you to be with me because Bart says it's okay. I want us to be together, free and clear. You're right about the family, too. If they are going to be happy for us, they need more time. I won't keep us a secret from anyone."

"Tom, no. They will get used to it. I know they will. I don't want to wait," Cait pleads. "Please don't make me wait." Thomas kisses her softly and holds her close to him.

"Sweet Cait, I'm not going anywhere. I hope we will keep hanging out, working together at the office, and having Sunday dinner. When the time is right, we'll know. If we rush this, we could ruin everything."

Cait sits quietly, thinking. Thomas is afraid Cait will go out and find someone else. Cait is disappointed and hopes she hasn't made a fool of herself.

"Tom, I don't know what I'm doing. I feel so many things. I love you, I'm sure of that. Being with you gave me relief from the agony I feel every day. Everything reminds me of Bart. I open a drawer in the kitchen, and there is a bottle cap from one of his beers. I used to yell at him about flipping those damn tops in the drawer. Now it's a treasured memory. Then I cry. I guess this grieving thing takes longer than I thought."

"It takes as long as it takes."

"I wanted you to take the sadness away. Using you to feel better is not fair. I understand. Being afraid to tell the kids means, despite what I want, it's too soon. When the time is right, I will be thrilled to tell them, and they will be happy for us. I don't know how long this will take, Tom. I'm afraid that if I take too long, you will find someone else. Someone like Sunny." She leans back against the couch cushions and sighs.

"None of us knows what the future holds. I worry about the same thing. What if you take up with the muscle-bound trainer at your gym? All I can say is, the way I love you is not something that has happened for me in a very, *very,* long time. I trust it, Cait. When love is real, it lasts. Take all the time you need. Let's do this right. Okay?"

Two steps forward. One step back.

17

Shaking the Foundation

Thomas finger-picks an original song on his guitar as he watches the Weather Channel.

According to the buzz in town, a hurricane is heading their way. Climate change has generated some weird storms, but a direct hit is not unheard of in New England. Thomas lived in Florida long enough not to underestimate the whims of a hurricane. After a week of dire warnings, a hurricane can end up being a nothing burger. Once, though, Hurricane Wilma surprised everyone. It made landfall in Mexico as a Category 5, causing it to weaken. Floridians, from years of experience, expected it to dwindle and become a Gulf shore rainstorm at worst. Thomas was working in Fort Lauderdale at the time, and no one expected Wilma to be a problem for them. She wandered around the Gulf of Mexico before literally getting a second wind. Wilma intensified, skipped off the Florida Keys, and nailed Fort Lauderdale. The Sheraton Inn, where Thomas was staying, provided a safe shelter. People huddled in an interior ballroom while the storm roared, walls shook, and the power went out. The hotel was built to withstand a hurricane. Thomas doesn't think his condo would fare as well with a direct hit. But this is New England. How bad could a hurricane be?

Thomas's phone rings. "Hey, Sam. What's up?"

"Can you come over?" Sam asks.

"Sure. What's going on?"

"You'll see when you get here." Sam is oddly mysterious. Thomas parks his Jeep and bounces up the stairs to Sam's second-floor apartment. Huffing and puffing, he rhythmically knocks on the door, *Knock, knockity, knock, knock.*

"Hey, Thomas. Thanks for coming over," Sam leads Thomas down a narrow hallway covered with framed photos of his band days. It's his hall of fame, he jokes. When they get to the living room, Thomas sees Sunny and considers bolting back down the stairs. Damn. Thomas can't believe Sam set him up, and he's in no mood for a confrontation with Sunny.

"Thomas. How ya been?" Sunny asks in her soft southern drawl.

"Good. I've been good. Where's Ellie?" Thomas stays standing, nervously toying with his keys.

"She's back home in Nashville. I always did think you cared more about my dog than me."

Thomas sighs in frustration. He will not let her bait him into a stupid argument. Sunny went back to Nashville. They're done. She can think whatever she wants, but, damn, it's hard for him not to vigorously defend himself.

"Sam? What's going on?" Thomas asks.

"Come. Sit. I'm sorry not to warn you, Thomas. Thought you might not come if ya knew Sunny was here. She has something to say." Sam gestures that he is giving Sunny the floor. It's been eight months without a word from her. What could she have to say? Thomas sits on the couch far away from Sunny. Sam takes a seat in the middle.

"Thomas, I came back to Connecticut to take care of some business. It has nothing to do with you, so don't even think I came running back for you. Of course, I had to see my old friend, Sam." Sunny smirks and dips her chin, nodding coyly in Sam's direction. "You know Sam, he can't stand conflict. He talked me into tryin' to clear the air between us. Not sure it's possible, but what the heck. I'm here—might as well see if we can bury the hatchet."

"We can do that, as long as the hatchet isn't buried in my back. I see your mean, passive-aggressive streak has been perfected. That's nice."

"And you have sharpened your sarcasm. Congrats."

"Great. Well, I'm clear." Thomas slaps his thighs and starts to stand, but Sam places a hand on his arm.

"Give the lady a chance. Sunny, behave yourself." Sam needs a whistle to referee this discussion. Thomas sits down, bracing for a further assault on his character.

"I'm not angry. I'm disappointed it didn't work out with us, but *c'est la vie*. How's Cait?" Hearing Cait's name from Sunny irritates Thomas.

"Cait is okay, if you really want to know. Bart died right about the time you left. It was tough on her and the family."

"Yup. I heard. No doubt your loving support carried her through. Were you as *kind* to her as you were to me? Did you offer her the solace of your bed? I am sure there is a part of you that's happy. Now you and Cait are free to carry on." Sunny's snark is like a sharp stick in the eye.

"Whoa, Sunny. This is how you clear the air?" Thomas shouts.

Sunny shrugs. "I'm sorry. You're right. Maybe I'm not as okay as I'd like to be." Sunny swallows hard. "I'm sorry about the way things ended. I was hurt. And angry. I thought things were different between us, but I was mistaken. You were good to me and Mama, and I thank you for that. I mistook kindness for love. It was a shock when you refused to go to Nashville. Sam has been explaining the situation to me. I thought you were a class-A bastard. I was wrong about that. Apparently, you're just an inept jerk. I apologize for acting up and not properly thankin' you for your kindness."

"Thanks, I think. I might be a jerk, but telling Cait how you *perceived* I felt about her was downright mean. Why did you do that?"

"I thought she should know. It was obvious you weren't going to tell her."

"Jeez, Sunny. That was not your business to butt into. Look, you were special to me. All I wanted to do was help. I know what it's like to lose a mother. I'm sorry my actions misled you."

"You wanted to help, but not mislead me? Thomas, *we were sleeping together.* Jesus, at least admit you were a selfish asshole. Or a coward. Don't make me do all the work here. You should have told me the truth," Sunny huffs.

"You're right. I should have told you the truth sooner. I did the best I could. I'm sorry that wasn't good enough for you."

"Listen, I think part of this is my fault," says Sam. "I asked Thomas to be kind to you, considering everything you were going through."

"Isn't that just *perfect!* You two good old boys, talkin' about me and figurin' out what I needed. I'm so damn lucky to have your pity." Sunny folds her arms across her chest and narrows her eyes. Sam shuts up. Sunny is pissed off with a capital "P." Thomas is irritated. If she hadn't thrown him out on Christmas, they would have talked, and this whole scene could have been avoided. He hates scenes. There were way too many dramas with women in his band days. Some of those were doozies, requiring police intervention. Thomas should have listened to his gut and not gotten tangled up with Sunny.

"Did you come here to rake me over the coals, Sunny, or to sleep with Sam?" Thomas can be nasty when he's riled up, and that was a zinger.

"Maybe both, asshole. Why do you care?" Good question, and the ball is in Thomas's court.

Sam groans. "Enough bickering. This is not accomplishing anything."

"You're right. I gotta go. You guys enjoy yourselves." Thomas stands to leave.

"Wait. Don't go," Sunny pleads. "I'm sorry. I get mean when I'm hurtin'."

"Yeah, no shit. I'm sorry this is going badly for you. I said I'm sorry. I didn't mean to hurt you. What more do you want from me?"

"Nothin' Thomas. I want nothin'." Sunny hangs her head, frowning.

Sam lifts his guitar and finger-picks the opening notes of James Taylor's "You Got a Friend".

"Don't mind me, I'll noodle here while you two sort out your business." Sam has a plan. He hopes neither Thomas nor Sunny will be able to resist music to break the ice. Before long, Sunny sidles up to Sam and sings along. Thomas rolls his eyes and tightly crosses his arms. There is nothing like music to open hearts and soften pain, but for Thomas, it will take more than this hokey performance.

"What the hell, Sam? You're into music therapy now?" Thomas asks, shaking his head.

"You know what they say: 'Music hath charms to soothe the savage breast.' You guys are pretty savage. I thought it was worth a shot." Sam shrugs.

"Speaking of music, Sam invited me to your band practice. Do you think you can stand to be around me without fightin'?"

"I have no idea. I used to love singing with you, Sunny. I don't want to fight. Do you think you can hold back on being snarky?"

"Maybe. I already spit out everything that's been festerin'."

"How long will you be here?"

"Not sure yet. I'm staying with Sam. I'll see how long he can stand me." Sunny looks at Sam and smiles. She extends her hand to Thomas in a gesture of peace. Thomas accepts it.

"Truce?" Thomas asks.

"Truce," agrees Sunny.

Let's hope. Because as this storm passes, there is another one brewing.

Tropical depression number eight is now a full-blown hurricane named Valerie. The storm meandered in the Atlantic basin and is now picking up speed and strength. Spaghetti models seem to agree it will skirt the Outer Banks of North Carolina and land somewhere in New England. Thomas got a note from the condo association that if Valerie threatens, they will be boarding up the doors and windows on the ocean side of the building.

At Sunday dinner, the family makes a plan. Cait's house is inland, and it has a safe, dry basement. It's surrounded by trees, which is a problem if wind takes them down, but there isn't anything they can do about that. It is decided that Thomas will store his valuable equipment at Cait's and hang out there until the storm passes. Sadie wants to be with her mother and will bring her husband Jack and young children. Barrett and his family will stay at Matt's in Stonington. Cait makes a to-do list, and the family divides up tasks. These storms pass quickly, but the aftermath can be a lingering problem. It might be days before Thomas can get back to his home to survey the damage.

Four days later, Valerie turns into a monster storm with projected landfall somewhere between Old Saybrook, Connecticut, and the Rhode Island border. The weather is already changing. The air is thick with tropical mugginess. In the past, hurricanes lost a lot of their juice traveling over the colder waters of the Atlantic. But ocean temperatures keep climbing. Valerie will weaken, but not by much.

Hours before landfall, Thomas locks up his condo, picks up pizza, and drives back to Cait's. It will be a long night. As he walks into Cait's house, his phone rings.

"Hey Sam, you set to ride this out?"

"Not exactly. We've been told to evacuate. Can we come to your place?"

"They evacuated my place, too. If anything gets destroyed, it will be my condo."

"Shit. Of course. What am I thinkin'?" Sam mutters.

"I'm at Cait's. Hold on." Thomas mutes his phone and asks Cait if Sam can join them.

"Sure, of course. He is always welcome. It will be fun. Tell him to bring his guitar."

"Okay. He might bring someone with him. Is that okay?"

"Sure. I wouldn't want anyone stranded in this storm. Tell them to come on over."

"Sam? Come to Cait's. Bring your guitar, sleeping bags, whatever you need. It will be a hurricane party." This is where it gets tricky, because Thomas never mentioned his encounter with Sunny. He has to tell Cait who Sam's plus-one is.

"Cait? Can I talk to you for a sec?" Thomas takes her aside for a private conversation. "Sam is bringing Sunny. She's in town on business and staying with him."

Cait groans. "Really?" Cait rolls her eyes and purses her lips. "I guess we have to let her in. What kind of person would I be to leave her out in a hurricane?"

Thomas breathes a sigh of relief. He figures there will be more to talk about after the storm blows over, but this is good for now.

"Thank you. I know it will not be the most comfortable arrangement, but they have to evacuate, and I'd hate for them to go to a shelter. It's only for the storm. As soon as we can get out, they will be on their way." Thomas puts his arms around Cait. Sadie chases after Gracie, running at full speed in Cait's general direction. She stops in her tracks when she sees her mother and Thomas, unsure of what she is interrupting. Thomas steps back. Cait makes a quick recovery, telling Sadie that Sam and Sunny are joining them.

"Thomas was trying to make nice. He knows I don't like Sunny." Cait laughs nervously, scowls at Thomas, and scoops up Gracie. Sadie accepts the explanation. For now.

The wind is picking up, and the eye is still miles offshore. Sam and Sunny arrive with sleeping bags and guitars. The TV is repeating constant updates. They go outside to move the cars and make sure everything is securely stowed. Ominous cloud bands, black as charcoal, speed across the sky.

"This is not going to be good," Thomas says. Before they are in lockdown, he plays a rousing game of tag outside with the kids. Cait fills a carafe with hot coffee and slides a pizza into the oven. Sunny approaches Cait.

"Cait, thank you for taking me in. I know we've had our issues. I was not expecting to be evacuated, and I'm grateful for your hospitality." Cait isn't exactly giving Sunny the cold shoulder, but she's reserved. It's hard to forget the confrontation outside CVS last January.

"It's okay. I had bigger things to deal with after you left."

"Yeah, Thomas told me about your husband. I'm so sorry. I lost a husband, too. I know how painful it is."

Cait's eyes mist over. "Well, thank you for your sympathy. You were married?" Cait is curious, which might be the first step toward reconciliation.

"Yup, married twice. My second husband died. He was the love of my life and the bane of my existence." Sunny chuckles. "Funny how a man can be both."

"I know exactly what you mean. What happened?" Cait asks.

"He was a musician in the Grand Ole Opry. He and some of the guys were in a van heading to a gig, and there was an accident. My husband was killed."

"I'm so sorry. I had no idea." This is a new side to Sunny, and Cait doesn't want to let it pass. "Please, sit. Want some coffee?" Cait asks.

"Sure. Thank you."

Cait pours two mugs of hot coffee, and they sit at the kitchen island. She rests her hand on Sunny's arm. "I'm not sure which is harder, knowing your husband is going to die, or getting a surprise phone call. They are both pretty awful. How long ago was that?"

"It's been years. Not as fresh as your loss."

"Yeah, I'm still pretty raw. I miss Bart. Let me show you something." Sunny follows Cait to a kitchen drawer. "You will laugh at me." Cait opens the drawer and shows Sunny the pile of bottle caps, telling her the story and explaining their significance. "I can't bear to part with them."

Sunny loops her arm through Cait's, patting her hand. "I'd never laugh at that, hon. My man used to leave guitar picks all over the house. Even in the bathroom, if you can believe that. It was a long time before I could bear to pick 'em up."

"Does it get easier, Sunny? Do you still miss your husband? I hate to think I will feel this lost for the rest of my life."

"Oh, yeah. With time. But everyone's different. I will always love him, and never forget, but after a while, I stopped crying every day, stopped blaming myself for God knows what, and started to enjoy life again. It was a gradual process."

"Well, I'm looking forward to not crying every day. Has there been anyone since then that you cared about?" Cait catches herself before saying more. "Ouch, look who I'm asking! I'm sorry, Sunny." Cait is embarrassed to bring up this uncomfortable topic.

"Yeah, there's been a select few. Thomas is the latest in that parade. Seeing him still stings some, but I don't blame you, Cait. People can't help who they fall for. He fell for you. My loss."

"That's kind of you, Sunny. I'm happy you are here. Really, I am."

The family eats pizza and monitors the storm on the Weather Channel. Bands of rain are coming through, and wind is picking up. Sadie and her husband Jack take the kids downstairs to get settled for the night while Thomas, Sam, Sunny, and Cait play a ruthless game of Monopoly. When the house goes dark, Cait reaches for a flashlight and runs downstairs to check on Sadie. The kids are asleep.

"Okay, that's it for me," announces Sunny. "I was in New Orleans during Katrina, and these storms freak me the heck out. I am going downstairs to hide in my sleeping bag." Cait hands Sunny the flashlight.

"I'll go with you, Sunny." Sam follows along. That leaves Thomas and Cait. They peer out the sunroom windows, watching lightning streak across the sky and tree tops being blown violently. Rain bands come and go. Thomas puts his arm around Cait.

"I saw you and Sunny talking today. Everything okay?"

"Yeah. It was good. We were talking about widowhood. I didn't know she lost her husband. It softened my opinion of her. A little. I blundered and asked her if she had been with anyone since her husband died. She doesn't blame me for your breakup, but I get the sense she blames you."

"Yeah. Sam roped me into a confrontation the other day. Sunny wanted to clear the air. But first, she needed to beat me up one more time. I think we ended up okay. Friendly enough to let her stay here with us."

"Well, I doubt she will ever be my best friend, but I did appreciate the conversation we had. Do you think this is as bad as the storm will get?"

"Not sure. Hope so." They sit on the couch, listening to updates on the computer. Cait checks her phone. The battery is full, and there is a signal. She calls Matt to check on them.

"Matt? How are things at your house?" They reassure each other that so far, all is well. A loud crack, followed by a ground-shaking thud, startles them. "Matt, we're okay. A big tree just came down out front, but missed us. We are heading to the basement. Love you. Be safe."

Even in the basement, the deafening noise outside keeps them on edge. The kids are the only ones able to sleep. Trees are coming down with resounding booms, lightning flashes, and wind gusts rattle the windows. The rain, driven sideways by wind, pounds against the house. Sam passes a guitar to Thomas and grabs another for himself. "

Time for a little music therapy," Sam says softly. He finger-picks the melody for "Amazing Grace" and sings softly. Thomas accompanies, and they all sing the song over and over.

Thomas plays a folksy version of Creedence Clearwater Revival's "Have You Ever Seen the Rain".

"Okay, I get it. We are going with weather tunes," Sunny whispers. "How about this one?" She borrows Sam's guitar and sings "Sunshine on My Shoulders" by John Denver. "Back to you, Sam." Sunny passes the guitar to him.

Sam plays the lullaby-like version of "Somewhere over the Rainbow" recorded by Israel "IZ" Kamakawiwo'ole.

"Okay, that's enough for me. I'm hiding my head under the covers." Sam yawns. "G'night"

"Goodnight, Sam." Cait pulls a quilt over herself on a couch. Thomas lays his sleeping bag on the floor next to her.

"Goodnight, everyone. Love y'all," Thomas says.

"We love you too," Cait echoes. She hangs her arm off the couch, resting her fingertips on Thomas's shoulder.

18

Clean-up

The next morning, the sun is bright and the sky is crystal clear, as if Mother Nature hadn't thrown a destructive tantrum the day before. The kids wake up talking and giggling. The adults open their eyes slowly, their aching backs reminding them they are sleeping on the basement floor. Upstairs, Cait throws open the curtains, revealing a shocking scene of destruction.

"Valerie sure musta' been pissed off," Sam comments.

"Lord, what a mess. Looks like we aren't going anywhere today with that huge tree blocking the road."

"Yup. That's the reason why the power's out. See how it pulled down those wires?" Sam notes.

"So much for getting the electricity back today. Cait, got any influence with the town to get this fixed?" Thomas teases.

"Absolutely none, I'm sorry to say." Cait frowns. "I hope they can clear the road soon, though. What if there is an emergency?"

"They would have to send in a chopper, I suppose. Let's try not to have an emergency, okay? I'm sure the town is doing the best it can. Probably a lot of damage to deal with."

Without the normal activity and electrical hum of appliances, the neighborhood is eerily quiet. The peace is broken when a neighbor starts a generator, followed by a chorus of chainsaws. The yard is littered with limbs and branches, but no windows are broken, and the roof, minus a few shingles, is intact. They are lucky. The cars, parked in a protected area behind the house, are safe. Sam's car is dented by a limb that came down on the hood, but overall, it could have been a lot worse. Up the street, a tree is lying across a neighbor's roof, crushing it like an eggshell. Breakfast is a cup of lukewarm coffee and bowls of cereal with milk that's on the edge of going bad.

"Damnit! I can't stop flipping the flippin' light switch," Sadie growls.

"I know. I just attempted to heat my coffee in the microwave," Sam commiserates.

"Old habits die hard. By next week, you'll be used to it," teases Thomas, ducking to avoid the pot holder Sadie throws at him. The natives are getting restless. While Cait has cell phone service, she gives her brother a call.

"Matt. How are things at your place? Everyone okay?" Cait asks, shushing the shenanigans in the kitchen.

"We made it through okay," Matt reports. "How about you guys?"

"Same here. We're stuck because so many trees are down. The power went out last night, and it looks like it will be out for a while. But the house is okay."

"I guess we're all lucky. Barrett has the kids outside cleaning up branches. Then we're raiding the refrigerator and eating everything before it turns. I hope it doesn't kill us. You have gas for your grill, I hope? Any word on mom's condo?"

"Yes, we have gas, big brother. We'll eat well today, but tomorrow who knows? We have lots of peanut butter," Cait jokes. "No word on the condo. Thomas is anxious to hear something."

"Yeah, I bet he is. Okay, well, we're set here. I planned ahead for once. Stay in touch, sis. Barrett will call later. Love you."

After a hearty meal of eggs, bacon, and leftover pizza, they get to work. The kids gather twigs for the fire pit. Gracie picks up a single twig, toddles across the yard, and carefully places it in the fire pit. She takes the job seriously and will be busy with that for a while. Neighbors walk up and down the street, stopping to chat and collect news. No one knows when the street will be open.

Supper is everything they can salvage from the freezer, tossed on the grill. Dessert is marshmallows roasted around the fire pit. When the little ones start to fade, they all go inside. Sadie reads stories to her children by flashlight. Her husband, Jack, is checking his phone for news. Everyone else is playing Scrabble by lantern light and arguing over which words are legal.

"Snork is not a word!" Sunny berates Sam.

"Is too. It's a cross between snark and dork. That gives me nine points! Ha! I'm ahead."

Thomas and Cait shake their heads and smile.

"I like that word, Sam. I'm going to start using it," Thomas says. Sunny gives Thomas a dirty look, and they move on to invent other words. Thomas's phone dings a text notification from the condo association.

"Shit!" Thomas exhales and slumps back in his chair. "The condo flooded. Of course. The place is a disaster, and FEMA is coming to look at the damage in town. I'll call the insurance company tomorrow. I pay through the nose for flood insurance, so the damage better be covered. It will be a long time before I have a place to live, though, so I'll need to rent an apartment while renovations are getting done." Thomas is ticking off everything that needs his attention.

"An apartment? Don't be ridiculous, Tom. You can stay here as long as you want. I have plenty of room," Cait says. Thomas would like to jump on that offer, but wonders if that's a good idea considering how he feels about Cait. The chance that being roommates could slip into something more is a risk Thomas would love to take, but if their timing is off, it could end badly. He doesn't respond to Cait's offer one way or the other. He'll wait to see how it plays out. Maybe she is just being nice, and the offer doesn't mean anything.

"I bet your Jeep can scoot around the downed trees, and we can get over there to see what's up," suggests Sam.

"You read my mind. How's our garage doing, Sam? Have you heard from Monte?" After Sunny sold her mother's house, the band needed a place to practice. Perry's friend, Monte, offered his garage in New London.

"It's cool. No flooding. Debris was blown around, but no major damage. Monte said power is out everywhere, though, and cell service is spotty. He heard Valerie knocked down a cell tower or two."

"I'm glad our equipment is safe. I guess that's one good thing." Thomas is glum, thinking about the moments in the condo with family, and his decision to move in. The destruction breaks his heart. It will eventually be repaired, but it will never be the same.

"Three good things, Tom. We are safe, and so is Matt. I feel sad about the condo, though," Cait shares.

"Yeah. Even though it's just stuff, it's still sad. I hope my dad's desk survived. I shoulda' moved it out of there."

"I hope it can be salvaged. I know how special that desk is," Cait reassures Thomas, resting a comforting hand on his arm. Sadie raises an eyebrow at her husband with a look that says, *See? Told ya.*

"Something is going on with those two," Sadie whispers to her husband. "I can feel it."

"Maybe. Would that be a bad thing?" Jack asks. Sadie thinks about that.

"No, I suppose not. It would be an adjustment, though, and I'm not ready."

"They aren't either, or they would be open about it. Leave 'em be, Sadie. Whatever is going on, they can handle it, and so will we."

On the second day post-Hurricane Valerie, the neighborhood has run out of patience. Armed with chainsaws, the neighbors go to work on the huge tree blocking the road. The team effort pays off, and a narrow passage around the tree trunk is opened. Thomas, unable to wait another second, gets his keys, announcing he is going to check on the condo. Sam volunteers to go with him.

"Be careful. *Please?*" Cait demands.

"We will. We'll stay in touch."

The route to the condo is circuitous around streets closed by downed wires and debris. The closer they get to the shoreline, the more damage there is. Boats lay on their sides in yards like beached whales. When they arrive at the condo parking lot, the grounds crew is clearing sand with shovels and a small bulldozer. Caution tape blocks the stair-wells. Neighbors survey the damage, shaking their heads. Thomas approaches them.

"Hey. How ya doin'? This looks awful. Have you been inside?"

"Not yet. It's bad, though."

"I'm on the ground floor, so I imagine my place is totaled. Are they letting people go in?"

"Ground floor? Your place flooded for sure. We're on the third floor and lost part of the roof. They're keeping us out until they inspect the stairs. You might be able to get in to grab stuff, but that's about it."

"I hope you can get in soon. Wish me luck." Thomas and Sam approach his front door, unlock it, and give it a push. The door moves a few inches before jamming up against wet sand. "We aren't getting in this way. Come on, let's look around back."

They pick their way through debris to the back of the building. The beach looks like a giant hand sculpted it into an unfamiliar new shape. Pilings, from docks torn apart by the storm, litter the shore like Lincoln Logs. On the patio, seaweed and sand are piled up against the soaked plywood covering the French doors. The storm surge buckled the doors and flooded the condo. It's a mess. Bess's heart would be broken if she could see this. Thomas clears sand with his bare hands and pulls on the soggy plywood to make enough space to squeeze inside.

"You got that flashlight, Sam?"

Sam hands Thomas his Maglite. A thin beam of light travels over the interior, revealing snapshots of destruction in the soggy gloom. The floor is thick with mud, and his belongings are scattered everywhere. The waterline is halfway up the walls. He sloshes his way through the living room to the bedrooms. His black lacquered bedroom furniture is ruined. Thomas inhales and girds himself to look in the studio. The only thing in the condo that cannot be replaced is his father's antique desk.

"Sam?" Thomas calls. "Can you come in here and help me? I'm in the studio."

Sam picks his way through mud and debris to where Thomas is trying to lift his father's desk.

"I have to get this out of here. It needs to dry out. If it stays, I will never be able to save it." Salt water has soaked the wood, making it impossible to open the drawers. The weight of it is too much for the two men. Thomas collapses to his knees. "It's hopeless, Sam. No way we can move it."

"Hold on, Thomas. Be right back." Sam approaches the grounds crew working in the parking lot. He explains the situation and asks if they can help.

Two strapping young men, with ropes, pulleys, and a dolly, wrestle the desk out of the condo and into the light of day.

"Now what?" the tall, skinny guy asks. Thomas hasn't thought past getting it out of the condo. He wants to get it to Cait's and tuck it safely in her garage.

"I want to get it to my friend's garage. I can't leave it out here in the parking lot. You guys got any ideas?"

"I got a truck. If we can load it in, be happy to drive it over for ya," Gus, a brawny man covered with tattoos, offers. "We were about to quit workin' here anyway."

"Really? That's fantastic. Thank you. I'm so grateful. I'll make it worth your while," Thomas pledges.

"Hey, we're happy to help. Besides, we needed a break from movin' sand," Gus says with a grin. "People helpin' people is what it's all about. Nothin' like a disaster to bring out the best in folks."

Once the desk is safe in Cait's garage, Thomas and Sam go inside the house.

"Cait?" Thomas calls.

"Yeah, what's up? How's the condo?"

"It's totaled. But we had help getting the desk out of there, and it's in the garage drying out." Thomas leans on the kitchen island. "Sam and I are going to go back out and see if we can find a store that's open. What do we need?"

"Milk and bread for sure. Ice, if you can find it. And whatever else that looks good to you. Be careful."

"We will. Be back soon. Come on, Sam, let's see if we can find a store that's open."

The Stop & Shop is dark and locked up tight. They drive around listening to the radio. Bradley Airport is open, so Sunny can get to her flight tomorrow. FEMA and Governor Lamont declare the shoreline a disaster area. Eversource and United Illuminating are working day and night to restore power, assisted by crews from half a dozen states. They say it will take time. Thomas pulls into a convenience store on Pennsylvania Avenue, where people are buzzing around. Generators are running to keep the lights and coolers on, but the gas pumps are not working. Bagged ice is long gone. They buy milk, bread, and snacks.

When they pull into Cait's driveway, four-year-old Connor runs out to greet them. Little Gracie trails behind, trying to keep up.

"Did you get us candy?" they ask excitedly. Thomas grins and opens his jacket pocket for Connor to reach in. "Oh boy. Sour Patch Kids!" He rips open the pouch and offers Gracie one.

Gracie spits it out. "Ooo, yucky."

"Here, honey, I have something for you." Thomas takes a KitKat bar from his other pocket. She grins, and Thomas lifts her into his arms, carrying her to the house.

"You made it. How are things out there?" Sunny asks.

"Good news and bad news," Sam says cryptically. "The airport is open. Streets are passable but tricky. My apartment looks okay, but we didn't go inside. Power is out everywhere. Sal's is open. He has a generator and wood-fired ovens." Sam sets two large pizza boxes on the island. "Cheese pizza only. No frills, and don't even ask! If his supplies hold out, he will be rich after this. The place was mobbed."

A crowd forms around the island, hands grabbing slices of delicious hot pizza.

"We got milk, bread, and snacks, Cait. Everything is picked over. I hope you like salt and vinegar potato chips and macadamia nuts." Thomas tucks the milk into the cooler of rapidly melting blocks of ice. He shows them pictures of the condo.

"The insurance company is overwhelmed with claims. I left a message."

"Oh, Tom. That's awful. I'm heartbroken." Cait frowns, side-hugging Thomas.

"On the plus side, anyone who wants to go home, it's possible. The radio said that power will start to be restored later today for a lot of folks and will take a week or more to get to everyone," Sam adds. Thomas's phone rings. It's his brother Andy.

"Are you okay? I just heard about the hurricane. Jeez, you'd think Montana is on the moon for all the news we get."

"Yeah. Just my luck after living in Florida to get hit by a hurricane in New England. We're fine. But the condo is destroyed."

"Oh, man. I'm so sorry, Thomas. What about Dad's desk?" Andy asks.

"I managed, with the help of some guys, to get it out of there before it was beyond repair. It's drying out in Cait's garage. It's damaged, but I'm hoping to fix it. I guess this is the risk of living on the shoreline." Thomas sighs.

"I'm glad you're safe. That's the important thing. Where are you staying? I imagine you will be condo-less for a while," Andy says. Thomas texts pictures to Andy and tells him he is staying at Cait's for now.

"You can always come to Montana, little brother. We'd love to have you close by," Andy suggests.

"Thanks, Andy, but I think I will have my hands full here for a while."

On the third day after Hurricane Valerie, the town and power company arrive before dawn with a caravan of trucks and heavy equipment. For the first time ever, Cait is overjoyed to be awakened by the sound of utility vehicles.

A few hours later, the power is on, and their lives head toward normalcy. Sunny thanks Cait for her hospitality, and Sam takes her to the airport. Sadie and Jack take the kids home. The house is finally quiet. Thomas and Cait are alone. They sit at the table eating a meal that Cait scraped together with bare essentials. Thomas lights a candle and turns off the overhead light.

"Tom, what the heck? Now we have power, and you turn off the lights?" Cait shakes her head.

"I like eating by candlelight. It's romantic. Sue me." Thomas watches the candlelight reflecting in Cait's eyes.

"What are you looking at?" Cait asks.

"You."

Cait smiles.

19

The Beat Goes On

Weeks after Hurricane Valerie blew through Niantic, life is returning to normal, minus a few trees. Many shops and restaurants are open again. The grocery store is restocking shelves. Reconstruction is ongoing. Miraculously, the foundation office only suffered minor flooding.

Thomas recovers personal items from the condo that survived the flood. Everything else is piled in grotesque heaps in the parking lot, awaiting removal. The constant sound of saws, hammers, and nail guns punctuates the air. Dehumidifiers hum full-time. Thomas's new doors secure a hollowed-out shell lined with studs. Now it's a matter of scheduling a contractor to rebuild. He stands in the middle of what was the living room, looking at the fireplace stripped of walls. The condo seems smaller without walls.

Thomas is considering design changes to modernize the space. Maybe an open floor plan with recessed lighting, a guest bathroom, and indestructible vinyl plank flooring would work. Thomas is afraid Cait won't like his ideas. She will want to make it exactly the same as it was. The condo holds fond memories of Cait's mother, and change is not her favorite thing. But unless another hurricane comes calling, this may be the only opportunity to create a home the way Thomas wants it.

In the meantime, he and Cait are living in her house. They're getting comfortable seeing each other first thing in the morning, without scrambling to look good and have fresh breath. They argue about what to watch on television and fight over the remote. After a polite goodnight, they go to their separate rooms. In the morning, they squeeze past each other getting coffee, touching briefly, and jumping away. Boundaries are strictly enforced like an electric fence. Chores are divided up, and they get into a roommate rhythm.

Thomas slips under the covers in his room alone. As he closes his eyes, he hears Cait scream. Like Superman in jockey shorts, he leaps out of bed and rushes to Cait's bedroom. She is kneeling on the bed, her eyes wide with fear.

"What's wrong?"

"There is a mouse in here. It ran over my foot and under the dresser," Cait says. "I know this is such a girlie thing, but I don't like mice," she tells him, looking embarrassed. "I'm sorry to wake you. I freaked out."

"Hey, it's okay. I'm afraid of clowns. If you see one of those warn me." Thomas teases. "We'll get some traps tomorrow. They just want to find a warm place for the winter. Do you want to sleep in my room tonight?" Thomas asks, expecting her to decline.

"Yes. Can I please? Are you sure you're okay with that?" Cait asks.

"Yes. I'm sure." For a quick second, he considers switching rooms with her. He's okay with mice. But on second thought, it would be nice to have Cait sleeping next to him. "Come on. We'll close this door and deal with Mickey Mouse tomorrow." Cait is wearing a pink Victoria's Secret nightshirt that barely touches her knees. Her graying blond hair is pulled up in a loose ponytail. She is the sexiest woman Thomas has ever seen. They get in his bed and turn out the light. He will be a gentleman if it kills him. He lies on his back, hands folded over his chest, eyes closed. Cait rolls toward him.

"Hey. Thanks for letting me sleep here."

"No problem."

"Okay. Great," Cait says, watching him.

"What?" Thomas asks. "I can tell you want to say something."

"I do. Yes, I certainly do. You must be psychic." Cait laughs nervously.

"Okay then. *What?*"

Cait snuggles up close. "I just wanted to say goodnight."

"Okay. Goodnight."

"It is customary in my family to say goodnight with a kiss."

Thomas's eyes snap open. He turns to face Cait. She kisses him gently goodnight. *Is that a friendly kiss or an invitation kiss?* He wonders. It doesn't matter, because he is already kissing her deeply, bringing her body close.

"Cait. I don't think this is a good idea. Remember what happened the last time?" he says between kisses. "I'll go sleep in your room."

"No, Tom. Please stay here with me."

"Okay, but behave yourself." Thomas cautions. "Goodnight."

"Okay. I'll try." Cait snuggles up against Thomas, softly kissing his ear lobe, cheek and working her way down his neck. "You smell so good." Cait whispers. Thomas groans.

"Cait, you need to stop. Remember our agreement." Thomas lies still on his back, trying to think of anything other than Cait's soft lips on his cheek.

"What agreement? I don't remember any agreement." Cait slips her hand under Thomas's T-shirt, tracing her fingers over his chest.

"Are you trying to seduce me, woman?" Thomas asks.

"Yes. How am I doing?"

"It's working." Thomas's resistance dissolves. He turns toward Cait, kissing her passionately.

He can feel her heart beating against his chest. If this were a horse race, they'd be off and running.

Thomas wakes up in the middle of the night, and Cait is gone. He pulls on his boxers and goes to the bathroom. Cait's bedroom door is open a crack, but she isn't in bed. Thomas pads quietly down the hall and peeks down the stairs. Candlelight flickers in the living room. He quickly debates whether to check on Cait or go back to bed. Maybe she can't sleep and doesn't want to bother him. Maybe something is wrong and he needs to help. Thomas grasps the banister and slowly descends to the first floor. Cait is sitting on the couch.

"Can't sleep? Can I sit with you?" Thomas asks quietly.

"Sure. Sit. Tom, we did it again."

"Yes, we sure did." Thomas grins and puts his arm around her, kissing her cheek. Cait exhales one big breath.

"What about Thanksgiving? And Christmas? I woke up wondering how I'm going to manage the holidays."

"What do you mean, manage them?"

"If we are together, how will the kids handle the holidays? It's the first one without Bart. Is it fair to move on so quickly? Just because I'm ready, it doesn't mean they are."

Thomas huffs. "I don't know, Cait. They're grown-ass adults. If you wonder how they feel, ask 'em."

"I suppose. But what if I ask them, and they don't want me to be with someone?"

"Do you need their permission? I'm positive they want you to be happy. If they are concerned about anything, they will tell you. Then we'll work it out." He pauses. "And what do you mean, *someone*? You wouldn't tell them it's us? Me? Or is it *not* me?" Thomas narrows his eyes.

"Of course it's *you*. I thought it would be good to first explore the idea generally."

"What are you afraid of, Cait? Is there something else besides concern for the kid's feelings? Do you want to sow some wild oats before settling down again? I would hate that, but I'd understand. You were married a long time."

"That's ridiculous. There is nothing to be afraid of. I can't wait for us to be together. I'm not interested in sowing anything wild unless it's with you."

"Uh-huh." Thomas bends forward, resting his forearms on his thighs, head down. He hears what she is saying, but he doesn't buy it. He turns his head to look at Cait. "Then what is it? Every time we move forward, you pull back. And tonight, you were the one who turned up the heat. What gives?"

"I know. I'm sorry."

"You're sorry? Look, as hard as it is, I want to be patient. I haven't pushed you because I understand you need time. You're right, it hasn't been a year yet. First holidays are tough. But tonight, you seemed ready to move forward. Now you're pushing me away. The back and forth is making me crazy." Thomas pauses, debating whether to say what he knows needs to be said. "I think it's best if I move out. Then you can take all the time you need to manage the holidays."

"What? *No!* Where will you go? We can figure this out," Cait pleads.

"I don't think so, not like this. I'll ask Sam if I can stay with him until I find a rental. I'm not mad, and I don't blame you for needing time. But I can't live in this house with you. Not like this. What happened tonight will happen again, and you know that. I don't want us to be a dirty little secret, passionate at night and inscrutable during the day. That hurts me, Cait. Do you understand that? Take care of your kids, take your time, and let me know when you're ready." Thomas walks up the stairs, back toward the bedroom.

"Where are you going?"

"Back to bed. It's the middle of the night and I'm tired." Cait rushes after him, following him to his bedroom.

"How dare you! You...you..." Cait sputters. "You *know* what I've been through and how hard it's been. You don't have children. You

don't know what it's like to be a parent. I have to consider my family."
Cait spins on her heels, ready to slam his door.

"Oh, I get it. I'm supposed to understand and empathize with your
pain and suffering. Which, in case you haven't noticed, *I do*," Thomas
announces in a voice a few decibels louder than Cait's. "What about
my feelings, Cait? Don't I deserve consideration too? We are living
here, side by side, pretending we are roommates. Do you know how
often I want to reach out and hold you? Kiss you? Do you know how
hard it is for me to pretend nothing is going on between us?"

"If you were more understanding, we wouldn't be fighting now."
Cait sticks out her chin, crossing her arms over her chest.

Thomas springs up off the bed and stands in front of her, nose to
nose. "Bullshit. We are fighting because you made love to me tonight.
Remember? And now you're scared and want me to put my feelings
aside and forget all about it. I'm supposed to say, 'Sure, Cait, no problem. Is there anything else you'd like?" Thomas's sarcasm is biting.
"How many times are we going to do this? Huh?"

"None of this would have happened if you hadn't asked me to sleep
with you."

"*Excuse me?* It wouldn't have happened if you didn't need protection from a tiny little mouse. Was there a mouse, Cait? Or was that just
an excuse to get into my bed?" Thomas glares angrily at Cait.

"Ach. You are impossible, Thomas Malcolm Ogilvie!" Cait stomps
her foot.

"I'm impossible? *I'm impossible?* How dare you blame me for tonight. I am careful every day not to cross the line, as tempting as it is. I
was a perfect gentleman, and then *you* crossed the line. I gave up a job
in music to help you with the foundation. Remember? How dare you
tell me I'm not understanding," Thomas growls in frustration, raking
his fingers through his hair.

"You are so selfish." Cait's face is crimson with anger. "It's all about
you. Whatever *you* want. Maybe I don't want what you want."

"Then, what *do* you want? All the benefits of a man around the house, to chase mice with an occasional fuck thrown in? You're the selfish one. You aren't afraid, Cait, you just don't care. I'm glad I finally know that."

"Don't be *stupid*. Of course, I care. Do you think I would sleep with you if I didn't care?"

"Honestly, Cait, I don't know anymore." Thomas shakes his head in disbelief.

"Argh. You are so infuriating." Cait leaves, slamming his door.

After a restless night, Thomas wakes up early and makes coffee. Last night's surprising events are consuming his thoughts. His anger made him say things he regrets. Maybe Cait feels the same way, but the bottom line is the same. Thomas needs to move out. He texts Sam asking if he has space for him temporarily.

Sam texts back: *Of course. You get the couch.*

Thomas thanks him, texting that he will see him later. Maybe he should have stayed with Sunny, the bird in hand, because Cait, the bird in the bush, is impossible. Sam knows Cait well—let's hope he has words of wisdom to offer along with his couch.

Cait walks past Thomas into the kitchen and pours a mug of coffee. No words are exchanged. She sits at the opposite end of the table, scrolling on her phone. The silence is deafening. Thomas stands, takes his mug into the kitchen, rinses it, and places it in the dishwasher. Without a word, he goes to his bedroom and starts packing. Cait is nowhere to be seen while Thomas loads his Jeep. He knocks gently on her bedroom door.

"What?" she says with a sharp edge to her voice.

"I'm sorry about last night. Can we talk?"

"I have nothing to say to you, Thomas."

"Okay. I'm going to Sam's. I'll pick up the rest of my stuff later."

No response. Thomas leaves, closing the front door tightly and hoping that isn't a metaphor for his future with Cait.

Thomas, guitar strapped to his back, thumps his suitcase up the stairs to Sam's apartment. Sam greets him, helping with his bag.

"Make yourself comfortable," Sam says. "You want coffee?"

"Sure. Thanks."

Sam pours two mugs, handing one to Thomas. "So, to what do I owe the pleasure? I thought things were going well at Cait's."

Thomas sighs loudly. "Cait and I had a fight. A *whopper*."

"I figured it was something like that. What happened?"

Thomas tells Sam the story, including the scary mouse, managing Christmas, and slamming doors.

"Every time we move forward, I get hopeful, and then she pulls back. Cait got up in the middle of the night. We talked for a bit, and then we fought. We have clamped down our feelings so much that this stuff was simmering and had to come out at some point. I'm sorry it came out with so much anger. I told her I couldn't do the back and forth anymore and was moving out. I'll find an apartment as soon as I can, Sam. I don't know if I did the right thing for *us,* but I know it's the right thing for *me.* She accused me of being selfish. That stung. Am I being selfish, Sam?"

"Nah. It sounds like you were both upset and said things you regret. Happens to all of us. I think moving out makes sense. That hurricane threw you together too soon. This hasn't been the easiest road to romance for either of you."

"That's true. I told her to let me know when she's ready, and then we'll talk. I'm afraid she will never be ready, Sam. I'll probably see her at a meeting or in the office from time to time. But no more Sunday suppers or hanging out. I will be cordial but distant. What are you thinking? You look worried."

"Not worried. Sad. Loving someone you can't be with is painful. Letting go and allowing what will be, that *que sera, sera* stuff, takes trust. Love sure ain't for the faint of heart. Hurts, huh?"

"Oh yeah. Hurts bad. Last night I was too angry to hurt, but now I feel awful. We said some pretty nasty things. I don't know if we can come back from this."

"If one fight is a deal breaker, then it wasn't meant to be. Everyone fights. But people who love each other cool off and work it out. This is good. I know it doesn't feel that way, but it is. You're finding out what kind of relationship this is. Can you get past this and feel better about each other? That's the question. If you can, then you're off to a good start. Trust me, there will be lots more fights."

"Maybe. I don't know. I'm going to focus on the condo, meetings, and throwing myself into writing songs for that album we talked about. Heartbreak works for Taylor Swift, maybe it will for me too."

"Good plan. Take care of yourself, and hope for the best. What else can you do?"

"Right. Will you go with me to pick up the rest of my stuff? I want to get this over with."

Sam slaps Thomas on the back. "Sure. Let's go."

Meanwhile, Cait broods in the living room, wrapped in the plaid blanket Thomas gave her for Christmas. She's afraid she blew it with Thomas. *Is she only concerned about her kids? Or is that her excuse to keep pushing Thomas away? That doesn't make sense. Why would she do that?* She was angry, but now she feels exhausted and confused. Her phone pings a text notification. Tom! Maybe he's changed his mind and is coming home.

Coming to pick up my stuff.

That's not what she'd hoped for. Miserable, Cait shrugs the blanket off her shoulders, folds it into a neat square, and goes to her room to hide under the covers. She does not want to see Thomas.

20

Missing You

The days in November are short. The nights are long and cold, especially without a loving companion to snuggle with. Thanksgiving is close, but Cait can't get excited about making plans. Over the past several weeks, Thomas has kept his distance, except for occasional all-business messages and random AA meetings. They avoid running into each other at the office. Thomas is protecting himself from further disappointment. Cait is battling demon guilt. They both have a dash of stubbornness, locking them in a standoff. One of them needs to take the first step toward reconciliation, but neither is ready to back down just yet.

On the Sunday before Thanksgiving, Cait makes lasagna for their family dinner. Thomas hasn't attended the dinners since their fight. Matt pulls Cait aside, asking her what's going on. After all, they were quite cozy in Cait's house, and now Thomas is nowhere to be seen. Cait brushes off her brother's concern, saying everything is fine, but Matt doesn't believe it. Something is going on. Dinner conversation flows around the table, and Sadie brings up the unavoidable conversation about Thanksgiving dinner.

"I don't know who's coming, honey. I haven't thought much about it," Cait says, eyes down, spearing a forkful of salad.

"Well, I have," Sadie announces, undaunted. "In addition to everyone at this table, I think we should ask Uncle Fred, Thomas, and Sam. No one should be alone on Thanksgiving, so if there are others, bring 'em on. Who else can you think of?" Sadie asks. Matt looks out the corner of his eye, observing Cait's less-than-enthusiastic response.

Barrett suggests they find out if Thomas's bandmates have plans. "It would be fun to have them here. The music last year was fun."

"Okay," Cait says. She wants to cut off this conversation before their Thanksgiving plans spin out of control. "I will make some calls if that's what you want to do. It's short notice, so they may already have plans. Are you sure you want a big gathering? I thought maybe, without your father here, it would be nice for us to have a quiet dinner."

"I miss Dad. Even though Dad was sick last year, he was in the holiday spirit. I'll never forget that," Barrett shares. "He loved the holidays. I don't think Dad would want us moping around. What do you think, Sadie?"

"I agree with Barrett. I can think about Dad around a table full of people I love better than at a small, sad dinner. Dad would hate that. What about you, Mom?"

That's a loaded question for Cait. "I'm having mixed feelings, I guess. Thanksgiving dinner is always wonderful, but I'm feeling sad celebrating without your father. I'm glad we are talking about it. I assumed we all felt the same way, which of course we don't." Cait feels guilty for having fun without Bart; for going on with her life as if his death didn't matter. But there's more. She can't shake off her feelings for Thomas, or the unhappiness she feels about him not being around. It all seems so complicated, and she wishes there was someone she could talk to about it.

"Who wants dessert?" Connor's hand shoots into the air. "I can always count on you, Connor." Cait smiles at her grandson. That was the end of the discussion. Whether she likes it or not, Thanksgiving is happening. Cait makes the promised calls inviting people to her reluctant holiday dinner. Fred, Bart's elderly uncle, accepts on the spot because he loves a festive meal with family. Sam accepts the invitation and will check with Jim and Perry. He didn't mention Thomas. Sam probably figures Cait will ask him herself. Thomas has to be invited to dinner. His absence would raise questions. Cait dreads the thought of answering questions. She calls Thomas, hoping she can leave a message.

"Cait! It's nice to hear from you."

"Yes, you too. I mean...I called you...you heard from me...I mean..." Cait babbles nervously. "Do you want to come to Thanksgiving dinner? We were talking about plans today."

"Oh, that's right. It was Sunday dinner. Thank you for the invitation, I would love to come."

Cait's heart leaps into her throat.

"But I made plans to go to Montana to be with my brother, Andy."

That knocks the wind out of Cait. She is disappointed and relieved at the same time. "Oh, okay. Have a good trip." Cait quickly hangs up to avoid conversation. Will she ever be comfortable around Thomas again?

Thomas found an apartment on the Boston Post Road in East Lyme, near where Sunny's mother lived. It was originally a mother-in-law suite added on to a spacious cape. It's semi-furnished, making it a perfect temporary home. The landlady, Ginger, has flaming red hair, a bubbling personality, and a contagious laugh. She's around Thomas's age and conveniently lives downstairs. Thomas picks up his keys and trots down the stairs to his car. Ginger bounds out of her kitchen door at the same moment, bumping into Thomas. She has reusable grocery bags under her arm.

"Hey, Thomas. How are things?"

"Good. No complaints. You heading to the grocery store?" Thomas points to the shopping bags.

"Yep, I've put it off long enough. Soon I will be fighting the mice for crumbs in the back of the pantry." Ginger laughs. "Where're you headed?"

"Same place."

"Wanna go together? I was planning on making a big pot of chili later, and I'd be happy to share it with you."

"That sounds like a plan. I'll make cornbread."

"Perfect." Ginger climbs into Thomas's Wrangler. They share a cart in the Stop & Shop, chatting amiably while they pile beans, tomato sauce, and Jiffy cornbread mix in the cart. Thomas adds the things he needs, partitioning off a section of the cart for his items. They have their heads together over Ginger's list when Cait pushes her cart around the endcap stacked with a dozen varieties of Cheerios. She stops dead in her tracks when she sees Thomas laughing with a vibrant redhead. She quickly backs up out of sight, crashing into a gentleman and almost toppling the display.

"Hey, lady. Watch where you're going," he grumbles, shaking his head at how inconsiderate some people are.

"Sorry." Cait spins her cart around to head down another aisle. She is tempted to spy on Thomas, but is afraid he will see her. She scoots to the checkout and escapes before they come face to face. The lines are short. She pays and pushes the cart out the door to her car. On her way out of the parking lot, she spots Thomas's red Jeep Wrangler. After loading the groceries into her back seat, she moves her car to a spot where she can watch unnoticed. Cait would be mortified if he saw her stalking him. She might end up hating what she finds out, but she can't help herself. Cait slouches down in the driver's seat to wait.

Before long, Thomas, and the fake redhead that Cait already hates, exit the store. They load groceries in the back of the Jeep and drive off. Cait puts her car in gear and follows them from a discreet distance. Her nondescript silver car, like a million others on the road, helps her blend in. Thomas turns onto Boston Post Road, and after a few miles, they turn left into a driveway. When Cait gets close to the driveway, she slows down, grateful no one is behind her. Thomas's Wrangler is parked next to another car. She knows that's where Thomas lives. She can't believe he's already entertaining a woman. Jealousy bubbles up, followed by deep hurt. *How can he move on so fast? Maybe he had Red on the side all along. The bastard.* She was right not to tell her children what was going on with him. Now, nothing will be going on. *Ever.* It's a good thing she followed him. Better to know the truth, even though it is a painful disappointment. When she gets home, she texts Sam.

Are you home? Can I come over?

"Can I get you anything?" Sam asks as Cait takes off her coat.

"No thanks, Sam."

Sam is a patient man, comfortable skipping mindless chatter until Cait is ready to talk.

"I'm not sure where to start," Cait says. "I love Tom and feel guilty as heck about that. We had a big fight, and he moved out of my house. You probably heard all about that. I'm afraid I screwed up and Tom thinks I'm a looney tune. But I'm also afraid my family and Bart will judge me if I am with Tom. That's my long story made short."

"Judge you? How? Why?" Sam asks.

"I don't know, maybe they'll think I'm desperate, needy, and can't be alone...maybe they'll think I'm moving too fast and disrespecting their father. Do I need to be alone, dressed in black widow's weeds, my whole life? The widow's union would probably be horrified by my thoughts."

"If there's a widow's union, I think they would understand."

"I want to be in love again and enjoy life. I want Thomas in my life. Then I feel guilty for wanting that. Tom says I do a back-and-forth thing. It's true. I want him close, then I push him away. That has to be frustrating for him. It's frustrating for me, too. I'm afraid that if it happens one more time, he will leave for good. Maybe he already has."

"So far, I'm tracking everything you're saying, and none of it sounds crazy. You seem completely normal for a woman who had a long and happy marriage to a man who passed away. Do you think you are rushing things with Thomas?"

"Yes. No. *I don't know.* I know what I want, but I can't get over the hump. And now there is the other woman. Did you know I was jealous of Sunny, and she and I fought about Thomas? Cripe, I feel like I'm in high school again."

Sam laughs out loud. "In some ways, we never graduate high school, Cait. I heard a little about what went on between you and Sunny. She was jealous, too. She sensed Thomas loved you, and, boy, did she hate that. But she's gone. I don't think Thomas is interested in going to Nashville, so voila—no other woman."

"Yeah, well, that's what I thought until today. I saw him in the grocery store with a woman, shopping and yucking it up." Cait frowns. "I wanted to spy on them but was afraid of getting caught and looking like a crazed stalker." Cait is too embarrassed to admit that she followed them home. "How could he? How can he love me and canoodle with *Red?*"

"They were canoodling? How did you gather that from seeing them in the grocery store? Her name is *Red?*"

"I don't know what her name is. But she has bright red hair that is obviously fake, so I called her *Red.*"

"*Oh.* I get it now. Honey, that's Ginger, his landlady. I helped him move and met her. She's a hoot. And gay. I met her wife, a lovely woman. Thomas rents an apartment upstairs."

Cait blushes a color as flaming as Ginger's hair. "Are you serious? Sam, I'm so embarrassed. I came close to making a complete fool of myself. Help me. *Please.* I don't know what to do."

"I'll tell you what I tell everyone looking for advice. Open your heart and share how you honestly feel. That means no bullshit about how you are supposed to feel or what people will think about how you feel. *Nada.* Simple, open communication. It never fails. Then you deal with what comes. If I could bottle that cure, I would make a billion dollars. Have you talked with your kids about your feelings for Thomas?"

"No. I've been waiting for the right time. I have a feeling they know something is going on. Especially Sadie—she doesn't miss much. People say I should mourn for a year. I hate that I am counting the days."

"Jeez, Cait. *Really?* Don't believe everything people tell you. Everyone is different. You have to do *you.* Love is something we should never put off. It is much too rare and precious. Only you know how you feel or what you're ready for. If you need more time, take it. But if you're counting the days...well...that's just a plain waste of days. Don't ya think?"

"I want to believe that, Sam. Tom thinks I have a deeper underlying fear."

"If he's right, what would that be? You have expressed a lot of fear in this conversation."

"I have?"

"Yup. So, what's the deep fear?" Sam asks.

"I know about a lot of little fears that pile up. Like, what will people think of me? What will my family say? I'm afraid to talk to them about it. I'm trying to protect my kids from feelings they may not even have. All that fear keeps me from thinking about the deeper fear. Know what I mean?"

"I sure do."

Cait's brow furrows, and she looks down at her folded hands. "I know what that fear is. I don't like it and don't want to feel it," she admits as she looks up at Sam. "I'm afraid something will happen to Thomas. I got lucky with Bart. He was a handful, for sure, but we had a good life—a good marriage. I loved him. Still do. His illness and death were just awful. When Bart and I got married, I was young. Too young to think about dying. Thomas and I are older, time is shorter, and we've both experienced losses. If I let myself love Thomas, sooner or later, something bad will happen. Maybe he cheats, lies, starts drinking again, or worse yet...gets sick and dies." Cait shivers. "I don't think I could survive that. It's safer to live without him. That's the crux of my back-and-forth problem, isn't it? I love him and I'm afraid of loving him. Damn, I hate it when he's right."

"Oh, Cait." Sam slides closer and puts his arm around her shoulders. "That's about as honest an answer as I've ever heard. Hearts feel everything, whether we like it or not. I had opportunities with some pretty stellar women in my youth, but I held back because I was afraid. I didn't let anyone get too close. Now I regret that. It's normal to protect ourselves from pain, and love is risky business. My hope for you, Cait, is that whatever you decide, you will have no regrets."

"Thank you, my friend. You always know exactly what I need to hear. It's not what I expect from an old rock and roll guy."

"Old? Hey, who are you calling old?" Sam chuckles.

"You know what I mean. I still don't know what I'm doing, but you've given me lots to consider. I'll keep you posted on my progress as I sort this out. Oh, and please keep this between us? I don't want Tom catching wind of any of this before I'm ready."

"You got it. My lips are sealed," Sam promises. Cait kisses Sam on the cheek and picks up her coat.

"Bye, Sam. See you on Thanksgiving."

21

Time Apart

Thanksgiving dinner is smaller and quieter at Cait's house this year. Classical Christmas music plays softly in the background as grandchildren watch the Macy's parade on television. Subdued conversation is punctuated by an occasional laugh. A crackling fire in the fireplace gives the living room a warm glow. Cait, however, is not glowing and needs to dig deep to find even a kernel of gratitude. She only wants to get through the day.

Dinner is the traditional turkey with all the trimmings. Ruby red cranberry sauce, herb stuffing, and jammy sweet potatoes dotted with tiny marshmallows are ready and waiting. The picture-perfect table is set with the good china, cloth napkins, and candles. It's a time of gratitude with family and friends. But, this year, everything is different. Cait stirs the fragrant, steaming gravy, going through the motions of the holiday. Last year, Bart said grace. He hated the attention, so he kept it short and to the point, which was so wonderfully Bart. The man was not one for embellishment. Cait smiles to herself. Sunny is back in Nashville. There will be no dinner drama this year, thank god. Thomas is her best friend, but he isn't around anymore. Cait is afraid he may be gone for good. Her mother's condo was gutted after the hurricane and will never be the place she remembers, ever again. Nope, nothing is the same. They say change is just change, whatever the hell that means. Maybe it's no big deal. *Then why does it feel so unsettling?*

"Mom? I think you can stop stirring the gravy before there is nothing left of it," Sadie says. "Are you okay?"

"What? Oh. Yeah, I'm fine. Just lost in thought. Help me pour this into the gravy boat, will you?"

Cait's kitchen is bustling as last-minute preparations take place. Side dishes are placed on the table. Pies and sweets line up on the kitchen counter. Matt dramatically sharpens knives to carve the turkey. It annoys Cait that a woman capable of roasting a turkey is not allowed to carve it. Apparently, like grilling, this is male territory.

Barrett goes around the table, filling glasses with champagne and sparkling cider for a kickoff toast. The grandchildren are starving and begging like puppies for morsels of food. Cait searches for something that will lift her spirits, but all she can think about is the huge cleanup coming later. After the plates are filled, there is a moment of silence around the table. Cait reaches for her children on either side of her, and everyone at the table holds hands. Cait bows her head.

"Dear Lord, this has been a hellova year. Pardon my language. Please bless us with your grace as we recover from the hurricane. Hold our hearts gently as we miss Bart, father and husband. Bless our family and friends. Bless those who aren't with us today and ease our hearts as we miss them. We give thanks for our health and the abundance of delicious food on our table. Amen." There is silence until Barrett offers a toast.

"Please raise your glasses. A toast to my mom. She is the glue holding this family together. She models resilience and shows us that we can have a full and happy life even after losing our dad. We love you, Mom. Cheers!" Well, that is a surprise. Bravo, Barrett. Cait hopes this will help push her over the edge, out of gloom and into a better mood. Uncle Fred taps his knife gently against his wine glass to get everyone's attention.

"I want to tell you all how grateful I am to be in this family of amazing, brilliant, warm, and loving people. And the food isn't too bad either. A shout-out to Bleu, Sunny's mother, in heaven or wherever she is. I'm grateful I got to hear her stories. *L'chayim*, to life!"

"Okay, so I see where this is going. Who else is grateful?" Cait asks. She was going to skip this ritual, but it looks like her family has other plans. One by one, gratitude is expressed.

"Mom, what about you? What are you grateful for?" Sadie asks. Cait sighs and takes a moment to reflect.

"Well, I'm grateful for you all, without a doubt. And I am grateful we got through the hurricane without too much hardship. Can we eat now? Please?" She smiles to soften the command, acknowledging to herself that it was a lukewarm expression of gratitude.

After dinner, dishes, dessert, and Sam's rendition of "Amazing Grace", people box up leftovers and prepare to head home. Sadie and Barrett linger with their families after everyone is gone.

"You okay, Mom?" Barrett asks.

"Hmm? Oh, yeah, I'm okay."

"Really? That doesn't sound very convincing," Sadie prods her mother.

"Honestly, I didn't feel much Thanksgiving spirit today," Cait shares. They sit on the couch in the living room, Barrett on one side of Cait, and Sadie on the other. "Everything felt so different this year. It was hard for me to get into the spirit."

"We noticed," Sadie says, giving Barrett a conspiratorial *I told you so* look.

"I'm not surprised. You two know me well. Since it's just us, there is something I want to talk to you about." Cait exhales slowly, calming her nerves.

"What is it, Mom? You can talk to us about anything. Right, Barrett? You aren't sick or anything, are you? You look so serious. I'm getting worried."

"No, not sick. Nothing bad. You know how much I loved your father, don't you?"

"Of course, we know that." Barrett tilts his head, questioning. It's time for Cait to trust her children with the truth.

"Okay. Good. And you know nothing will ever change how I feel about you, or how important your father was to this family. Right?"

"Yeah. We know. What's going on, Mom?" Sadie asks.

"How do you feel about me seeing someone? A new relationship? I'm not talking about serial dating or anything like that. I'm talking about a relationship with someone important to me. Please be honest, if you are not ready for that, I want to know."

"We want you to be happy. Don't we, Sadie?"

"Yes, we want you to be happy. I think Dad would want you to be happy, too. But it depends on who we are talking about. It sounds like you have someone in mind. And what kind of relationship? Are you thinking about getting married again?" Sadie asks the big questions. Cait pauses, looking at Barrett and then her daughter. It's time to take a leap of faith.

"Yes, I do have someone in mind. Thomas." There it is. Out in the open. Cait braces for pushback.

"That explains the backroom whispering you two do. I wondered what was going on," Sadie says.

"I figured you were picking up on something." Cait smiles at her daughter. "I'm sorry to keep a secret from you. I didn't want to talk about it unless I was sure. I'm still not sure, but I need to get it off my chest. I've always felt close to Thomas, maybe because of our shared experience with alcoholism. Then, when your father got sick, he was kind and helpful. He took over running the foundation for me, even though I knew he would rather do other things. He and I have talked about our feelings, but I keep putting him off. I didn't want to betray your father or move too fast." Cait's words come pouring out.

"Is this why Thomas hasn't been to Sunday dinners? Why he isn't here for Thanksgiving?" Barrett wants to know.

"Yes. Sort of. Partly. I mean, he was always welcome, but he felt it would be best if we had time apart. He was right, but I miss him terribly. After the hurricane, we fought while he was living here. He wanted us to be open about our feelings, but I wasn't ready to go public. I was afraid people would judge me. I was afraid of how you would react. Shit, I was even afraid your father would be mad at me throughout eternity. That hurt Thomas, so he moved out. He said when I was ready, we would talk. Sam knows us, so I went to him for advice. He helped me see that I pushed Tom away because I'm afraid. What if I let myself love him, and then I lose him like I did your father? That would be unbearable. I don't know what will happen now, and I'm afraid of that, too."

Sadie smiles. "I love Thomas. I'm glad you aren't talking about dating a bunch of internet weirdos."

"Hey! Who are you calling a weirdo?" Barrett says. "I met my wife online, and we are not weirdos."

"Yeah, I know, but you have always been an outlier, Barrett." Sadie gives him a look that says *Shut up if you're not being helpful.* Barrett settles back.

"Mom, Thomas is kind and supportive. I will never forget him letting me cry on his shoulder after Dad died. My kids love him too. Whatever you two decide, I think it will be okay."

"Yes, well, we'll see. It's a relief you both know what's going on. I hated keeping this from you."

"I'm glad we know, and if we can help in any way...you know we're here," Barrett adds.

"Thank you. Both of you."

"I do need to bring up one little detail." Barrett gestures by making a tiny space between his thumb and forefinger. "Technically, Thomas is your stepbrother. I know there isn't a blood connection, but will people think it's weird? You didn't grow up together. I didn't get to know him until a few years ago, so he's just a guy to me, but I'm wondering what you think about that."

"I wonder about that, too. People will think whatever they think, not that it's any of their damn business. They always think something, don't they?" Cait huffs, frowning. "Another thing about this is that Thomas and I would sort of be repeating history. Mom and James fell in love at about the same age as we are now. They lived in the condo, which, if things work out, we may too. Sometimes it feels as if I'm walking in my mother's footsteps, and I don't know how I feel about that. Is it good? Is it weird? I don't know." Cait smiles. "Now *that* would get people talking."

"I didn't think about that, Mom. You're right. It sounds like a movie plot."

"Yes, it does. I hope it has a happy ending." Cait thinks back to the morning with Thomas in the condo—the morning when she freaked out. It was such a strong déjà vu moment she wondered whose life she was living.

"Well, I admit I'm surprised by this news. I haven't been paying close attention like Sadie has." Barrett cocks his head toward his sister. "It's strange to picture you living with anyone other than Dad. Have you talked with Uncle Matt about it?" Barrett asks.

"No. Not yet. I wanted to speak with you guys first." Cait's secret is out. The gloom she felt all Thanksgiving Day finally lifts, and she is deeply grateful for her children. They wrap their arms around each other in a group hug.

"We love you, Mom."

Cait's eyes fill with tender tears of relief. "I love you, too. So much. Be patient with me as I figure this out, okay? And let's keep this between us for now."

Suddenly, rosy-cheeked grandchildren, burst into the room, jumping on the couch and into Cait's lap.

"We're hungry. Can we have pie, Mema?" Connor asks.

"We sure can." Cait smiles at the children, her heart finally full of gratitude. "Who wants leftovers?"

Time moves slowly, like molasses in January, as Cait's grandmother used to say. Christmas comes and goes, and the long, dark winter days tick by. Cait and Thomas keep their distance, only communicating via polite work messages and not much else. Occasionally, she and Thomas have an awkward encounter at an AA meeting. Sometimes she will show up at an Old Guys show, keep a low profile, and slip out unseen.

Cait isn't accustomed to so much time alone, focusing solely on herself. Her life has been about caring for other people, like her husband and kids. Floundering on her own, she starts seeing a grief counselor. The counselor reassures Cait that this uncomfortable time alone is not selfish or unnecessary. It's a time for her to discover who she is and to grow into this new, unfamiliar stage of life. Cait devotes herself to the foundation, takes an art class, joins a gym, and connects with old friends.

By spring, Cait feels better, lighter, happier, and more herself. Spending time alone wasn't exactly in her plan, but it has been useful. It turns out there is life after Bart. Cait tosses out his bottlecaps and rearranges the kitchen so she won't be constantly reminded of the past. The sharpness of grief has softened into poignant memories. Cait still thinks about Thomas, but she doesn't need him to rescue her anymore. She is perfectly capable of taking care of herself. But she still misses him.

Thomas misses Cait too, and he tries not to think about what she might be doing or with whom. He's been wanting her input for remodeling the condo, but it doesn't feel right to ask, especially after he walked out on her. Condo renovations require a million daily decisions, from selecting light fixtures to faucets to tile. Thomas will never look at a faucet the same way ever again. He and Sam continue polishing tracks for the album he wants to record. Thank God for the band.

It keeps him sane. Trying out arrangements and arguing with Sam over this riff, or that solo, absorbs him for hours. But no matter how busy he is, Cait is never far from his thoughts. He tries not to run into her, but when he does, his heart thumps.

By April, the condo is almost complete. The bright, open floor plan, the music studio, and the added guest bathroom are perfect. It resembles the home Bess lived in, but it's opened up and modernized. Thomas sorts through old family pictures of Bess and his father when they lived there. He will get them framed and arrange them on a wall after he moves in. Cait will like that.

It's a warm day in May, and Cait is relaxing on her newly constructed patio. After thirty years of marriage, she never thought she would enjoy time alone. Her house has been painted inside and out, giving it a fresh look. The furniture has been rearranged the way she likes it. Bart's worn-out recliner has been moved to the basement to make space for new furniture. Window treatments, which Bart would have criticized as too girly, brighten the living room. Her house feels fresh and all hers. Selling the house and downsizing has been in the back of her mind for a while. Cleaning and fixing it up is a step in that direction.

Cait's phone rings. It's Thomas. She freezes, unsure if she should answer it or let it go to voicemail. Before she can decide, the phone goes silent. What did he want? Maybe he will leave a message. She waits for the familiar ding of a voicemail notification. Nothing. Maybe it was a butt dial. She should probably call him back. The phone is clenched in her hand, waiting for a decision. No, if he has something to say, he will call back. She doesn't want to seem eager. But dammit, she is eager. *What* does he *want?* Curiosity gets the best of her, and her call goes through to voicemail.

"Thomas here. Thanks for calling. Leave me a message." Cait smiles at the sound of his voice, and her heart flutters.

"Hey, Tom. It's Cait. I saw you called. Call me back." Cait cradles her phone, waiting for a call back. *He is taking his sweet time with that,* Cait thinks. *Maybe it was a butt call. He could still call me back, though.* It would be rude not to. Cait checks the time. She has to get moving and change her clothes before meeting friends at the Spice Club for an early supper and then a movie. Thomas will have to wait.

The restaurant is busy, as usual, and the three friends stand together by the door waiting for a table.

"So, he called and didn't leave a message? And then you called and left a message?" her friend Deb asks.

"Yup."

"And you have no idea what he wants? How long has it been since you two talked? I mean, *really* talked," Linda prods.

"No idea what he wants. We haven't talked in—" Cait counts on her fingers the months since the hurricane "—about seven months. We've had contact, just not conversations. Mostly texts and work email, stuff like that. Don't look so shocked. We agreed to time apart, and it's been good. Got me hanging out with you two troublemakers again."

The hostess ushers them to a table by the windows. Cait's favorite is the East Lyme roll, but she looks over the menu anyway.

"Seven months? Okay, you gotta call him."

"Now?"

"Yes. *Now.* Call him. We will be your moral support, just in case it's something bad," Deb commands.

"Bad? Like what? Now you're scaring me." Cait lays down her menu. Their server approaches, asking for their order. "I'll have an East Lyme roll and the avocado salad. Thanks."

"What's your name?" Deb asks the server.

"Theresa. What would you like?" Theresa smiles cautiously, unsure if this table is already unhappy with her service.

"Theresa, if you loved someone, and hadn't spoken to them in seven months, and they called you but didn't leave a message, what would you do?"

"Um...I'd call them back?" Theresa hopes that's the right answer.

"Exactly! That's what we're telling her. I'll have the massaman curry. Linda, what do you want?" Linda orders, and Theresa rushes off.

"Do it! Do it!" Deb and Linda chant together. Cait looks around to see if they are causing a scene. So far, no one seems perturbed by her friends' behavior.

"I'm not sure this is exactly the time and place for this, but if it will get you to stop bugging me..." Cait digs her phone out of her purse and finds Thomas in her contacts.

"Put it on speaker!" Deb demands.

"I will not!" Cait rolls her eyes.

"Cait!" *Now* Thomas answers his phone. Why couldn't it go to voicemail this time?

"Tom, hey. You called. What's up?" Cait waves at her giggling friends, signaling for them to pipe down.

"It's good to hear your voice. It's been a long time."

"Yeah, a long time. Shhh," Cait shushes Linda.

"Did you shush me? What's going on?" Thomas asks.

"No. No, not you, Tom." Cait sighs. "I'm out with a couple of dear but very pushy friends. They insisted I call you, right this minute. We're at the Spice Club."

"They sound like great friends. Good for them. However, I wanted to chat without a cheering section, if that's okay with you."

"Of course. Can I call you when I get home?"

"Yes, please. I look forward to it. Give your friends my best. Later." Thomas hangs up.

Her friends high-five each other, grinning.

"That wasn't so bad now, was it?" Deb asks.

"For *you,* maybe." Cait shakes her head.

After the movie, when Cait gets home, she picks up her phone. Her heart is beating fast from a combination of excitement and nerves. After a couple of deep breaths and a few Whoppers malted milk balls leftover from the theater, she places the call.

"Cait! Thanks for calling. Are you alone now?" Thomas chuckles.

"Ha. Yes, you're safe. I'm wrapped in the throw you gave me. What's up? Please don't tell me anything bad. Okay?"

"Promise. Nothing bad. The condo is finished, and I've moved in. I wondered if you would come over to see it. Sometime. I mean, not right now, but sometime. Soon, maybe? I hope you'll like it."

"Yes. Okay. I'd love to see what you've done with the place."

"When? Do you have time tomorrow?"

"Yes, I think I can do that. What time?"

"Why don't you come for dinner? I'll grill something. Is that okay?"

"Sounds good. See you tomorrow." Cait pulls the throw tight around her and falls back into the couch cushions, smiling.

22

Hearts and Flowers

Cait tosses and turns in bed, thinking about tomorrow's dinner with Thomas. The reunion is scary. She can't wait to see him, but there are many unknowns. Like Scarlett O'Hara, she will think about that tomorrow. Tonight, she only wants to imagine a grand romantic gesture sweeping her off her feet and back into Thomas's life. That first look—their eyes meeting as she enters the condo—will tell it all. Cait sighs. She's probably watched too many romantic comedies. Mentally, she inventories her wardrobe and decides to dress casually in jeans, a linen blouse, and strappy stiletto sandals that kill her feet but are super sexy. Maybe she will bring an offering, like pastries from Sift Bakery. But what if he has moved on and only wants to show her the condo as a kind gesture? Maybe this invitation means nothing. Cait's breath catches in her chest. *Push that thought away. Far away. Please, God, don't let tomorrow be a disappointment. Please, please, please,* Cait prays. Worn out from overthinking, Cait finally falls into a deep sleep.

The next day, at five o'clock, Cait parks her car in front of the condo. She lifts the pastry box from the seat next to her and murmurs, "Okay, here we go."

Thomas sprints out of the condo to greet her. "Cait. Thank you for coming. I'm so excited. I can't wait for you to see the condo." Thomas takes her hand and leads her toward the front door. "Ready? I'd ask you to close your eyes, but in those amazing shoes, it might be dangerous."

"Ha. Ha. Very funny." Cait follows him to the front door.

"Tah dah!" Thomas swings the door open wide and welcomes Cait into the huge space. White floor-to-ceiling bookshelves are on either side of the fireplace. Ceiling fans whir slowly overhead. Vinyl plank flooring in shades of gray is dotted with colorful area rugs. A horseshoe-shaped sectional sofa surrounds a round marble coffee table in front of the fireplace. The color scheme is beachy with sand grays, blues, touches of orange, and dramatic black accents. It looks like a masculine beach house, which it is. Cait is speechless. It's so different, she isn't sure if she loves it or hates it.

"Wow! It's...different."

"Yup, it is, but I tried to keep the beach vibe going for Bess. If she haunts this place, I want her to feel comfortable. Come on, let me show you the kitchen." Thomas still has Cait's hand, pulling her along.

"Remember how you had that déjà vu thing in the kitchen with pancakes and all?"

"Yes. I do." Cait looks around, wide-eyed.

"I changed the kitchen so that wouldn't happen again. We need to make kitchen memories of our own. What do you think?" The black pearl granite countertops remind Cait of pebbles on a beach. The cabinets have a whitewashed finish. Brand-new stainless-steel appliances shine.

"Tom. This is...amazing. It's like my mother's, but different. You put a lot of thought into this."

"I did. I imagine it will take a little getting used to. But what do you think? Can you live with it?"

Cait holds her breath. Is Thomas dropping hints about their future by asking if she can *live with it* and make *kitchen memories?*

"Show me the rest."

Thomas gives Cait a tour of the added guest bath, the master bedroom suite, and the music studio.

"It's gorgeous, Tom. I think my mother would want to haunt this place. Oh, there she is now." Cait points toward the fireplace.

"What?!" Thomas spins around.

"Just kidding. Made ya look." Cait laughs.

"You scared me. Not that I wouldn't be happy to see your mother. Come on, supper's ready. Let's eat on the patio, and we can catch up. I can't tell you how happy I am to be back in my home. The renovations took forever. And happy to see you, Cait. Very happy."

Dinner is simple and delicious. They chat about what they have been doing over the last seven months. Thomas asks about her friends. Cait wonders how Thomas is doing with the new album. It's easy and enjoyable, like no time has passed. This man still makes her heart beat fast.

"Cait, can we talk about us, now that we've covered everything else?"

"Yes, I think that would be good." Cait twists her napkin nervously. "You go first."

"Okay. I don't want to live without you. I'm done. Your turn."

Cait's heart thumps. That was as close to a grand romantic gesture as she could want. Now that her wish is coming true, her mind goes blank. She isn't sure what to say. *Cait, get it together, don't leave the man hanging.*

"I...I...need a minute. Can we finish this inside?" Cait asks.

"Sure can." They pick up their plates, set them on the kitchen island, and get comfortable on the sectional. "Want tea? I can turn on the fireplace?"

"That would be nice." Some things haven't changed. Talking by the fire will always feel like home. Cait kicks off her sexy killer shoes.

"You looked shocked. I'm sorry. I was pretty blunt. Maybe I assumed too much. You want to talk, yes? I want to listen." Thomas hands Cait a mug of tea.

"Yes, I am a little shocked. In a good way, though." Cait sips her tea and collects her thoughts. Where to begin? "I've been talking with Sam. A lot. That man has a gift for knowing exactly what to say."

Thomas nods in agreement. "Yup. I call him the Yoda of AA. He's always helpful."

"Yoda?" Cait chuckles. "That's him. He helped me dig down into why I was back and forth so much. It wasn't what I thought, or about my kids, as you already suspected." Cait looks into Thomas's light hazel eyes, noting flecks of green and gold glinting in the firelight.

"I wanted you to magically take all my pain away. I was angry when you refused. Now I understand why you left, and it was the right thing to do. I have learned so much about myself in the months we were apart. I was back and forth with you because I was afraid. Letting myself love you, and then watching you die, would be unbearable. We are in our fifties, and at some point, something will happen to one of us." Cait pauses and takes a deep breath.

"When I married Bart, I was twenty-two and didn't think about dying. Everything felt like forever. But it's not. Losing my mother and then Bart made me very aware of how fragile and impermanent life is. So, I had to make a choice. I could take a chance and live life to the fullest, or be alone, and maybe get a couple of cats. I have no control over what happens beyond that. After you left, I focused on my side of the street, as they say in AA." Cait smiles thoughtfully.

"I started paying attention to my needs. I got comfortable being alone and discovered there is peace in that. I'm okay. But it's not enough to just be okay. I want a full life—with you, if that's possible. No more back and forth. Fear is not going to stop me, if I can help it. There's one more thing. I talked with Sadie and Barrett. I told them how I feel about you, about our fight, and that I wasn't sure what would happen."

"How did the kids take it? What did they say?" Thomas asks, holding Cait's hand in both of his.

"They were fine. They want me to be happy. It also helps that you've won them over. Sadie loves you. Tom, you were right. Sneaking around wasn't fair to anyone."

"I love you, Cait. That's never changed, no matter how many times you've pushed me away. It did piss me off, though." Thomas smiles. "I have to admit, I'm relieved. I had no idea what would happen tonight. For all I knew, you met some internet dude and you were heading off to live on a luxury yacht in Bali." Thomas slides closer to Cait and kisses the hand he's holding. "What does this mean for us?"

"No internet dude for me, thank you very much. Sadie was worried about the same thing. What's wrong with you people?" Cait laughs. "I worried that you met someone, too. I figured you were a hot commodity in town and the ladies would be chasing after you." Cait tells Thomas about seeing him in the grocery store with Ginger.

"I freaked out, backed up into a guy, and almost landed in a pile of Cheerios. I made a run for it out of the store, and I'm embarrassed to admit that I followed you. I thought you were seeing someone new, and it flipped me out. Sam talked me down off the ledge. He told me she was your landlady. Thank God I didn't do anything more stupid than follow you."

Thomas is snorting with laughter.

"I'm glad you think it's funny, Tom! Jeez. Give a girl a break."

"I love that you were jealous," Thomas says.

"I was not jealous!" Cait loudly insists. "Okay, maybe I was a teeny tiny bit jealous."

"Hopefully, I won't make you jealous ever again. So, back to the question. What about us? What now?" Thomas asks.

"I guess we have to figure that out. Let's spend lots of time together. I want to get to know you as a partner and do normal dating things with lots of sleepovers." Cait grins

"I like the sound of that, Cait. After our fight, Sam told me that a good relationship survives bumps in the road and gets even better. I feel that way right now. We got through a major bump, didn't we?"

"Yes, we did." Cait beams. "It's a relief not to hide how I feel about you."

"Hold on. Be right back." Thomas goes to the music studio and comes out holding a flash drive.

"I finished writing all the songs for the album, and they are all about us—our story." Thomas presses the small device into Cait's palm, closing her fingers around it. "Please listen to this. Let me know what you think. It's still rough, but we are getting closer to recording time. Music was how I tended my side of the street, and it kept me sane during our separation." Thomas brushes hair away from Cait's face and moves closer. "Does this mean I'm not banned from Sunday dinners anymore?" he whispers in her ear, kissing her cheek.

"You were never *banned*. You chose to stay away, so I would miss you. I'm aware of your dastardly plot." Cait turns her head slowly, until Thomas's lips meet hers. He stretches out on the couch and pulls Cait down, cradling her under his arm. "This feels so good. I've thought about this moment ever since I moved out of your house. No more separations if I have anything to say about it."

"And no more ambivalence from me." Cait snuggles against Thomas. "Just don't say until death, do us part. I'm still a little sensitive about that."

"How about in sickness and in health? Is that okay?" Thomas kisses Cait.

"I can deal with that," Cait whispers. "I don't have a cat, so I don't need to go home tonight. What do you think about a sleepover?"

"I think you read my mind. Come." Thomas pulls Cait up from the couch.

Cait and Thomas enjoy time together over the next few months. Thomas is welcomed into the family on a trial basis. In October,

Thomas goes to Montana to visit his brother. He wants Cait to go with him, but she refuses. Time with his brother is important, and there will be other trips together. While he's gone, she and her friends go to Vermont to tour covered bridges, do a little shopping, and admire the colorful leaves. It sounds odd, but she likes missing Thomas because it makes their reunion that much sweeter.

Cait is picking Thomas up at the airport, imagining their reunion like a scene from a movie. Cait will park the car and meet Thomas at baggage claim. She has been planning a surprise welcome home for days. As she gets dressed, a framed photo of Bart on his Harley catches her eye. Cait picks it up and smiles. In the message circle, he said he wanted her to be happy, and she is taking him at his word. No one ever said love was a limited quantity, and she is lucky to have another shot at it. Cait kisses the photo and tucks it into the top dresser drawer. She decides to wear jeans and her favorite pale-blue cashmere sweater. Her blond hair is freed from its messy bun, falling in soft waves around her shoulders. Cait thinks about bringing a red rose but decides against it. A rose has become a cliche ever since the television series *The Bachelor*. A big, red, heart-shaped mylar balloon is more her style.

If all goes well, Thomas's flight will land at four-thirty in the afternoon. Cait drives to T. F. Green Airport early because she can't wait any longer. She gets a parking spot in the lot across from the terminal, checks her lipstick, and sprints to arrivals. The balloon is an attention-getter, and people smile at her, no doubt remembering their romantic airport moments. Thomas will be surprised to see her waiting for him at the bottom of the stairs. She can't wait to see his face. He expects her to circle the airport like a shark waiting for him to appear.

She takes a seat near the baggage carousel. The flight information display reassures Cait that he is on time. One more hour to wait. An older gentleman sits near her, glancing in her direction several times until he finally says hello.

"Meetin' someone special, eh?" he asks. The man wears a plaid flannel shirt, jeans, and an Eddie Bauer jacket. His thatch of white hair and wire-frame glasses give him a retired professor vibe.

"Yes. I am. I'm being pretty obvious, aren't I? I hope it doesn't embarrass him."

"If he's embarrassed by a display of affection from a lovely woman, he needs to get over it and realize how fortunate he is." The man chuckles. "I remember, years ago, my Hattie greeted me at the airport. I was coming back from fightin' in the Korean War. She met me with a delicious heart-shaped cake she made herself. She wrote, 'I knew you were coming!' in frosting. There was a hit song in those days called 'If I Knew You Were Coming, I'd Have Baked a Cake'. It was the sweetest homecoming I ever got, and I'll never forget it. See, I'm still talking about it. Hopefully, your guy will feel the same."

"That's a wonderful story." Cait reaches out to shake the gentleman's hand. "My name is Cait. Did you and Hattie get married? I hope I'm not prying."

"Nice to meetcha, Cait. I'm Joe. And you're not prying at all. I love to talk about Hattie. Yes, we got married and stayed that way for almost fifty years. Sad to say, she passed a while ago from cancer. I'm meeting our son here. He lives in Denver and is coming to visit his old man."

"I'm sorry about your wife. My husband died too. We were married for thirty years. I loved him dearly, even though it was tough sometimes. I was unsure about starting over again, but I feel so lucky to have Tom in my life. It's nice that your son is coming to visit. Is he married?"

"He was. They got divorced two years ago. He is coming with his daughter, Charlie, who just turned twelve. I can't wait to see her. Youngsters grow so fast."

Arriving passengers are coming down the stairs. Joe waves to a younger version of himself. They hug and walk to the baggage carousel, with Charlie talking a mile a minute. Joe turns to Cait, patting his heart to wish her luck. What a dear man. Cait checks her watch and the arrivals board. The flight is still on time. Thirty more minutes to go.

Finally, Cait's phone pings a text message from Thomas.

Wheels down. XOXO

Yay. Welcome home, Cait texts back.

It will take a while for him to get off the plane, but Cait can't wait any longer. She stations herself at the bottom of the stairs, scanning the crowd, looking for him. Finally, she sees Thomas gliding down the escalator, looking at his phone, not paying the least bit of attention. When he sees her, a huge smile spreads across his face. He waves and races down the moving stairs, taking her in his arms.

"What are you doing in here? I thought you would meet me outside."

Cait hands him the balloon. "I wanted to surprise you, like in the movies. I hope you aren't embarrassed by the balloon." Cait laughs. "I'm so happy to see you." Cait kisses Thomas. They are oblivious to the log jam they create in the stream of people moving around them. An elderly couple bumps into them. The woman mumbles something about getting a room, but the man winks and gives them a thumbs up. Thomas puts his arm around Cait, steering her toward the baggage claim.

"I love the balloon. I love that you went to the trouble to meet me. That's never happened before, and I'll never forget it. Come on, let's get my bag and go home."

While they wait for his bag, Cait tells him about Joe and Hattie. When they get to the car, Thomas tosses his bag and backpack into the back seat. After Cait starts the car, Thomas gently strokes her cheek, turning her face toward him.

"I love coming home to you. Someday I might be sitting at the airport telling stories about you."

"Aww, that's sweet. Does that mean I'll be dead?" Cait muses.

"Oh. Not necessarily. Maybe you're doing time at the state penitentiary." Thomas laughs so hard he snorts. "Sorry. I couldn't help myself. Dying will be when we are very, *very* old. Maybe we die together doing something fun like skydiving."

"Can we not talk about dying, please?" Cait begs.

"No problem. Let's get back to kissing." Thomas tenderly kisses Cait, passion building on both sides of the Subaru console. He whispers, "I love you, Cait."

"I love you, too, Tom. Let's go home."

23

Father Christmas

The morning after Thanksgiving, Cait and Thomas sip coffee and eat leftover pumpkin pie for breakfast. Thanksgiving filled them to the top with joy and gratitude. Of course, great food didn't hurt either.

"Tom, let's get a Christmas tree today. I discovered a beautiful tree farm not too far away. Do you want one for your place too? Maybe we could get a twofer deal," Cait suggests.

"I don't need a tree this year. I'll live vicariously through yours. How's that?"

"That's fine by me. As long as you help me decorate. How about we get a nice wreath for your door? You have to do something festive, don't you think? Then we'll get some eggnog, start a fire in the fireplace, and play Christmas music. It will be you and me decorating our first beautiful Christmas tree together."

"Sounds perfect. What else is on your Christmas wish list? Besides a tree," Thomas asks. He already has a plan, but is curious about what Cait is thinking.

"I have everything I need." Cait kisses Thomas. "Having you here with me is the best gift I could ever have. But we should make a list for the kids. I'll check with Sadie and Barrett and see what the grandchildren are into this month. It will be fun to go shopping together. We will send something to your brother, too. Maybe it will snow. Wouldn't that be wonderful?" Cait asks with excitement.

"It would. Christmas is probably the only time of year I want to see snow," Thomas agrees.

The Cosgrove Christmas Tree Farm is busy. People wander through the rows looking for the perfect tree.

"Did you bring the saw?" Cait asks as they park the Jeep.

"We need a saw?" Thomas teases. "Of course I remembered. However, for a hundred dollars, I think they should cut it for us, deliver it to your house, and decorate it. The last tree I bought cost me ten bucks."

"Ten bucks? Are you kidding? Was that like thirty years ago? Welcome to the twenty-first century, Mr. Scrooge." Cait punches his arm playfully.

Cait, and Thomas, walk past the groups of people and find a quiet area. They examine the Frasers, balsams, and spruces. Every tree is perfect. They finally decide on a six-foot Fraser fir. Thomas gets down on his knees, sawing the trunk while Cait holds the tree steady.

"Oh my gosh, Tom! It's snowing! How perfect is that? My Christmas wish came true." Light, fluffy flakes drift down from a steel-gray sky. After the tree topples over, Thomas stands up, his face flushed from exertion.

"You have snowflakes in your hair," he tells Cait. "It makes you look like a Celtic snow faerie. It won't amount to much, but it sure is pretty on you." Thomas kisses her.

They drag their tree to the attendant and settle up. The tree is bagged and secured to the top of the Wrangler. The red Wrangler and the green tree make a perfect Christmas card photo. Cait and Thomas pose as the attendant takes their picture.

"Thank goodness they don't charge for photographs, too," Thomas mutters under his breath. Cait rolls her eyes.

"Don't be a grinch, Tom. It's our first Christmas together, so there's no holding back."

When they get home, they drag the tree inside and secure it in the stand.

"It's beautiful, isn't it? Even naked," Thomas remarks. "I guess it was worth the price."

"It sure is. Just wait till we get lights on it."

Thomas helps Cait bring the Christmas decorations up from the basement. Cait cues up Christmas music on the Bluetooth speaker and pours eggnog while Thomas gets a fire started.

"Cheers, my love!" Thomas holds up his eggnog in a toast.

"Merry Christmas, Tom. If I get much happier, I will burst."

The tree sparkles with hundreds of colorful LED lights. Ornaments are tucked in every nook and cranny of the Fraser fir. Thomas reaches up to place a star on the top of the tree.

"It's beautiful! I am so happy we got this done today. When the kids come to dinner on Sunday, they will be so surprised." Cait threads her arm through Thomas's as they admire their work.

"We're cooking dinner again?" Thomas teases. "It was just Thanksgiving. Shouldn't we get this Sunday off? It seems like we are always feeding those kids. *Not* that I'm complaining, you understand."

"Oh, but you *are* complaining. Speaking of food, I'm hungry. Want to get a pizza?" Cait asks.

"Sure. Let's go to Sal's." The original Sal passed away, but the shop is expertly run by his son, Angelo, and nothing has changed, not the ambiance or the menu. After sharing a pizza, they step out into the clear, cold night. Arm in arm, they walk down Main Street, admiring the garland-wrapped light posts and the twinkling lights in the tree branches.

"My mother loved this town. This time of year, it's like a Hallmark card. Do you think our parents are happy for us, Tom?" Cait pulls her hat down over her ears against the cold.

"I hope so. I'm positive my dad is thrilled I'm sober and finally settling down. I know *I'm* happy for us." Thomas puts his arm around Cait as they stroll. "If it's fate that we're together, we have no choice but to surrender."

"That's true. There is something mystical about falling in love with you." Cait agrees.

The days fly by for busy adults shopping, decorating, wrapping gifts, and baking cookies. The children can't stand to wait another minute. They are out of their minds with anticipation, causing parents to lose their minds too.

"How many different kinds of cookies do we really *need?*" Thomas asks with a wry smile. His sleeves are pushed up as he rolls out the chilled sugar cookie dough. Cait and Sadie frost and decorate cookies in a production line that would make Santa proud. Thomas's red Christmas apron is dusty with flour, and a Santa hat is perched jauntily on his head. He has never been happier in his entire life. In his youth, he thought fame, money, and being chased by throngs of women was the ultimate success. Thank goodness he has learned a little something about what is important. Sadie pokes Thomas in the ribs, startling him out of his reverie.

"Are you getting grinchy, Thomas? Just keep rolling that dough, man. We have lots more cookies to make," Sadie commands.

"Yeah, yeah. I know," Thomas mutters as Cait brushes flour from his beard.

"Don't let Sadie push you around. She can be a tyrant in the kitchen."

"No shit. I'm familiar with her ways." Thomas hip-bumps Sadie. "She makes Chef Ramsey look like a pussy cat." Sadie gives Thomas a disapproving side-eye, and they laugh. Gracie and Conner chase each other into the kitchen, whining for presents. They calm down with a freshly baked cookie, but not for long. They will be back.

"Hey, don't forget the elf is watching you. Better be good. Did you find him yet?" Sadie asks. Connor's eyes get big, and he pulls Gracie along to search the house for the tattle-tale elf. "That should keep them occupied for a minute." Sadie opens the refrigerator.

"Hey, is this eggnog alcohol-free? Can I give some to the kids?"

"Of course. Help yourself," Cait tells her daughter.

Later, the kids watch Christmas movies. The house smells like a bakery. Mulled cider warming on the stove adds spiciness to the air.

"It's beginning to feel a lot like Christmas," Thomas sings, pulling Cait into a twirling dance step they clearly did not practice.

"Hey, you two! Get back to work," Sadie scolds, grinning. This is the happiest she has seen her mother in a long time. Two more days until Christmas Eve. The Christmas tree sparkles, and electric candles flicker on the windowsills. Most of the gifts are wrapped and under the tree.

"Okay, you guys. I'm leaving the rest in your capable hands. I have things to do." Thomas removes his apron and hat. "I'll bring the keyboard over tomorrow for our carol sing. Text me if you need me to pick up anything." Thomas kisses Cait on the cheek, moves the elf to another location to keep the kids on their toes, and heads out.

Thomas answers his phone. "Cait, what's up?" It's the day before Christmas Eve, and Thomas is shopping for last-minute gifts.

"Are you going to do it?" Cait asks.

"Do what?"

"Be Santa! Don't you remember? I asked you to dress up for our grandchildren," Cait huffs.

"Oh, that! Did you say *our* grandchildren? Have I been promoted, or do I now have squatter's rights?"

"Don't change the subject. Will you do it?"

"Well, I would, but I don't have a thing to wear." The teasing is non-stop.

"I have a suit for you to wear, Mr. Smarty-pants. *Please?* The little ones get so excited, even though they know you're not the real Santa Claus. If you won't do it, I'll have to cram Matt into the suit, and I'm afraid he will split the seams. Maybe I could ask Sam."

"Of course I will do it. How could I refuse?"

"Bless you! You're the best. Can I bring the suit over for you to try on when I go to the grocery store? I think it will fit. We may have to stuff it with a pillow, though. No one trusts a skinny Santa."

"Sure. I'm almost finished shopping. Meet me in an hour? Do you want help at the grocery store? I can protect you from the Cheerios."

"Thanks," Cait says sarcastically. "You're all heart. I don't need protection, but would love the company. I'll see you later." Cait disconnects and smiles. It amazes her how resilient the human spirit is. Two years ago, she was heartbroken, caring for her dying husband. This year, she is happy. Cait trots downstairs to retrieve the Santa suit from its hiding place. Ever since her kids were little, she has managed to coerce a family member into wearing it. When Barrett was around eight, he started to catch on and announced that his father was Santa Claus. When Bart walked into the room behind Santa, Barrett was shocked. The look on his face was priceless. Cait felt sad when her kids were too old and savvy to believe in Santa anymore. She wants her grandchildren to enjoy the magic while they can.

Christmas Eve is a festive event filled with good food, gifts, music, and Santa Claus. The sound of jingle bells alerts the children that Santa is close by. Their faces are pressed against the windows, searching for the jolly man in the red suit. When Thomas bounds into the living room, pockets overflowing with candy, they shriek. He hams it up, asking the tattle-tale elf to whisper in his ear who has been good. All those years in a band made him quite the entertainer.

"What's that you say? Everyone has been good? Oh my. Well, Ho, ho, ho. In that case, presents for all."

The children squeal as Thomas pulls gifts out of his bag. Wrapping paper flies. When Santa's sack is empty, he turns his attention to the adults.

"Ladies and gentlemen. Each of you will get one Christmas Eve gift to open." Thomas knows which gifts under the tree are marked for Christmas Eve and, one by one, he passes them out.

"Wait. What is this little box hidden under the falling pine needles from the very expensive Christmas tree?" Santa raises an eyebrow at Cait. "Looks like this one is for you, young lady." Thomas cradles it in his gloved hands, holding it out to Cait. She is surprised because she thought she knew every gift under the tree. How did she miss this one? Cait carefully unwraps the box and opens the lid. There, wrapped in tissue, is Thomas's great-great-gram's brooch.

Cait gasps. "Oh my, Tom. I can't believe it. It's the heirloom brooch your father gave my mother." Cait holds it, tenderly running her finger over the burnished gold. She looks up at Thomas. "I remember when your father gave it to my mother. Do you?"

"I'm Santa, so I know everything. I heard a story about a family tradition." He smiles. "Let me pin it on you."

"Thank you, Tom—I mean Santa." Cait pulls the white beard down and kisses Santa Tom on the cheek. She doubts her children would know the significance of the brooch because they were young when James gave it to her mother. He presented it to Bess when they were

216

leaving for a family reunion in North Carolina. He downplayed the significance at the time, and Bess was put on the spot when excited family members thought they were engaged. Cait knows what this gift signifies and is thrilled.

"Ho, ho, ho. Merry Christmas! Santa has to get going. It's a busy night." The kids crowd around him, jumping up and down and pulling candy from his pockets. Thomas ducks out and meets Cait in the basement to change clothes.

"Tom, you have given me the best gift ever. It brought back a flood of memories."

"Last year, when I went to Montana for Thanksgiving, I asked Andy about the brooch. I mentioned my hope that you and I would finally get together, and Andy insisted that I take it for when the time was right." Thomas holds her close. "I hate to let you go right now. How much longer do you think this party will last?"

"Get yourself changed and we will move things along." Cait gives Thomas a quick kiss and hurries up the stairs before the grandchildren get suspicious. Thomas carefully folds the red suit and closes it in its box. He tiptoes upstairs and makes an entrance into the living room.

"Hey, Merry Christmas. Did I miss anything?" Little ones gather around him, talking fast about Santa and showing him their gifts. He raises his eyes and sees Cait offering cookies to the family. Considering his history, being in a family like this was never on his radar. Coming home was the best decision he ever made. Second chances are possible. After everyone leaves, Thomas and Cait sit in the glow of the Christmas tree, sipping hot mulled cider.

"Tom, you surprised me with this gift." Cait touches the brooch pinned to her sweater.

"Good. I was hoping you would be surprised. You know what it means, right?"

"I think so. According to my mother, it is a pre-engagement agreement of sorts. Is that what you think it means? Just checking. I don't want to assume anything."

"That is exactly what it means. What do you think? Will you consider marrying me?" Thomas asks.

"Are you kidding? Yes! Absolutely. *Yes.* Are you sure this isn't too déjà vu-y for you? We are walking in our parents' footsteps again."

"You're the one creeped out by déjà vu. I'm fine with it. Consider it a family tradition. Walking in their footsteps is how that works. I never thought I would get married again, and then I fell in love with you. It feels right. Coming home, getting sober, and falling in love is about the rightest I have ever been."

"Merry Christmas. My fiancé is beautiful in the morning."

Cait opens one eye to see Thomas smiling down at her. "No need to butter me up, I already said yes." Cait yawns. "Did it snow?"

"Nope. Not yet, anyway. I'm going downstairs to make coffee. I gave the elves the day off."

"That was generous of you. What do they get? One day a year?" Cait softly kisses Thomas. "I'll get up in a minute. Don't start Christmas without me."

Red poinsettias, holly, and bayberry candles are artfully placed on their Christmas table. Thomas turns on the tree lights, puts on classical Christmas music, and goes to the kitchen. Cait left a new bag of spicy Christmas coffee on the counter. He doesn't much care for flavored coffee, but for her? For Christmas? She can have anything she wants. As the pot gurgles and the aroma of cinnamon-fresh coffee fills the kitchen, Cait walks in.

"I see you found my special Christmas coffee."

"Yes, I did. You were pretty obvious about it. What's for breakfast? I'm starving."

"Belgian waffles with strawberries and whipped cream, bacon, breakfast sausages, and I can make eggs if you like. I have been making that Christmas breakfast ever since the kids were small. They hated waiting until after breakfast to open their presents, so I enticed them with whipped cream."

"You are enticing me as well, in many ways." Thomas smiles. "You want help?"

"I don't need help in the kitchen, but I would love it if you made a fire. You might need to get more wood from out back."

"You got it."

"Tom?"

"Yeah?"

"I'm so happy. It's going to be a wonderful Christmas."

"It already is, Cait."

After a leisurely breakfast, they share special gifts. Cait hands Thomas boxes wrapped in red, green, and gold striped paper.

"These are for you. I hope you like them. I had an elf helping me."

"Are you referring to Sam?" Thomas asks. "He's kind of elfish."

"That's the guy. Open. I can't wait any longer."

Thomas rips off the paper, revealing professional wireless headphones paired with the exact microphone he has been searching for.

"Thank you so much, Caity. I've been wanting that mic, where did you find it?"

"Sam and I went to New York City. It wasn't easy keeping the secret from you. I got you something else, too. I know what an excellent musician you are. I also know how you want to record that album with the Old Guys. Here. Merry Christmas." Cait hands Thomas an envelope. He carefully opens the seal and slides out a gift card. Thomas's jaw drops in surprise.

"Wow, Cait! This is unbelievable. It's too much." Thomas grabs her in an embrace, still gripping the gift certificate for recording time at The Power Station New England in Waterford. The studio has the same design as the original Power Station in New York City.

"It's not too much. You deserve every minute I could afford in that place. I went there to see it and talk to the guys because I know nothing about music production. They were really helpful and so nice. Of course, much of what they said was Greek to me, but I picked up on the important stuff. Did you know they have vintage equipment once used to record John Lennon and Nirvana?"

"I did not. That's very cool. Cait, it's the best gift I've ever gotten. Not only because it's an amazing place to record in, but because it's from you, and you support my music. You believe in me."

"Tom, I don't just *believe* in you. I *know* how talented you are. The songs you wrote for the album are crazy good. I listen to all of them over and over. That album needs to be recorded. It's about time you got a break."

"Well, I can't wait to check it out. We'd better get busy polishing up the tracks. There will be a lot of rehearsals this year."

"Wouldn't it be great if your album was a huge hit?"

"Frosting on the cake, that would be. I can't even think about it. One step at a time." Thomas pulls Cait to her feet, spins her around, and grabs her in a classic Ogilvie bear hug.

"Thank you! Now you have to open your present." Cait settles back on the couch as Thomas dives under the tree and pulls out a large box topped with a red bow. "Merry Christmas, Caity."

"Wait. I thought you already gave me my present? Last night?" Cait touches the brooch pinned to her Christmas nightshirt.

"Oh, my dear, there is more! I couldn't help myself. Open!" Thomas urges.

Cait rips the paper off and opens the box. Inside is an assortment of wrapped gifts. A pair of red Darn Tough Vermont socks with white snowflakes along the top, a can of spray snow, Vermont maple syrup in a maple leaf bottle, a Vermont hoodie, and a selection of cheeses.

"I'm picking up on a theme here, Tom. You hooked on Vermont?"

"Keep digging in there, Caity, there's one more thing." Thomas is grinning like a Cheshire Cat.

Cait pokes around in the tissue and finds an envelope. Carefully, she opens the flap, revealing a gift card for a romantic weekend at a five-star inn.

"I know how much you love snow. I thought a romantic weekend in snow country would be perfect. I booked it for the middle of February. If that isn't good for you, we can change it. In the meantime, you have snow in a can!"

"Tom, this is perfect! I love Vermont. Thank you! Let there be snow!" Cait pulls the heather gray sweatshirt over her head. "How do I look?"

"You are beautiful! As usual. When does the open house start? Do we have time for a Christmas snuggle in the bedroom?" Thomas asks while kissing Cait's neck. "I'll put on the Santa outfit if you like." Thomas's kisses work their way toward Cait's lips. She surrenders completely as he pulls her down on the couch.

"Mmm, Tom. You taste like strawberries, whipped cream, and a hint of cinnamon. Give me another taste."

"Maybe we should lock the doors and get more comfortable. What do you think? No one can get in if the open house isn't open." Thomas nibbles Cait's ear.

"I like the way you think. I never knew Santa was such a hot and sexy guy. Don't tell the children!"

Cait rolls off the couch and locks the doors. When she gets to the bedroom, Thomas has the covers pulled up to his nose, wearing his Santa hat and little else. "Santa! You devil." Cait tips her head down and coyly looks at him through her eyelashes. She pulls off the sweatshirt and slips into bed beside him.

24

All That Glitters Isn't Snow

Except for an occasional flurry, Connecticut has no snow throughout January. That disappoints Cait. But, on February thirteenth, the day of Cait and Thomas's drive to Vermont, flakes magically started to fall. Big, fat, heavy flakes of snow quickly cover the ground. It is a beautiful sight.

"See! Santa is powerful. A late Christmas present for you, Cait." Thomas tosses their bags in the back of his Jeep. "Do we have coffee to go?"

"We do!" Cait holds up two insulated travel mugs. "Have you got the address and reservation number?"

"Yup. Is everything secure in the house? Sadie knows where we will be?"

"Yes, heat is turned down, and the house is buttoned up tight. Sadie knows where we are going in case of an emergency. Dear God, please don't let there be an emergency. I want this weekend so much."

"Me too. Since it's finally snowing, do you have snow gear? Boots and all?" Thomas asks. He wasn't a Boy Scout, but he knows it's best to be prepared.

"I think I have everything. I can't wait to get there. It will be so beautiful if this snow continues. Did you check the weather?" Cait asks.

"Last I checked, a decent snowfall is predicted. I want to get to Manchester Center before driving gets bad."

They pile into the Wrangler and head off on their adventure. In good weather, it takes three hours to get to Vermont. Thomas wants to take the scenic route, but considering weather conditions, he decides to stay on Interstate 91 as long as he can.

When they get past Hartford, heading toward Springfield, Massachusetts, the weather gets worse. Heavy snowfall is making visibility difficult. Snow is piling up on the roadway. Cars creep along in a line. The sticky snow cakes up on the windshield wipers, smearing melting snow with each pass. The defroster is on full blast, but visibility is still poor through the windshield. Traffic slows to a crawl. The conversation between Cait and Thomas becomes tense and focuses on getting to Vermont in one piece.

"I think Santa overdid it on the snowfall. I guess we need to be more specific with our wish list," Thomas says as he grips the steering wheel, staying in line with other cars, lights, and flashers on. The speed is down to thirty-five, and even that feels risky. Getting towed out of a ditch is not on his list of preferred weekend activities. They pass several cars off the road. Tow trucks with flashing lights struggle to get to the disabled vehicles. It's a mess.

"I just checked the weather, and it will snow all the way. Be careful, Tom. No rush. We get there when we get there." Cait is tense. "Maybe we could find a place to get something to eat and wait for conditions to improve."

"We can keep that in mind, although it looks like we are in the middle of nowhere."

Cait checks her phone. "No cell signal here, Tom. It must be a dead spot. I will let you know if a signal comes back."

Hours later, exhausted, they finally arrive at the inn. They pull in to what they hope is the driveway between two snow plow markers. The plow has made a pass through the parking lot at least once, but the snow continues to pile up. They park near the front entrance of the inn and scramble out of the Wrangler. With luggage held high out of the snow, they mush to the front door of the inn. The innkeeper, Henry Brown, welcomes them at the door, showing them where to put their snowy boots and coats.

"Ya made it. Good for you. I wasn't sure we would see you tonight. Let's get you checked in so you can warm up. Snow is welcome in these parts, but it's a problem when we get it all at once, if you know what I mean." Henry chuckles and suggests they hunker down for the night because the nor'easter will dump a lot more snow on them before it's done.

"Sounds good to us. The drive was not fun. Roads are awful. Is anything open around here? We need to get something to eat," Thomas inquires.

"There's a convenience store close by that's probably still open. You can walk to it. It's not far. They have a pretty decent deli. If that plan fails, we'll rustle up something for ya."

Henry guides them through the colonial living room, around the corner, and down a hallway. Antique bookshelves that line the walls of their room are filled with bestsellers, and some classics original to the old house. Cait can't wait to look them over. Upholstered chairs sit close to the fireplace. An ensuite bathroom has an inviting jacuzzi tub. The king-size bed has a plaid down comforter that matches the curtains. A flat-screen television hides behind the doors of an armoire that also houses a small refrigerator and a microwave.

"This place is perfect! Very romantic," Cait calls from the bathroom. "There are candles in here. I love it. Hey, after we eat, let's soak in the tub by candlelight." Cait throws herself down on the bed.

"Ahhh, this is heavenly! Come try this out, Tom."

Thomas flops down on the bed with a sigh. He turns to face Cait. "You like?" He smiles. "I did a bunch of research, and this place got high marks. Comes complete with snowmageddon, no extra charge."

"I *love* it. We could make coming here a regular thing."

"That would be nice. Maybe in the summer. Hungry?"

"Starving. You know what?" Cait asks. "You are the only person I want to be snowed in with. Snow days are my favorite days, and this is so romantic." She is grinning. Seeing her happy makes this worth the effort.

"Let's get this trek done. My pants are soaking wet, and I can't wait to get them off and warm up."

"Ooo. I can't wait either!" Cait flirts. "Come on. Let's go."

They bundle up and set out in the direction the innkeeper suggested. The snow is blowing into drifts, making for strenuous walking. Up ahead, they see lights glowing like an oasis in the blizzard. Thomas and Cait go inside, stomping the snow off their boots.

"Hi. Quite a snowfall we're having," Thomas says.

"Ay uh. What can I getcha? We're out of roast beef, but there's turkey. Ya got here just in time. Me and the missus were just about to close up. Only idjits would be out on a night like this." The man squints and frowns at Thomas.

"Turkey sounds good. Let's get two turkey grinders. What do you have to put on them?" Thomas asks.

"We only make 'em one way. You get what you get. If you want fancy fixins' go to Subway, but they're closed, cuz of the weather. Bunch of nervous Nellies." The man isn't interested in small talk. Meanwhile, Cait roams the store, filling a basket with drinks, chips, Vermont cheese, and crackers. The minute they step outside, the store lights go out.

"We just made it. That guy was not much fun," Thomas comments.

They walk through the blizzard, clutching bags of groceries, snow clumping on their eyelashes. Back in their room, they strip off wet clothes and start a fire in the gas fireplace. Cait has her Vermont sweatshirt and warm wool leggings on. Thomas digs sweatpants out of his bag and pulls on a Fair Isle wool sweater.

"Nice sweater! Did you get it especially for this ski trip?' Cait asks.

"I did. It seemed Vermont-ish. Skiing? Are we skiing?" Thomas pulls a small table by the fire and unpacks the sandwiches and drinks.

"The sweater is perfect, whether we ski or not. You are very handsome." Cait kisses Thomas. "Maybe we will go cross-country skiing. Ever tried it? We certainly have enough snow. Maybe too much, actually." Cait rips open a bag of Cape Cod potato chips.

"No, can't say that I have. I spent a lot of time in the south, where such a thing is unheard of." Thomas laughs. The TV is tuned to a local weather channel. They unwrap their sandwiches, and suddenly the power goes out, and the inn is silent. After a few minutes, there's a knock on the door.

"Hi folks, ya probably noticed the power is out from the storm. Lines are down. Not sure when it will come back on, but we're hoping for the best. I brought you a flashlight and a battery-operated lantern. We like to be prepared. The fireplace will keep you warm. Yell if you need anything. Oh, if you want a shower, take it now while the water is still warm. G'night."

"Henry seems to take things like this in stride. What else can happen? Not exactly how I pictured this weekend." Thomas frowns.

"So much for the jacuzzi. It's okay, Tom. It's an adventure. Besides, we will be here for a few days. I'm sure the power will be back on soon. Let's jump in the shower together to conserve water." Cait raises her eyebrows flirtatiously.

"I'm all for conserving water. Last one in is a rotten egg." Thomas pulls off his sweater as he walks to the bathroom. After a quick shower, they wrap themselves in luxurious white terrycloth robes provided by the inn.

"Oh my, I love these bathrobes. They are so soft and fluffy. I could live in one. Who needs clothes?" Cait gushes. "I wonder if they sell them here."

"Maybe. We will ask Henry. Let's eat before I faint." They sit by the fire, grateful for the warmth. If they can get past the inconvenience, their getaway is very romantic. After supper, they climb under the covers. It's been a long day.

"Tom, I know this isn't how we imagined our weekend, but I think this is wonderful. I feel like we are all alone in a romantic snow globe. It's magical. However, it would be nice to have electricity. I have my eye on that Jacuzzi." Cait pushes damp curls off Thomas's forehead. "You have to admit, it's memorable."

"That's one word for it," Thomas grumbles. "But now might be the perfect time to make it more memorable. Don't move." Thomas swings his legs out of bed and rummages through his backpack. "One more surprise, Cait." Thomas slips back under the covers, facing Cait, looking into her eyes. "I feel like I have loved you for multiple lifetimes. The past six months have been all I ever hoped for. Do you know what tomorrow is?"

"Um, Saturday?"

"It's Valentine's Day. I planned this trip around that. It isn't exactly turning out the way I imagined it."

"It has been a long time since I celebrated Valentine's Day. That's so sweet."

"I planned to have roses waiting for you, but the florist is snowed in. But I do have this." Thomas pulls a small box out from under the covers. "Cait, I want to spend my life with you. Will you marry me? Please? I am making this official." Thomas flips open the box, revealing a single perfect diamond set in a gold band of entwined Scottish thistles. "I had it made for you. The thistle is the national flower of Scotland. It represents bravery, courage, and loyalty. Those are qualities I admire in you, and it's how I want to be when I'm with you. And because a thistle is a prickly plant, it also symbolizes protection. I pledge love, loyalty, and protection, Cait. Always. Forever." Thomas holds his breath, waiting for what feels like an eternity.

"Tom, it's beautiful. Yes. *Yes.* Of course, I'll marry you. I already said yes at Christmas." Cait holds Thomas's face, kissing him. Thomas slips the ring on Cait's finger.

"I know, but this is beyond the brooch promise and is really *official.* Caity, I will not disappoint you. I was going to do a dramatic presentation at a classy restaurant, but they're closed too. I couldn't wait until a spring thaw to ask you to be my wife. But maybe this is better, yeah?"

"Oh, Tom. This is so much better! Have you had this planned since Christmas? Now I *have* to steal this robe, because it will always remind me of this moment." Under the covers, Cait moves close to Thomas. "This is the most romantic snow day I have ever experienced. And one I will never forget."

In the morning, the sky is blue, and the sun, reflecting off a blanket of white, is dazzling. The scent of fresh coffee lures them out of their warm bed. Thomas flips on the light switch, and the power is still out. But, unless the inn has bacon aromatherapy, a hot breakfast awaits them.

"Good morning!" a ruddy-faced woman in an apron welcomes them in the dining room. Strands of gray hair escape the bun on top of her head, and there is a good chance she is Mrs. Claus. Cait expects that at any moment she will awaken from the best dream she's ever had. "I'm Henry's sister, Charlotte. I do the cookin' here. He and his wife, Evie, are out clearing a path. We got over two feet of snow. Bromley Ski Area will be giddy. Coffee?"

"Nice to meet you, Charlotte. Yes, coffee, please."

Charlotte hustles off to the kitchen.

"Doesn't she look like Mrs. Claus, Tom? Are we in a dream?" Cait pokes Thomas.

"She does. But my dreams have electricity, so nope, not a dream." Thomas holds Cait's hand under the round oak table covered with a cheery yellow tablecloth. In the center is a seasonal arrangement of holly, pine branches, and pinecones with a ceramic snowman in the center. Charlotte sets a carafe of coffee and mugs on the table.

"Breakfast this morning includes freshly baked cranberry walnut muffins, scrambled eggs, bacon, and breakfast potatoes. We have two kinds of toast: whole wheat and rye. The butter and homemade jam are on the table. Thankfully, we cook with gas, so the power outage hasn't slowed me down." Charlotte hustles back to the kitchen. Cait and Thomas sip the delicious coffee when a man probably in his sixties, wearing jeans and a well-worn Virginia Theological Seminary sweatshirt, joins them.

"Okay, folks. Help yourselves." Charlotte places the family-style breakfast on the table. "Enjoy. Yell if you need anything. I'll be in the kitchen."

Cait and Thomas chat with the gentleman as they linger over coffee. His name is John Parsons, and he is an Episcopal priest visiting his sister and aging mother in town. That explains the sweatshirt. He grew up here and remembers snowstorms like this happening all the time.

"Now it's a national disaster, and everything shuts down. Strange, isn't it, how things change?"

"It is. So many things are strange these days. How long will you be staying here, Reverend?" Thomas asks. "In case we need a priest." Cait shoots Thomas a disapproving look.

"Please call me John. I will be here till the end of the week. I am getting my mother settled in assisted living. She and my sister live together, and Mom is getting to be more than my sister can handle. Mom has always been more than any of us could handle, but that's another story. It will be good for both of them to have their own space." He sets down his mug. "On that note, I'd better get going. They're gonna need me to dig them out. Nice to meet you folks."

After breakfast, Cait and Thomas go out to explore. Red-faced people in snowsuits are shoveling or blowing snow. The plow came through already, making the street passable.

"Hey, Henry! Beautiful day, eh?" Cait waves to the innkeeper as he pushes snow off the sidewalk. "Heard anything about the electricity?"

"Hey, good morning. I haven't heard anything definite. I expect now that the snow has stopped, it'll be fixed soon." Henry leans on the handle of his upright shovel, breathing hard. "Where ya headed? I think some of the shops are starting to open. Not much slows down a Vermonter."

"We're going to walk around and see what's here." They wave goodbye to Henry and start down the street, snow crunching under their feet. Thomas sings the old classic "Winter Wonderland" as they walk.

"In the meadow, we can build a snowman, then pretend that he is Parson Brown. He'll say, 'Are you married?' We'll say, 'No man. But you can do the job when you're in town."

"It's our song!" Cait sings with him as they stroll hand in mittened hand. "Later on, we'll conspire, as we dream by the fire, to face unafraid, the plans that we've made, walking in a winter wonderland." She laughs. "This is a winter wonderland, Tom. Look, a coffee shop is open. Let's go in."

They sit at a table in the shop, sipping rich hot chocolate topped with a mound of whipped cream. They can hear a generator running outside, which explains how the shop can operate. Gingham curtains hang at the frosty windows, and Vermont-made gifts and postcards fill shelves and racks.

"Singing that song makes me think. Are you aware that our innkeeper is Henry *Brown* and the priest is John *Parsons?* Coincidence, you say. I think not. It's a sign, Caity," Thomas says.

"A sign? I didn't know you were into that kind of thing. A sign of what?" Cait sips her cocoa, getting whipped cream on the tip of her nose.

"I'm not into a lot of woo-woo stuff, but I do believe in signs." Thomas dabs Cait's nose with a napkin. "It's a throwback to my Scottish heritage. We're a superstitious bunch. The snow, the romantic lack of electric lighting. Henry and John. It is all screaming, *for God's sake, people, get married already!* Can't you hear it? "

"What are you talking about? You want to get married here? Now? Are you serious?" Cait is incredulous.

"You said it yourself, Cait, this is a romantic winter wonderland. It's perfect! If we are going to do it anyway, what better time than now? We aren't getting any younger. We have the perfect location. And a priest in residence." Thomas squeezes Cait's hand, grinning.

"That's so impulsive, Tom. What will the family say? Don't you think they would want to be at our wedding?"

"They will yell *congratulations* and probably throw confetti at us, if I know them. We can have a party to celebrate when we get home. Think about it. It would be fun, and talk about memorable! Yeah?" Thomas's eyes are big, and he is nodding yes like a bobblehead doll.

"Memorable for sure. We would need a license," Cait muses.

"You mean you're considering it?" Thomas's Cheshire Cat grin is back.

"I'm thinking about it. It would be romantic, and maybe you're right about signs."

Thomas, and Cait, walk around town, stopping in various shops and chatting with the locals about the snow. Cait wants to know where they can cross-country ski. Thomas is wondering where to get wedding rings. By afternoon, they head back to the inn to warm up with tea and warm scones, fresh whipped cream, and homemade strawberry jam.

"Wow. These scones are delicious." Cait devours the tasty baked goods. "I have been thinking about your idea. How would we do it? We would need to stay here longer. Since we need a license, we would have to wait for the town hall to open. Right?"

"Yeah, that's true. Let's talk to Henry and see what he suggests. Then you take your time deciding. No pressure."

Thomas and Cait check into extending their stay at the inn. Henry fills them in on Vermont laws and where to get a marriage license. They can get the license on Monday morning and get married any time after that. Henry and Evie are excited about the prospect of a wedding. Everyone looks at Cait, waiting for her decision.

"Stop looking at me! Jeesh. No pressure, my ass. I'm going to call Sadie and Barrett and see how they feel about this. If they are okay with it, then I will consider going ahead." A cheer goes up from the innkeeper and his wife. The lights suddenly turn on in the parlor.

"See. It's another sign," says Thomas. Cait talks to her children and is surprised by their enthusiasm for a Vermont wedding. Cait is dismayed and a little sad that it doesn't bother them to miss it.

Saturday night, as Cait snuggles with Thomas in bed, she is finally ready to make her decision.

"Tom, Sadie thinks the idea of a Vermont wedding is very romantic. I feel bad that she won't be here, but like you said, we can celebrate when we get home. And we'll have lots of pictures. It seems to be coming together effortlessly before my eyes, so how could I refuse? Count me in. Let's do it."

"Really? That's great! This is going to be the best wedding ever. Just us and this charming inn surrounded by snow. If you ask me, this is how everyone should get married. You and me, Caity, happily ever after."

Sunday morning at breakfast, they ask John Parsons to officiate, and he readily agrees. They will have a candlelight ceremony Monday evening. Charlotte agrees to make them dinner, including a special wedding cake. On Sunday afternoon, they bought simple wedding bands at a jewelry store in town. Evie is taking care of the flowers. The last issue is what to wear. Thomas is fine with his jeans and sweater. Cait is thinking about something a little fancier. Evie takes Cait to a boutique owned by a friend.

"Ohhh yes! This is it." Evie pulls a dress off the rack and shows Cait. It is a pale blue cashmere sweater dress, mid-calf in length, with a scoop neckline and a flattering A-line shape. It's perfect.

"I love it, Evie." Cait takes it to the dressing room for a try-on. The dress fits Cait like it was made for her. She steps out of the dressing room to show Evie, and the two of them agree—it's the perfect dress.

"I'll get the florist to make you a bouquet of forget-me-nots that will be perfect. And I have a string of pearls you can borrow that will be beautiful. Then you will have something borrowed and something blue covered."

"I have the antique brooch Tom gave me for something old, and everything here is new. We will have tons of good luck."

"Not that you need it, honey." Evie winks at Cait. "I got a good feeling about you two."

They browse the shop, and Evie comes across a pale blue button-down shirt of soft cotton. "This is for your sweetheart! He can still wear his jeans, but this will dress him up a bit, and the color matches your dress."

"Sold!" This is the easiest wedding Cait has ever planned. "Thank you so much for helping me, Evie. You're making my day very special."

"Are you kidding? I'm having a blast. I love weddings."

Monday afternoon, Cait and Thomas are helping Henry and Evie set up for the ceremony. They place candles, flowers, and folding chairs around the room.

"That seems like a lot of chairs, Tom. Are we bringing people in off the street as witnesses?" Cait jokes. She no sooner gets the words out of her mouth when she hears the tiny voice of Gracie calling to her. Cait wheels around.

"Oh my god! What are you doing here?" Cait picks Gracie up, hugging her tight.

"Thomas invited us. Well, actually he said we should get our tails up here, pronto. He knew you wouldn't want to do this without us, and we wanted to surprise you."

"Well, that you did. I'm so happy you're here. No wonder you were so enthusiastic about us eloping. It never even occurred to me that you would be able to drive up." Cait looks over Sadie's shoulder at Thomas and mouths *Thank you. I love you.*

"We wouldn't have missed it, Mom," Barrett says while hugging his mother. "Besides, I heard the skiing is great."

Candles are lit. Reverend John Parsons replaces his sweatshirt with official priestly attire. Gracie drops rose petals around the room. Sadie and her husband Jack attend the couple, standing on each side of Thomas. Cait walks into the room on the arm of her son, Barrett, carrying the promised bouquet of forget-me-nots. Instead of the wedding march, Bing Crosby's "Winter Wonderland" plays through the speakers. Henry Brown and his wife, Evie, stand poised to help. Charlotte peeks out of the kitchen, dabbing a tear from her eye with the corner of her apron. Saul, a local photographer and friend of the Browns, takes pictures of the simple ceremony. Thomas takes his phone from his pocket and video calls his brother Andy.

"Andy! It's happening! Hang on." Thomas hands his phone to Barrett. "Barrett, will you hold my phone so Andy can see the ceremony? Thanks. Okay. I'm ready now." Thomas beams at Cait and takes her hand.

"When I arrived here in Manchester to help my mother move, I had no idea I would be called on to perform a wedding," Reverend Parsons says. "But here we are, gathered today to join Thomas and Cait in holy matrimony. The good Lord sought to bring these two together, and I just happened to be having breakfast with them. He works in mysterious ways. It is my honor to bless this union. Do you have your vows ready?"

"Yes, Father." Thomas turns to look at Cait. "I, Thomas Malcolm Ogilvie, promise to love, honor, and cherish you, Cait, for all the rest of my days. I've never felt my Scottish heritage as much as I do now, with you. Maybe that's our parents at work again. My ancestors have wed with these words for centuries. Cait, I promise you the first cut of my meat, the first sip of my wine—symbolic of course—and from this day it shall only be your name I cry out in the night and into your eyes that I smile each morning." Thomas slides the ring on Cait's finger. "With this ring, I thee wed."

Cait brushes a tear from her cheek. "Thomas, I can't stop smiling. This day, and everything you have done to make it special, means so much to me. I promise to love, honor, and cherish you for the rest of my days. I don't know about the meat and the wine, but I do vow that your name will be the only name I cry out in the night, and into your eyes I will smile each morning. I love you now and forever." Cait slips the gold wedding band on Thomas's finger. "With this ring, I thee wed."

"Bear with me, folks, while I drone on. I don't get a captive audience very often. There is something magical about how this wedding came to be. Does that make it special? Maybe. Lasting? Possibly. When the Lord lines things up, miracles happen. There's a huge snowfall, a warm inn, a master baker in the kitchen, and the surprise of loving family members. That's magic. I have officiated many weddings in my time. Not all of them are ones I had faith in. But this one? This one feels right. It brings to mind that very overused wedding reading from Corinthians. I'll paraphrase. Love is patient. Love is kind. It doesn't boast. It isn't loud or rude. It doesn't keep score. Love always protects, trusts, hopes, and perseveres. People don't always do that perfectly, but we try. Without further ado, I now pronounce you husband and wife. Congratulations." Thomas kisses Cait. Barrett hands Thomas his phone.

"Andy, did you see that? I'm a married man!"

"I did see. Wow. Em and I are in tears here." Andy holds up a glass of his father's Talisker Scotch. "Dad's here with you, Tom. *Slàinte Mhath*, my brother. I am so happy for you. Where's my new sister-in-law?" Thomas walks over to Cait, showing Andy the wedding party as he goes.

"Cait, congratulations and welcome to the family! We are so happy for you both. Honeymoon in Montana?" Andy suggests.

"Thank you, Andy. This is a surprise, but I couldn't be happier. I haven't even had time to think about a honeymoon, but Montana sounds great. Hey, everyone?" Cait calls out. "Say hi to my new brother-in-law." Cait has another potent déjà vu feeling. She isn't sure what that means, but for now, she is simply going to enjoy her wedding day to the man she loves.

Epilogue

Afer a couple of days romping through snow with Cait's family, they drive back to Connecticut. Thomas and Cait are tired and happy. The reality of what they've done is starting to dawn on them. It was a perfect wedding ceremony, and having her children there meant everything to Cait. Thomas's thoughtfulness is one reason, among many, why she loves him. Now, alone in the car, there is a lot for Mr. and Mrs. Ogilvie to think about. Thomas is excited to be married to the woman of his dreams and can't wait to get into the recording studio. Cait is wondering what married life will be like with Thomas. Once their relationship came out of the closet, it seemed to progress at warp speed.

Cait and Thomas are still basking in the honeymoon stage. But she knows from experience that it will change. For the better, she believes, or she wouldn't have married Thomas. But anything can happen. She wonders about that déjà vu feeling she keeps having. Cait takes a deep breath, exhaling noisily.

"You okay, wife?" Thomas asks, keeping his eyes on the road. "I love calling you that, by the way."

"Yeah, well, don't overdo it, husband. I think I'm still sort of spinning. Between the snow, the kids coming up, and all the excitement, it's like a dream, ya know? Still catching my breath. You?"

"Couldn't be better." Thomas grins, glancing quickly at Cait. "That was the best trip I have ever been on. We need to go back there every year."

"That would be nice. In the meantime, we have a lot to do and things to figure out. This happened so fast." Cait looks seriously at Thomas.

"Yes, but wasn't it fun? And we have our whole lives to figure things out." Thomas says, bringing Cait's hand to his lips. "Let's go to Montana to celebrate with Andy."

"Okay. And we want to plan a party with our friends, remember?" Cait looks down at her beautiful engagement ring and smiles. "Tom?"

"Yeah?"

"You don't expect me to be a sitcom wife, all dolled up with dinner on the table at five every night, do you? I've done enough of that."

"Hell no. Look at me? I'm the least trad person I know."

"That's a relief."

"All I want is for you, *us*, to be happy. Whatever that looks like. And for now, it looks like going to Montana and throwing a party."

"Yes. Yes, it does." Cait smiles.

Acknowledgements

I have deep gratitude for everyone who made this story come to life. That includes my writing buddies Joanne Moore and Patty Chaffee. I could not have done this without your support and continuous cheerleading! I so appreciated your feedback when I was sweating over the synopsis. We have so much fun and have accomplished things I never believed possible.

Thank you to my dear friends, Wendell, Katherine, Mark, Gina, Monica, and Julia, who willingly read rough drafts and offered insightful feedback. I am grateful for your enthusiastic participation.

Thank you, John Oat, artist and creator of my constantly changing cover vision. I appreciate your artistry and patience as I threw ideas at you. I think you nailed it.

Thank you to my editor, Francesca G. Varela. I am so fortunate to have found you. You are a brilliant wordsmith and made this story the best it can be. Please don't retire.

Finally, last but not least, I am thrilled to have found Steven Porter of Stillwater Publications. His experience in the publishing business and his patience while I asked question after question, was just what I needed. His expertise made the process effortless and professional.

A Note from the Author

Over two years ago, a friend asked if I would like to join a writing group. Our intention was to support each other in finishing our novels. I jumped at the chance. A whole cast of characters filled my head, my days, and the pages. The result was *It's About Time*.

I had no intention of writing a sequel, or—horrors—a series. My muse had different ideas about that, however, and Thomas Ogilvie started to tell his story, *Thomas's Second Chance* was born. I hope you enjoy it. I'm grateful to my readers and love hearing from you.

Please, please, please take a moment to share a review on Amazon. Reviews keep the Amazon machine rolling and make my books visible. Thank you.

You can reach out to me anytime.

Sign up for my sporadic mailing list at my website:
https://hillaryoat.com/

Find me on Facebook at Hillary Oat Author

Or shoot me an email: hillaryoat@gmail.com

Slàinte Mhath
Hillary

About the Author

The Basics: I'm a mother of three and grandmother of five. I love dogs, but don't have one right now. I grew up in Schenectady, New York, and I am always surprised when people have heard of it. I've lived in Southeastern Connecticut for many years and love it. My novels are set in Niantic, Connecticut.

The Scotland Connection: There are two kinds of writers—plotters and pantsers. I am a pantser, meaning I write by instinct rather than plan. I have no idea what's going to happen, but something surprising always does. I didn't know there would be a Scotland connection, but it does make sense. When I was a kid, my father dragged me to the Scottish Games in upstate New York every year. Several years ago, I went to Scotland, and it blew me away. The Highlands are rugged and gorgeous. The people are tough, determined, but also kind. It felt like home. It makes sense that it would seep into my story.

Fun Fact: When I was writing *It's About Time,* I Googled the name of a popular Scotch in Scotland, and I settled on Talisker, made on the Isle of Skye. I had never heard of it, but when I went into the package store to buy a bottle of wine, there was Talisker on the shelf. I had to buy it.

Another Fun Fact: I love books and cannot pass a little free library in town without taking a peek. I have stacks of books waiting to be read.

I've discovered a whole new life passion and purpose as an author. Book three in the Ogilvie Family Series is in the works. Thank you for reading.